MW01614755

THE LIES
I TOLD HIM

the spellbinding domestic thriller

VANESSA GARBIN

Published by The Book Folks

London, 2021

ISBN 978-1-913516-03-1

www.thebookfolks.com

To my loving parents

Prologue

He had been ignoring her of late. Distant, even when in the same room. Irritated by her mere presence. It was as though her very existence bothered him.

Anna wasn't certain if this was a good or bad thing.

Her head knew it was good. Because the less he cared about her, the less he watched her. And the less he obsessed about her every move like he used to, the more likely she would be able to escape his clutches.

Still, the sadness came, seeping into her heart and making it heavy, so that it hung inside her chest like a dead weight.

For the past few weeks, Anna had noticed that he was coming home later than usual, and he almost always entered the front door smiling either to himself or at his phone. She guessed that this meant he'd found someone new. That she had become tiresome enough that he no longer cared with whom she spoke, or what she wore in public, or what food she ate.

And yet despite all of this, she loved him still. She wondered if she'd ever stop loving him. And this shamed her to no end.

But was it love? And did he love her in return? Anna had no way of knowing. No experience or standard of love by which she could compare. She was not certain that she had ever been loved in all her seventeen years. Not even on the day that she had been born, for it was then that she was discarded for the first of many times in her life.

Maybe she'd never discover what being loved felt like – certainly not with him.

No. This was not love. It couldn't be.

In truth, the relationship exhausted her. He'd drained her of not only her happiness and hope – what little she'd had before she met him – but of her very life force; to the point she often felt empty, soulless and unable to make the simplest of decisions for herself. Maybe because there was no 'self' left.

She wondered, as she rubbed at her bruised wrists, if she would ever find the courage to escape.

1

Daphne

I nurse my second glass of wine as I relax against the spongy cushions of the outdoor sofa in our backyard. My skin prickles at the coolness of the autumn night. I like the crispness of the evening breeze. Makes me feel tingly and alive.

The sky is crystal clear and filled with stars, a spectacular sight. But, as always, my mind is crammed with thoughts. No. Worries. If worrying were a profession, I'd be the absolute master at it.

Mainly, I wonder how Gabriel is going at his first 'cool' party – a fellow classmate's sixteenth birthday. My heart flutters with nerves... he's such a gentle, trusting soul, my sweet Gabriel, and I hope that the more streetwise kids don't offer him alcohol or drugs.

I also briefly wonder what my husband, Joe, is jerking off to in his study. Because that's his after-dinner routine. In fact, do I really want to know? No. No I don't. Just thinking about that website on his laptop makes my skin crawl and sends me into a mild state of panic. I've gotten used to it in a sense. I've learned to somewhat control the fluttery fear in my heart by concentrating on the simple in and out of my breath, whenever Joe disappears into his study.

Once, I sat behind a man on a bus who, unabashedly, logged onto that same site and proceeded to watch various videos, sound up, while he ate a soggy taco that dripped orange sauce onto the white sleeve of his shirt. He only turned it off when a small, curly-haired child from across the aisle leant over and said, 'Can I watch too?'

I can still remember the anxiety I felt as I watched that man casually peruse the menu after he'd logged on. The sweat on my palms, the flush of heat at the base of my neck, the erratic heart palpitations in my chest.

I'm no prude. I love sex. But that site, and the many others like it, will never let me forget the darkest, most shadowy time of my life, a time of fear and shame. A time before Joe and Gabriel.

A time when I foolishly surrendered my heart to a monster.

The wine has grown warm in my cradling hand. I take a sip and force my mind to other, more banal things.

Dinner. We have plenty of leftovers from our lamb roast tonight and I think about sending Gabriel across the road tomorrow morning, to our elderly neighbour, Glenys, with a plate. Yes, that'll be nice. I adore Glenys. She reminds me of one of my foster grandmothers, Mary – the only adult in the foster system who was truly interested in me and seemed to genuinely care – whom I sadly only knew for a little over a month when I was eight before she passed away suddenly from a stroke. Even Glenys's house smells the same as Mary's did. I'll never forget it. Lavender. Such a comforting scent.

A breeze stirs up the dried leaves scattered across the pavers and I take another sip of my merlot, enjoying the soft, plummy flavours. The zephyr lifts the hem of my skirt a little and reveals my toned thighs. Toned thanks to the long, early morning walk I take each day. It's a pity my husband doesn't appreciate my thighs in a physical way. Aesthetically, yes. He loves my body. Calls me 'perfection on legs'. But I'd wish he'd reach out and touch them once in a while.

I sigh. The wine is working its way through my veins. Warming me from head to toe. Wine always gets me in a certain mood... a mood that makes me wish my husband didn't have porn-addiction-related impotence.

Joe and I have the house to ourselves tonight. It would be heaven to walk inside and have him take me, in a moment of passion, on the dining table, make the vase of flowers at its centre tremble and shake along with us.

But actual sex hasn't happened for us in a very long time.

My thoughts return to my son, Gabriel. When he announced that he'd been invited to a party this weekend I had to restrain myself from jumping for joy. He hasn't been invited to a party, a proper party with both girls and boys attending, since primary school. Sure, he'd been invited to a few sleepovers with his two closest friends over the years, but this is different This is very exciting. I mean, I'm not worried about him being antisocial in the grand scheme of things or anything. He is only sixteen and he is a gamer and has many online friends, as well as his two close friends he's known since kindergarten. But I am extremely happy for him to be getting out of the house and actually physically hanging out with kids his own age.

My heart warms. I'll have to remember to go easy on him when he returns. Not to demonstrate too much enthusiasm, or pepper him with too many questions, or he'll clam up and tell me nothing. Teenagers are like cats. They'll come to you when they're good and ready.

There is always tomorrow morning, my favourite day of the week.

Sunday.

Hot chocolates, blankets and chats on the couch together has been a routine of ours since my son was a toddler and rose early each morning to watch *Peppa Pig* on ABC Kids.

Gabriel is still an early riser, like me, even on Sundays, which I thoroughly enjoy now that he's a teenager and spends a lot of his time online.

My husband, Joe, likes to sleep in on his days off, which is fine by me because it allows time for me to catch up with Gabriel alone.

But Joe does spoil us with a fully cooked breakfast once he wakes up. His scrambled eggs and crispy bacon are to die for.

When I first met Joe, he was a chef at a modern Italian restaurant where I'd started working when I first moved here just shy of eighteen. He used to sing while he cooked. That's how I noticed him – I think I fell in love with his voice first.

Oh, how I miss that Joe. Passionate Joe. Joe with the sparkle in his eyes. Joe who used to touch me with those sensual hands of his. Joe who used to growl into my neck with the promise of a night of ardent lovemaking.

I sigh and swallow down the dregs of my wine while my eyes drink up the inky sky.

There's something about the sky that I've always loved. I've always thrilled at the vastness of it. Even as a little girl, I would wake up in the early hours of the morning and stare out my window to watch the sky change colours as the sun came up with the promise of a new day.

But it's the silken black night sky that's always been my favourite.

The stars make me think of my parents – my real parents, whom I never got to meet seeing as they both had passed away before I'd turned eighteen, the age I was legally allowed to make contact if I wished. Both drug addicts.

Are they up there? Are they proud of me? Do they even know me? Do they know about that time in my life I'd rather forget? Do they watch Gabriel grow? Do they laugh and cry with me? Or are they up there, finally at peace with themselves, leaving me to work out life for myself.

When I was a child, I'd make up fantasies about my birth parents. I'd imagine them both tall and beautiful with long fair hair and dark chocolate brown eyes. They were so young, with such promising futures, that their parents had forbade them to keep me. But they spent every waking moment searching for little baby me after I was taken away from them, until their sadness at being kept apart from their only child caused them to turn down the dark path of drugs and to eventually overdose together, in an almost romantic Romeo and Juliet manner, their last waking thoughts of me, their beloved daughter.

The truth, of course, is that they simply walked out of the hospital, without giving me a name and without ever looking back. But I've told myself that fantasy enough times over the course of my lifetime that it has become my own version of the truth and feels as real as if it had truly happened.

I smile and whisper an 'I love you' to them and decide to go inside and find my husband. Maybe he's up for a cuddle and a movie. One thing I can say about Joe is that for what he lacks in the marital bedroom, he certainly makes up for with cuddles and loving affection. He's like a big soft teddy bear in that regard and I can't get enough of it.

* * *

Ten minutes later we're both sharing a blanket and I'm encased in Joe's strong, warm arms while we watch *The Shining*.

A large bowl of microwave popcorn rests on my lap, and for now, this is enough. I am satisfied, I tell myself. I am loved. And it feels wonderful. As wonderful and as comforting as the lovely, buttery scent of the popcorn on my lap.

That is, until somebody knocks on our front door. Quick, loud, frantic knocks.

Joe glances at his phone. 'Gabriel's not due back for another two hours.'

A boy from Gabriel's class, Leo, not one of his usual friends, is dropping Gabriel home.

I met Leo for the first time earlier this evening. Turned out he was invited too and needed a lift to the party and asked Gabriel if he could get a ride. Of course, Gabriel had said yes. He described Leo as a loner with not a single friend at school. He'd been kept down a grade and many of the kids at school chose to remind him of this frequently according to Gabriel, who felt bad for Leo. Anyway, I was happy to pick the kid up and deliver both boys to the party.

But something about the boy once I met him... his vibe in the car... it felt off. Call it mother's intuition, but despite his politeness and his neat outward appearance, something about this boy seemed not quite right. I kept catching his pale green eyes fixed on me, unblinking, from the rear-view mirror. I mean, he's just a kid, a harmless, pimply teenager. But it was still unsettling.

I even messaged Gabriel after I'd dropped them off at the party to ask if he wanted me to pick him up from the party myself, instead of Leo's mum or dad – people I've never met since Leo had asked to be picked up from a cafe near his home instead of his actual house, which of course had me suspicious that the boy was hiding something or perhaps ashamed of where he lived.

But Gabriel hasn't answered my text. And maybe I'm just being the worrywart that he's always calling me.

The knocks on the door turn into incessant bangs.

'Who could it be?' I whisper, setting my mug of tea on the coffee table, my heart pounding. In an instant my mind is conjuring up the horrible possibility that the police may be at our front door and that something terrible may have happened to Gabriel. That he's perhaps at a hospital getting his stomach pumped right this very minute.

'I'll get it,' says Joe, standing up, shoulders back and chest out as he approaches the front door. 'Probably just kids mucking around.'

'Mum. Dad. Open up!'

'It's Gabriel!' I jump up from the couch as Joe unlocks the front door.

As I step into the hallway Gabriel bolts into the house and slams into me. His skin is hot and sweaty through his T-shirt. A shirt we'd shopped for together, last weekend, especially for the party.

'Hey.' I gently touch his arms. I can feel his lean muscles coiled tight beneath his skin. 'Slow down. Hey, are you okay?'

'Sorry,' he says, head down, his mop of dark curls, like his father's, falling over his eyes so that I can't see them. 'I'm fine. I'm just tired, okay. I'm going straight to bed.'

'What do you mean? It's only nine o'clock. Why are you home so early?' I start to follow him but Joe puts a gentle hand on my shoulder as I watch Gabriel disappear into the hallway.

'Leave him for a minute. Something's happened. Maybe he got embarrassed in front of a girl. He had no marks on him so he hasn't been hurt physically. Maybe we should leave it. He is a teenager after all.'

I turn around and Joe shrugs. We often joke that we have to lie to other parents about the whole eyeroll-rebellious-rude-teenager thing. Because Gabriel has never given us any kind of stereotypical teenage grief.

Maybe Joe's right. Maybe it's time for Gabriel to start behaving like a real teenager. And for us to step aside and allow it.

But now my pulse is a deafening roar in my ears and I know that I can't leave it at that. I just need to know. I need to know what happened to my sweet, cheery boy to make him race into his room like that.

I also need to know... oh God, that he hasn't seen it.

My heart races in panic while Joe stares at me like I've lost my mind. But of course, he doesn't know my greatest fear.

Since Gabriel got his first digital device at age twelve, I've taken great care to ensure that various parental locks prevent him from watching porn.

But teenagers these days, they're so tech-smart, they know their way around these things. And even if he hasn't managed to unlock it at home, there's nothing to stop someone from showing it to him. Someone at the party for instance.

Oh God.

As my panic levels rise, I remember what I've learned from one of my favourite YouTube therapists.

I close my eyes and take a deep breath, several of them in fact, and slowly but surely, my heart relaxes and my fears fade... a little.

Nobody would recognise me as that girl from the video. I look completely different now. Plus, only a few of Gabriel's friends have met me face to face. A lot of his new gamer friends are teenagers from across the globe that I may never even meet.

Joe raises his brows at me and smiles. He knows me too well – well, not that well. At least, for all the porn he watches he's never given me any indication that he's ever stumbled across that video. But he knows how much I worry about Gabriel. He knows that sometimes I can wrap him up in a little too much cotton wool.

He gently strokes my cheek then kisses my nose.

'Give him ten minutes. Just to cool down. Then you can go in.'

I sigh. 'Okay.'

After ten excruciatingly long minutes, I take my mug of now lukewarm tea, tip it down the kitchen sink and then go directly to my son's bedroom.

I brace myself and gently knock on his door.

No light beams out from beneath it and he doesn't answer me.

'Gabriel, can I come in?' I ask.

After a few long, drawn out seconds, I get a response.

'Okay. But I'm trying to get to sleep.'

As soon as I enter the dark room, I can tell that Gabriel has been crying. The hallway light is all I need to see that his face is blotchy and damp.

'Are you okay?' I ask softly. The mattress creaks as I sit on the edge of it.

'I'm fine, Mum. Just tired.'

'Did something happen? You can tell me. You can tell me anything, love. You know that.'

Gabriel sniffs and he sinks lower beneath the doona so that I can't see his whole face.

'It just finished early. That's all.'

I know this isn't true. Teenage parties don't typically finish at 9pm. But I can't push him. What happened has obviously shaken him.

'Oh, well... that must have been pretty disappointing for you.'

I notice that his phone is face down on his bedside table. He's never put it face down before. It keeps vibrating.

'Would you like me to put your phone on charge?'

'No! I mean, sorry, but... no. It doesn't need charging. Just leave it. Now can I go to sleep? Please?'

The phone continues to vibrate and I have to resist the urge to just pick it up and check the notifications. But I could never betray my son's trust.

I reach out and stroke his hair and brush a stray curl away from his forehead. He doesn't recoil in disgust at my touch.

I sigh with relief.

He hasn't seen it. Gabriel doesn't know my horrible secret.

But still, I feel selfish for feeling relieved. Something is deeply troubling Gabriel and I just wish that I could fix it for him. But of course I can't push him now. That would be cruel. I need to give it a rest. He'll tell me when he's ready. The main thing is that he's home and back under our roof, safe and sound with the two people who love him most.

'Okay, love. You have a good sleep and I'll see you in the morning.'

* * *

Later that night, after I remove my coloured contact lenses, I peer over the dark rims of my prescription glasses and spy pale blonde roots coming through at my

11

scalp, so stark in contrast to my glossy raven waves that it almost looks as though I'm going bald or at least thinning. Damn. Since I've been taking these new skin collagen vitamins, my hair has been growing a lot faster. The bonus being that my skin has never looked so radiant. I look ten years younger – at least. But I'll have to open up another box dye a week earlier than usual.

Nobody has seen my natural blonde hair in over twenty years.

He was the last person to see it, to touch it. And the memory of it still turns my blood, my body, my skin cold.

Brunette me is the new me – the only me that exists now. The determined girl with the fresh box-dye job who arrived over twenty years ago in Perth with two hundred dollars in cash in her pocket and the name of an Italian restaurant, situated in the port town of Fremantle, who were looking to hire her – me – as a waitress.

Brunette me is a capable, confident woman named Daphne. Talented with numbers, bookish, observant, a horror-movie-lover... she keeps to herself but loves her husband and son more than anything in this world.

Blonde me – Anna Trinovic – the girl who presented her body, mind and soul on a platter for her narcissistic ex to feast on, is long gone... a grainy, poorly shot video is all that remains of her.

Daphne Dubois is here to stay.

And I want to keep it that way.

For the safety of my family, I need to keep it that way.

2

Gabriel

If only I hadn't said yes to that stupid party invite, I wouldn't be in this position. Now I can't even shut my eyes without seeing it. Without seeing her. If only I could unsee it.

Part of me is kind of glad that I was there. Because at least I covered her up before everyone barged into the room. But still. I can't handle this feeling. I feel sick, like I want to vomit every five seconds even though there's nothing to bring up. I can't eat. I can't sleep. I can't do anything except replay that night over and over.

What bothers me the most is that she may not even be aware of what happened to her. I mean, I'm not sure exactly what happened either. I just know it was bad.

And I feel sick every time I picture him leaning over her like that and seeing her face when she turned her head towards me... her dead eyes and her drooling mouth, the way her words came out slurred when she attempted to speak. She was so helpless. It makes me shiver and shake, and cry when I think about it too much.

I wish I had done more. I should have overcome my shyness and just gone up to her earlier on in the party and warned her to stay away from him.

I wish I'd known that he was one of those guys – whatever that means... I still don't know what actually happened. But it didn't look good. It felt wrong the moment I stepped into the room. Heavy. Bad. I'll never forget that smell of sweaty bodies, vomit and bourbon.

My stomach churns.

I wish I'd never turned up to the party with him. If only he hadn't asked me for a lift.

Yesterday I sat in front of my Xbox, the TV screen black, and my mum came and asked me what was wrong, for the millionth time, and I realised that I must have been sitting like that for hours.

My mum knows something's up. She's worried. And she's acting weird. But then again, my mum's always doing weird things. Like her hair. She dyed her roots again yesterday. She thinks I don't notice her trying to cover up the blonde bits every two weeks.

Mum's such an enigma. I can never work her out. Like she loves me and she loves Dad, and, as far as a mother-son relationship goes, ours is a pretty good one – we're much closer than most of my friends are with their mums. But there is still so much I don't know about her.

Most of the kids at school have their mums on Instagram... I suppose it's their parents' way of keeping tabs on what their kids are posting. But not my mum. She has nothing. No Facebook, no Instagram, no Twitter... she has zero social media.

Anyway, I'm glad she doesn't. I'm glad she doesn't know how bad social media can be. That she doesn't see all the crap that gets posted. That there are guys who find girls who are out of it and vulnerable like Catelyn was that night and take pictures of them and post them, or worse, take advantage of them in that state.

Great. Everyone saw me and Leo show up and leave the party together and they're going to think that I'm friends with him. That I was somehow involved with whatever it was that happened in that room.

Fuck. Fuck. Fuck.

My phone has been going crazy. But I've let it run flat. I'm too gutless to charge it, to look and see the messages, to see who has been texting me so incessantly and why.

I just want to forget that night. Pretend it didn't happen.

And why did I have to drink? I'm such an idiot. I've never even had a full drink before. Only half of Dad's beer once after I helped him mow the lawn. And on Saturday night I suddenly decide that I can handle tequila shots? I mean I only had a few and thought I felt pretty decent and not too drunk or anything. But now I'm not so sure.

It's made my memory of the party so foggy. That is, the events leading up to the room. What I saw in the room sobered me the hell up right away. That I can remember. But everything else before is hazy.

When I try to think too hard about it my heart feels like it's going to beat its way right out of my chest, just come tearing out through bone and flesh and skin. I'm that fucking scared. More scared than I've even been in my life. Of what I don't know.

I think it's the not knowing that scares me.

But then I think of Catelyn and hate to imagine how scared she must have felt when she woke up, and I feel worse for her. I should have done something. I should have maybe got onto her phone and called her parents. Asked them to come and pick her up and get her the hell out of that house.

What's she thinking right now? Does she even remember what happened?

Oh God, I hope she doesn't think I had anything to do with whatever happened. That I'm in any way friends with Leo.

My heart rate goes into overdrive again and I'm sweating. And my head is thumping so hard I feel like my brain is going to explode.

To tell you the truth.

I kind of hope it does.

Because right now, I just don't want to be here.

3

Daphne

I'm worried about my son. He's not himself.

I've tried everything. Even letting him game on non-gaming nights. But he just sits there staring into space whilst ignoring all the game party invites flashing up onto the television screen that his friends keep sending. Last night he didn't even bother turning the console on and just stared at the blank screen. I had to force a casual smile on my face to mask my concern as I passed him on the way to my bedroom, my heart fluttering in panic and my mind imagining the worst possible reason for my son to have been turned into this shadow version of himself.

Since Saturday night I haven't slept much and I've hardly eaten. I haven't even been able to work properly. I keep screwing up numbers because my mind is only on my son. All I can think about is the terror in my son's eyes when he rushed through the door that night. And the tears he tried to hide later.

Something happened that night. At the party. Something that has changed Gabriel.

Instead of our Sunday morning hot chocolate and chat on the couch the following day after that dreaded night, Gabe had stayed in bed, ignoring his vibrating phone until the battery died and it finally grew silent.

Since then, things have gone from bad to worse. The light has dimmed inside my sweet, sunny Gabriel... and it's getting dimmer with each passing day. I haven't seen his smile all week. I've missed it so much.

He has lost weight, too. This week I've discovered that he's a lot like me. When something is worrying him, he doesn't eat or sleep well.

Unlike Joe who has the ability to switch off no matter what.

Once, back in his chef days, Joe witnessed a fight between two kitchen hands – he'd even managed to wrestle the bloody knife out of the aggressor's hands.

That night, after a quick visit to hospital on his way home to be sure that the staff member who'd been rushed there was going to be okay, he arrived home, ate a bowl of leftover chocolate self-saucing pudding with vanilla ice cream, and then proceeded to flop into bed and snore himself silly for nine hours straight.

If only I could sleep so heavily after dramatic events.

I take a sip of my first coffee of the day, and shift around on the couch until I'm comfortable, then Gabriel enters the room, his dark hair dishevelled and his olive skin looking pasty.

'Can I stay home today? I'm not feeling the best.'

For a moment I'm speechless. It's the longest sentence my son has spoken to me since Saturday night. I clear my throat.

'Yes. Yes, love, of course you can.' I nurse my coffee in the palm of my hand, savouring its warmth and beam a smile at my handsome son. 'We can spend the day together. You can game if you like. Or we could watch Netflix and make some popcorn.'

I throw a glance outside the living room window and shiver at the gloomy-looking clouds looming. 'Looks like it's going to rain, too. Perfect for staying in.'

Gabriel stares at me for a few seconds, looking even paler than a moment ago, and I know now that I've scared him away with my enthusiasm.

'Actually, I think I have a test today... science. So, I should go.'

There's an awkward silence. It's so foreign to me. My son and I have never done awkwardness in the past.

'Of course,' I say, smiling brightly. 'You wouldn't want to miss out on the marks. I'll send some Panadol with you in case you need it.'

He nods, even though we both know he won't be needing the paracetamol as he isn't sick at all, and disappears down the hallway to get ready for school.

I guess he'd rather face another day at school than leave himself open to a heart-to-heart talk with me. Though it hurts, I understand completely. Whatever it is that has happened is obviously so horrific in his mind that he can't share it with me just yet. I'll just have to give him time.

After I rinse out my coffee mug and let it drain on the sink, I decide to get dressed and meet the new client who's booked a meeting to discuss having me manage his finances. Though I'd initially dreaded it when I first opened my eyes in bed this morning, I know that it'll be good for me to get out of the house. And it's not as though I'll have to do much – just introduce myself and explain what I can do for him. Half an hour of my time at the most.

It might do my head good to think about something else. And my stomach could do with a break too. All it's been doing is burning and twisting beneath my ribcage.

Gabriel refuses my offer of a lift to school and after I confirm via text the name of the coffee shop where I'm meeting Mr Ben Maxwell, I grab my briefcase and leave the house. Though I technically work from home, I've never had a client visit my private residence. I only ever meet them in public places and when I started my business several years ago, I specifically chose a cute little coffee shop in an entirely different suburb to conduct my business at. Much safer that way. I guess there's always a fear, in the back of my mind, that he, my ex, will book an appointment using an alias one day. And honestly, I'm not sure what I would do if I came face to face with him after so many years.

* * *

I'm greeted at the coffee shop with a big smile by the barista Sally, and the delicious, earthy aroma of my favourite beverage.

'The usual?' she asks with a wink.

'Thank you!' I smile and slip into my favourite booth seat by the window, which also gives me a great view of whomever I'm meeting as they enter. That way I can do a dash out the back door, via the restrooms, if my ex ever shows.

Sally brings me my coffee and after a bit of chit-chat about how her university degree is going, she leaves just as a handsome gentleman enters the cafe and glances around quickly before zeroing in on me with a single raised brow.

'Daphne?'

I stand and nod.

'Lovely to meet you, Ben,' I say, holding out my hand for him to shake.

He takes it and gives me a firm yet gentle shake, all the while staring at me intently.

'Have we met before?' he asks, drawing his hand back and rubbing at his chin. 'You look so familiar.'

Immediately the hairs on the back of my neck prickle and I feel the blood drain from my face. It's my default reaction whenever anybody asks this seemingly innocent question.

'No. I don't believe we have. I'm not originally from here.'

He smiles and waits for me to take a seat before he does.

My heart is pounding like mad. I'm certain he can hear it.

I look over at Sally and give her a nod and within seconds she's taking Ben's order for an almond milk latte, glancing at me from time to time, silently asking me if I'm okay. I smile at her briefly and it seems to satisfy her enough to leave us to go and make my prospective client's coffee.

Sally doesn't know why I'm the way I am, why I'm skittish around new people, around men especially; why I fear being recognised on a daily basis. But she and the other staff have known me long enough to perhaps sense my body language and recognise the way that I tense up whenever I meet someone new.

'I'm sure I know you,' he says, grinning now, almost flirtatiously. 'Or maybe you just look like an actress or something.' He shakes his head. 'Oh... I swear...'

Oh God. This is it. It's finally happening. He's about to recognise me from the video.

Abruptly I stand, the whoosh of my pulse in my ears louder than the sound of the cafe's coffee grinder.

'I'm so sorry, Ben,' I say, while he stares up at me looking completely puzzled, his dark eyes wide. 'But I'm going to have to leave. I haven't been well lately and I feel like I'm going to be sick. Tummy bug,' I add, before hastily scooping up my briefcase, my phone and my keys.

'Hang on, are you okay to drive?' he asks, calling after me as I rush out the door and onto the tree-lined street, leaving behind a bewildered-looking Sally and an even more bewildered-looking Ben.

Later that night, while Joe is in his study and Gabriel is in his bedroom listening to what can only be described as depressing music – not that I can talk as it's not dissimilar to what I used to listen to as a teen – my phone lights up with a text.

I freeze for a moment, wondering if it's Ben, declaring that he's finally remembered where he's seen me from.

But when I look, it's a number I don't recognise at all. I click on the text and read it.

> *Hi Daphne, I hope you don't mind me*
> *writing to you. But I just thought you*
> *needed to know.*

I set down my glass of wine.
My heart pounds as I punch out a reply.

Know what? Who is this?

It's Leo. Gabriel has been weird at school. He doesn't sit with his usual friends and just wanders around with his AirPods in. Something isn't right with him.

Leo. Leo from school. Leo who Gabriel attended the party with.

Maybe I can finally find out what happened that night.

Thank you, Leo. Thanks so much for reaching out.

No problem :-)

Has he been like this all week?

Pretty much. I've actually been wanting to write to you all week, but just wasn't sure if it was the right thing to do.

It is the right thing to do, Leo, and I can't thank you enough.

You're welcome :-)

May I ask how you got my phone number?

There was a business card on the floor of your car the other night. I picked it up and was going to give it to Gabriel, but forgot. I'm sorry.

It's okay. I'm just glad you reached out. It's so kind of you. I've been

*worried about Gabriel since Saturday
night. Do you know what happened?*

*Not really. Just that he suddenly
wanted to go home. I'm sorry Daphne,
I wish I could be more helpful. I'm
probably just wasting your time.*

*No, no. Not at all. Honestly, I'm just so
glad you reached out. It's very mature
of you to do so. And kind.*

He takes a while to respond.

*Nobody has ever said that about me
before.*

I'm not sure what to say to that. He sounds a bit
lonely, and maybe needy, to be honest.

*Well, I'm sure your parents are super
proud of you.*

*They're never around, so I wouldn't
know.*

Oh, I'm sorry to hear that.

I'm not sure how to end the conversation. I mean, I'm
glad that he has reached out and it's good to have a bit
of a window into the side of Gabriel's life to which I
have no access. But I feel a bit weird chatting to Leo.
Almost like I'm betraying Gabriel by speaking to a boy
he claims he doesn't know well despite attending the
party on Saturday night together.

*Don't be sorry. I'm fine. I'm pretty
good at looking after myself and I'm a
pretty good cook.*

He sends a long stream of food emojis. I smile at my
phone. He seems like a nice kid. And the fact that he
reached out with concerns about my Gabriel warms me

to him. I almost feel guilty for thinking there was something off about him when I first met him.

'Maybe you can teach Gabriel to make something one day,' I text, adding an egg emoji and a chicken leg.

He sends me a blushing smiley and I decide to wind up the conversation.

> *Well, I'm off to bed. Thank you so much for reaching out, Leo. I appreciate it so much. Please let me know if you hear anything about the party or what it is that's bothering Gabriel. Again, thank you so much.*

> *Oh. It's only nine o'clock. That's pretty early to go to bed. But okay.*

I decide to leave it at that and open up my Kindle. I've got so many books on my to-be-read list, I should make a start. A good psychological thriller to take my mind off things. Or a perhaps a nice romance.

But five minutes into the book, my phone lights up with a text again.

It's from Leo and simply says, 'Goodnight.'

At that moment Joe emerges from the study, shuffling down the hallway in his pyjama shorts and his favourite old, ripped T-shirt which still bears yesterday morning's coffee stain.

'You okay?' I ask, when I see him frowning and rubbing his forehead.

'Headache,' he says, but he's staring at my phone. 'Who's that at this hour?' he asks.

For a moment I freeze as though I've been caught having an illicit affair. I lie all the same. Because something doesn't feel quite right about texting a seventeen-year-old boy.

'Oh, the client from this morning. I had a bit of a tummy bug and I cancelled on him,' I say, my skin growing cold at the memory of Ben today, the way he'd tried to recall where he'd seen my face. The man will probably be resting his head against his pillow as he's drifting off to sleep tonight and it'll finally come to him. He'll know where he's seen me before and then at least one person will know. And that's one too many.

Joe keeps staring at my phone. 'What does he want?'

'Oh, just to reschedule.'

'Are you going to text him back?'

I look at Joe, really look at him. It's unlike him to behave like this, almost jealous... or at least suspicious.

'I've already sorted it. He's just confirming a new time. I'll text him in the morning.' I spring up from the couch and give Joe a quick hug and rub the back of his neck gently.

'Let me get you some paracetamol.'

His shoulders relax and he sighs. 'Thanks, love. I'm so lucky I've got you looking out for me. I don't know what I'd do without you.' He pulls back and shakes his head. 'Sometimes I don't even think I deserve someone as perfect as you, Daphne.'

I try my best to hold his loving gaze, but inside my head a voice is screaming. Reminding me that I'm far from perfect and that I'll never ever truly be Daphne, the woman my husband loves so much.

Because Daphne is only a mask.

And after so many years, why am I beginning to feel her slip?

4

Catelyn

Ever since the party, I've had a strange feeling that other people, or someone, knows something that I don't. I almost get the feeling that I'm being watched. But here I am in the hallway at school and nobody's eyes are actually on me – everyone is far too busy either talking to their friends or peeking into their blazers, trying to hide the fact that they're on their phones.

My cheeks flush at the memory of Saturday night – or lack of it. All I know is that I woke up in Jack's little brother's bedroom. It was dark and I was alone. I could smell a boy on me and I felt dizzy and ran out of the room and just made it to the bathroom in time to throw up in the bathtub.

Exactly who I'd been with I wouldn't know. I can't recall who I'd been chatting to or anything. Nothing. I can't even remember walking through the front door despite being completely straight when I'd done so.

The worst part is I'm not sure how I ended up in the bedroom and I hate that I've given everyone all the more reason to agree that yes, I'm the whore they've always thought I was.

So much for changing my ways. I'd sworn only the night before that I'd give up drinking. But then, that morning, I'd decided to allow myself one drink at the party. Just one drink to banish the nerves and to boost my courage. And bam... I'd obviously decided to keep drinking and had hooked up with God knows who.

The funny thing is, nobody has claimed it. Most guys talk about their conquests, so who is this guy that scored and isn't sharing. I'm almost intrigued by the fact that he's not bragging.

The worst part is, and it's the part that terrifies me, is that he didn't use protection. And even though I've slept with a fair number of guys since I lost my virginity last year, we'd always used protection. Why not with this guy? What on earth possessed me to okay raw sex?

I wonder if he's from school or if he's just a party rando.

That familiar prickle of shame climbs up the back of my neck and I inwardly curse myself for drinking and allowing myself to get so out of it that I had another one-night stand.

Because I just want to do better. Treat myself better because I deserve more respect than this.

Of course. Sex is okay and I enjoy it enough, and I haven't regretted my sexual awakening and all the good times that have come with it. But I want the intimacy and the romance with it too. I've got so much more to offer than just my body. I want more now. I want a friend. A companion. Someone to snuggle up with and talk into the early hours of the morning. Someone to laugh with. Someone to love. Not a guy who is okay sleeping with a girl who is so out of it that she can't remember the act the next day.

It's just not right.

I walk into Maths, feeling like crap, and wait for any tell-tale whispers or looks, but my heart stops when I catch eyes with Gabriel Dubois.

Oh my God. I remember his face. In the dark. Wait... and then a flash. Had he taken photos of me?

Gabriel?

He just does not seem like the kind of guy to do that.

My face heats up but I'm betting I'm not as red as his face has just turned now that he's seen me.

Okay, so, he's just as embarrassed.

Maybe he knows something.

Or maybe…

The teacher calls for quiet and yells at us to sit down, but Gabriel does the opposite. His eyes to the floor, he picks up his bag and rushes out the classroom, the teacher calling after him.

I want to follow him. I want to ask what happened. I want to know if it was him and I want to know what I drank and how I got so wiped out.

But our teacher is furious now and shaking his head and I don't want to test him. I'm one note of concern away from a Friday afternoon detention and I've got work at 4pm so it's a no-can-do.

I'll just have to wait. Maybe I'll message him later. If I get the guts.

More flashes of the night return. Seeing his face seems to have triggered them, triggered hazy memories. I recall the scent of someone, a boy, mostly pine-scented deodorant, and the burning taste of something acidic in my throat. I remember the heat of my skin too, my whole body, the feeling that my brain was on fire, and then, the drowsiness.

But I can't remember any other visions of Gabriel other than his face, his eyes wide, peering down at me in the dark.

But Gabriel?

He just doesn't seem like the type. I honestly don't even know much about him other than that he's completely obsessed with gaming. I don't think he's ever even dated a girl. And to be honest, Saturday night was the first time I'd ever seen him show up to a party.

I shake my head and open my laptop and try to concentrate on what the teacher is saying, but all I can think about is Gabriel.

Gabriel Dubois.

Why was he looking down at me?

Did we?

Or did we not?

5

Daphne

It's 5pm and I'm sauteing minced garlic and bacon in extra virgin olive oil for a quick pasta.

Joe messaged half an hour ago to say that he'll be home late tonight and will grab a bite to eat on the way home. It's very unlike Joe. He never works late and I'm unsure how I feel about this latest turn of events.

He was funny with me this morning; stand-offish, almost. And last night his strange hostility to seeing my phone light up with a message was more than odd. Very un-Joe-like.

My stomach growls as I pour in the thickened cream and stir the bubbling sauce.

'Gabriel,' I holler across the living room from the kitchen, excited at the prospect of dinner alone with my son.

I've got a bottle of white wine on the table and I plan to allow him a tiny bit mixed with water, like my foster grandmother used to mix for me with a wink when I was a teen.

My phone, which is currently playing *The Killing Moon* and is sitting in a large soup mug doubling as a speaker, pings as a message comes through.

It's from Gabriel. He's been doing this ever since Saturday night. I call out to him from the hallway, or ask him a question, and he responds via text.

> *I'm not hungry. I think I do actually have a bit of a bug... from this morning still.*

I sigh at my phone and turn the music up. So much for the heart-to-heart chat I'd been hoping for.

I pour myself extra wine and set to work draining the pasta.

I'll just have to keep trying. Because there is no way I'm giving up on my son.

A warm cloud of steam caresses then stings my face as I upend the hot pasta into the strainer, during which my phone pings again, then again and again.

I set down the saucepan and, with a fluttery hope in my heart, pick up my phone, hoping that Gabriel has had a change of heart.

My breath catches in my throat, and then disappointment weighs my shoulders down.

The messages are from Leo. Asking if we can talk. Three times.

My stomach swirls with dread. I don't know why. But I'm torn between wanting to know what happened on Saturday night, but also being frightened of what I'll hear.

> *Hello, Leo. Is everything okay?*

Though it's nice to have somebody looking out for Gabriel, especially while he's not saying much to me, I'm hoping once things get back to normal and Gabriel is back on his feet that this texting stops. It feels like a betrayal to my own child to be speaking behind his back like this. It's just not right.

> *Kind of. But kind of not. I need to speak to you. I need to tell you something. It's about Gabriel.*

> *Okay. Yes, please tell me.*

My heart thuds loudly in my eardrums.

*Can you meet me at that cafe where
you picked me up before that party?
Let's say 8pm?*

A prickle of apprehension creeps up my spine.

What about your parents?

*They are both away on business.
Conferences. I'm home alone. Unless
you'd prefer to come to my house? I
can make a pretty good cappuccino.*

*No. Without your parents there, it
wouldn't be right for me to come to
your house.*

*Okay. Well, I suppose it will have to be
the cafe with its bitter coffee. But
that's okay I guess.*

He seems a bit miffed that I'm not coming to his house.

My skin grows cold. This absolutely doesn't feel right. I mean, I know that Leo means well, but, again, this feels like such a betrayal to Gabriel to be meeting Leo behind his back, to discuss him.

But he's my son and I'll do anything to help him, even if it means meeting this strange friend of his, so I quickly tap out a quick 'Yes. See you there', and take another gulp of wine for courage.

I'm not sure if I want to know the truth about Saturday... but there's no backing out now.

I stare at my phone, willing Gabriel to message that he's had a change of heart and is coming out to join me at the dinner table. Because then I could cancel on Leo and it can just be Gabriel and me tonight. Mother and son, working together to make things right again.

But the minutes tick by and before I know it the pasta has cooled and I've been staring at my phone for ages while a myriad of possible explanations for

Gabriel's behaviour Saturday and post Saturday night flicker through my brain.

I sigh and give the strainer a shake and loosen up the pasta before tipping it into the sauce and gently heating it all up together.

At least in an hour's time, I'll be closer to the truth.

6

Daphne

'Where are you off to?' Joe asks.

It's 7.45pm and I'm in the bathroom winding my raven hair into a low bun. Joe just got home and he smells like beer.

'How was work?' I ask, trying not to sound like I doubt that he's been at work, and also carefully deflecting his question.

'Good. Really good. We just discussed some new plans for the business. Some new ideas.'

'Oh.' I adjust my blazer and appraise my reflection. It is actually a strange thing, choosing what to wear, and quite difficult at that. What do you choose to wear to a clandestine meeting with a teenage boy you don't really want to be meeting up with?

I appraise myself in the full-length mirror and I'm happy with my blazer and blue jeans combination.

'What kind of ideas?' I ask, turning to face him.

He shrugs. 'Oh, nothing worth mentioning. It'll bore you, to be honest.'

'Okay. Well, I'm off. Just a quick coffee with the girls.'

'Oh, I thought Linda was at dinner with Geoff tonight?'

'Yeah, she is. These are book club girls.'

'Right-o. But you haven't touched that new book you've got. Not since Saturday anyway.'

I look away. He's just as perceptive as me.

'Oh, yes, well, I'll just quickly google the summary when I park,' I say with a wink.

'Cheeky girl,' he says and I detect a hint of sadness in his gaze.

Something is not right with my husband and I almost feel like cancelling. But I can't very well keep a teenage boy waiting. It could be dangerous for him being out at night, especially while his parents are away. And I need to find out what's up with Gabriel so that I can right it.

'Let's watch a movie when I get back. I won't be long,' I say, stretching up on my tiptoes to give him a peck on his nose.

'Sounds lovely,' he says, and for a moment, he looks as though he's going to tell me something, but then he shakes his head. 'Okay. Well, you go off and enjoy yourself and I'll see you when you get back.'

'Okay. There is a whole heap of pasta in the pot for you. Gabriel hasn't come out of his room to eat. Maybe you can try and lure him out. He might feel more comfortable sharing whatever's bothering him with you.'

'I'll try.' He kisses me back, on the lips, and smiles. 'Now go.'

I feel marginally better now that he's smiling. But still. Something isn't right with Joe. Could it be work stress? Or something else?

Maybe after I've spoken to Leo, and hopefully I'm able to help Gabriel, I can start focussing on Joe and our marriage.

When I arrive at the cafe, there's only one customer inside, and it's Leo, hunched over his phone in a corner booth, the blue light illuminating his face. He really needs to improve his posture and sit up straighter otherwise he's going to muck up his spine.

Leo steps out of the booth and stands when I enter – he's extremely tall – and waits for me to slide in before he sits back down. Very old-school manners. It's nice. It can't be too bad at home if his parents have brought him up with such lovely manners.

'Shall I order our drinks?' he asks, sliding the menu towards me.

'I'll just have a latte, thanks.' I take out my purse and hand over a $10 note. 'My shout.' But he waves my money away and proceeds to the counter.

What a strange boy, I think. So adult but also so... something else I can't put my finger on. Just different.

Beneath my blazer I shiver a little. But I'm not sure if I'm actually cold or just dreading what I'm about to hear.

Leo returns and over the busy sounds of our coffees being made, he asks me how I am.

'I'm doing okay, thanks.'

'How are you?' I ask him.

He sighs and spreads out his long-fingered hands in front of him. 'I'm okay, but... but I'm worried about Gabriel.'

I nod, encouraging him to continue even though my heart is in my throat.

'He's getting worse. I think he really needs a friend.'

The coffees arrive and we thank the waiter in unison.

'Jinx,' Leo says, smiling at me over his hot chocolate.

He holds out a pinkie finger.

'Come on, we need to make a wish together.'

'Oh.'

I put down my coffee cup and reluctantly entwine my pinkie with Leo's. His finger is icy cold. This feels strangely intimate and I glance out the window half-expecting Joe to be standing out there, or worse, Gabriel.

Leo closes his eyes while he wishes and I decide to do the same. My wish is of course for Gabriel to be okay and, whatever the problem is, for me to be able to help him through it.

Leo tightens his finger around mine and I open my eyes and find him staring at me intently, before I tug my finger free from his grasp.

'Okay. Back to Gabriel,' I say, unable to hide my full-body shiver. 'You mentioned he needs a friend. I know that several of them have been trying to reach out, on the Xbox and on his phone but he's refusing to answer it.'

'I know. That's why I asked you to meet. I have an idea how I can help Gabriel.' He takes a sip of his hot chocolate and puts it back down, his elegant fingers trembling a little.

'I thought it might be nice if I come over... maybe tomorrow afternoon. I can hang out and maybe help you to cook dinner and try to get Gabriel talking.'

My stomach contracts a little. I know Gabriel would hate it if Leo came over – he hasn't even wanted any of his close friends around, let alone this boy that I've never heard Gabriel mention until recently. He had told me himself, before the party, that he'd only agreed to give Leo a lift to the party because he'd felt sorry for him because he doesn't really have many friends.

'Well, I'll see. I'd need to run it by Gabriel first, of course. But it's so lovely of you to want to give up your time to help him to get better. I really appreciate it.' I take several long gulps of my coffee, burning my tongue. I want this clandestine meeting over and done with. I want to get back to Joe and Gabriel. Even though Leo is being kind, I just know my son too well. He's not going to say yes.

I shiver again. This whole meeting and Leo's future plans to hang out with Gabriel are starting to feel intrusive and claustrophobic.

'Okay, well, text me later tonight after you've asked him,' Leo says, his green eyes glowing with intent.

I nod, take another long gulp of my coffee and notice that Leo frowns and takes a tiny sip of his hot chocolate, which is mostly full still.

'I might not get a chance to ask him tonight, but I will in the morning,' I say, then I drain my coffee cup, so quickly that a tiny drop of coffee escapes my mouth and dribbles down my chin.

Leo watches me wipe my chin and then shifts his gaze down to his hot chocolate.

'I'm a slow drinker. Sorry. I was actually going to ask you for a lift home, but I can see you're in a rush.'

I detect a hint of disappointment in his voice and I feel bad all of a sudden. Here he is trying to help my son, and with no parents at home. My motherly instinct kicks into overdrive.

'Oh, I'm sorry, Leo. How rude of me. You take your time and enjoy that hot chocolate. And of course, I'll drive you home. It's the least I can do.'

Leo smiles into his hot chocolate and I detect a hint of blush in his cheeks.

He's not so bad, just a little shy and introverted.

'You know, Gabriel loves hot chocolate too. We drink hot chocolate every Sunday morning. It's our little ritual... a way to catch up on the week.' I sigh and wonder if we'll ever do that again. The way Gabriel's been since that party, I find it hard to imagine us going back to that level of closeness.

'I wish I could drink hot chocolate with my mum.'

I clear my throat. Feeling bad now for rubbing my and Gabriel's relationship in Leo's face.

'So, what do your parents do for a living?'

Leo visibly stiffens and sets his mug down a little too hard.

'Can we not talk about them please?' His voice catches a little.

I give him a sympathetic glance. He's just a kid really. A vulnerable child. And he's staying at home alone. Life must get pretty lonely for him.

'It must be tough being on your own while they're away.'

He shrugs. 'You get used to it.'

'Yes,' I say absentmindedly, thinking back to my own childhood and the aching hollow I often felt inside, the pangs of loneliness.

He takes another long sip of his hot chocolate and I wonder if I'm the one making him uncomfortable now. I glance away as he takes several long gulps until the mug is drained. He sets it down with a sigh and looks at me, his head hanging down a little, his shoulders drooping as though he wants to just shrink into his body, into the booth and just disappear.

'It's nice that you care. It's nice to be cared about.'

My heart squeezes. The poor kid.

'I'm sure your parents care about you very much. They must be so proud of what a kind young man you've turned out to be.'

He shrinks into himself even more.

'Maybe.'

The barista, who's been sweeping beneath the other tables, heads our way with a broom and I wonder if it's closing time soon.

I clear my throat. My head is already back home with Gabriel and Joe.

'I think it's time we head home,' I say smiling.

He stares down at the table and picks at a piece of chipped laminate.

'Okay.'

Part of me wants to sweep him up into my arms and invite him to stay at our home and give him the full-blown family experience, but the other part of me knows how horrified Gabriel would be to find Leo in our home.

Besides, I'm sure his parents love him very much and they are working so hard to provide for him. Sure, it must be hard to be home alone for a lot of the time, but imagine how wonderfully independent he must be at such a young age?

I've always wondered if working from home has allowed me to baby Gabriel a little too much. Maybe I need to take a leaf out of Leo's parents' book and not be so available.

Leo stands and I'm struck again by how tall he is. Leo's height reminds me of my ex and I shudder as I recall how I used to feel in his company towards the end of our relationship. Vulnerable and small. Like I didn't matter. Like I was a pest he could crush between his thumb and index finger.

We exit the cafe and step out into the vast, empty carpark, and I smile at how fast the barista managed to lock the door behind us and flip the OPEN sign to CLOSED.

The black night is emphasised by the closed, unlit supermarket next door, and surrounding shops. I shiver. The autumn air has a chill to it and I quickly unlock the car and get in.

Leo smiles as he climbs into the passenger seat and buckles his seat belt. He rubs his hands up and down his long, slim, denim-clad thighs.

'I like this car,' he says. 'It smells nice.' He taps at the little vanilla-scented tree swinging from my rear-view mirror.

'That's Gabriel's favourite scent,' I say, grinning.

The smile vanishes from Leo's face and he turns to stare out the passenger window, almost morosely. I notice how cramped his legs look.

'You can slide the seat back if you like. You look so uncomfortable.'

His hand disappears down the side of the seat and after a couple of clicks, he slides back a few inches and smiles, staring into his lap. 'Thanks.'

'Do you have any siblings, Leo?' I ask as I pull out onto the main road. It's not that late, but the streets are virtually empty.

He remains quiet for half a minute before he nods.

'Yes. A brother. But he died.'

'Oh.' My heart drops. 'Oh, I'm so sorry, Leo.'

Poor Leo in his lonely house with the ghost of a brother who has died. A huge sadness weighs down upon my heart for this boy. No wonder he's so shy, so strange, so introverted. He's been through a harsh loss already and he's not yet an adult.

'It's okay. It happened when I was little. I hardly remember him.'

'Still, I'm sorry.'

We drive for about a minute in silence until I realise that I need directions.

Leo must have also realised this.

'Turn left up ahead. Then it's a quick right and a quick left.'

I follow his directions.

'That's my house, number eight,' he says as I slow down and pull into the driveway of a grand, modern, triple-storey home.

'What a beautiful home, Leo. You must love it. I bet it's stunning inside.'

'You can come in and have a look if you like?' He smiles at me, his eyes lit up in hope.

'Oh, I'm sorry, I'd better get home before Gabriel and Joe worry about me.'

Leo looks like a kitten who's been kicked.

'But how about I come in and have a look next time?'

'Next time?' He nods and seems satisfied with that. 'Maybe you can come over with Gabriel.'

'Maybe. And if your mum and dad are home you can introduce me to them.'

He frowns. 'If they're ever home.'

I smile sympathetically and he nods, his hand on the open passenger door.

'Thanks for the lift, Daphne,' he says, holding my gaze.

I smile.

'You're most welcome, Leo. I'll wait in the driveway until you've gone inside.'

'Okay. And I'll text you after I've checked all the rooms to be sure there's no murderer waiting for me.'

'Oh God. Yes. Please text me to say that you're safe and sound. And maybe you could text me your mother's number, too. So that I can introduce myself. I don't want her thinking that some random woman is texting her precious son.'

He smiles softly as he bends down to look at me from outside the vehicle.

'Precious,' he says, with a small laugh. 'I really like that. Even if I'm far from it.'

'Of course you're precious. Every child is precious to their parents.' I smile and grip the steering wheel. 'Well, take care, Leo. Thanks for the coffee and the update on Gabriel. I really appreciate it.'

'No problem. Say hi to Gabriel and remember to ask him about me coming over tomorrow.'

'Will do.'

Leo watches me as I reverse a little way out the driveway before I reach the end and hover. Then he walks to the front door and lets himself in, turning on the hallway light and waving at me from the front door.

I beep and drive away, knowing already that there is no way that Gabriel is going to allow me to invite Leo into our home. Not tomorrow or ever. Even if he wasn't going through a tough time like he is now, he still wouldn't want it.

When I get home, Joe is in the shower so I go and check on Gabriel.

The lights are out in his room and I knock on his door and then gently twist it open only to find him under the doona, looking far too stiff to be sleeping.

'Goodnight, Gabriel,' I whisper, praying that Joe had managed to reach out to him while I'd been gone, seeing as I didn't really get much out of Leo tonight.

I close the bedroom door and return to the kitchen where Joe has left his phone resting on the benchtop.

It lights up and I quickly glance at it.

The initials N.F. pop up.

I haven't heard him mention anyone with a name beginning with N at work before.

Another message pops up from N.F.

Why the initials? It seems so strange.

I know Joe's password, but years ago, very early on in our relationship, we made a promise that we'd never snoop on each other's phones, as we both agreed it's an invasion of privacy. We also agreed that if we ever felt the need to want to check, we'd air our urges to each other and discuss the reason behind it like mature adults. Trust is huge in our relationship. And yes, I know

40

that he has a porn addiction and impotence relating to that. But I'm worried if I bring it up that it'll worsen the issue and there'll be no chance of us getting our intimacy back.

So, I'm going to assume N.F. is a work colleague and leave it at that.

A yawn escapes my lips. I'm exhausted and I don't have the energy to deal with a heavy conversation after my meet-up with Leo. And to be honest, I hate that I've shared more words with Leo today than I have my own son. I feel... irritated all of a sudden.

And now that I think about it. Leo didn't exactly enlighten me tonight. He didn't offer any new information that can enable me to help Gabriel. All he really did was invite himself over to our house, which I've already decided is a big fat no. I'm not even going to bother asking Gabriel as I know what the answer will be. I know him too well and I take comfort in that at least. It makes me feel close to him still, my beautiful boy.

I make myself a cup of tea and, unable to wait for my turn in the shower, because Joe takes forever, I slip into my favourite pyjamas – dark blue flannelette dotted with tiny white stars, a Mother's Day gift from Gabriel two years ago – and sit up in bed, cradling the warm mug in my hand while I tell myself that tomorrow will be a better day.

But then my phone lights up and I remember Leo saying that he was going to text me.

I open the text. It's an image. A selfie.

Leo sitting up in bed with reading glasses on and a book in his hand.

> *All safely tucked in bed. Thanks again*
> *for tonight :-)*

Oh Leo, I think. You should be sending this message to your own mother, not me.

I text back a quick 'Goodnight', but inwardly groan when I get a text back almost a second later.

*Did you ask Gabriel about me coming
over tomorrow after school?*

I sigh and tap out a reply.

*I'm sorry, Leo, Gabriel still wants to be
alone so I think we should respect his
need for space right now. But thank
you so much for being such a kind
friend to him. I really appreciate it.*

'That's a shame,' he writes back. 'And you're
welcome,' he adds, with a blushing smiley.

I hit 'like' on the message, because it's the easiest
way to terminate a conversation and turn my phone
upside down, hoping he doesn't send me any more. As
much as I feel for him, with his parents being absent, I
can't replace them. I have my own family to worry
about.

I quickly peek at my phone, but regret it instantly.

Three messages from Leo.

I put my phone on do not disturb and pray that some
normality returns to my family when I open my eyes to
a brand-new day tomorrow.

7

Gabriel

I'm sitting in my new usual spot, behind the old sports shed – the one that isn't used anymore because it had to get sprayed for white ants or some other kind of insect.

I'm hiding. From Catelyn. She's been making eye contact with me and one time, between classes, she even slowed down as though she wanted to talk to me. I was like... shit, shit, shit and I started inwardly choking, like I was unable to breathe, and turned and walked the other way. I spent the next class in the boys' toilets: firstly, so that I could hide from her and, secondly, so that I could be sick in the toilet bowl and finally breathe.

The worst part is I don't know what to do about this. What I want to do is tell her the truth, tell her what I saw, what I think I saw. But at the same time, I've been getting psychotically incessant texts from Leo saying things like, 'Nothing happened. I found her like that, just like you did.' And part of me doesn't know what to believe. Of course, this had to have happened on the first night I decided to drink alcohol – only three shots but still enough for me to question everything about that night.

On autopilot, I unwrap the turkey and salad sandwich that my mother so carefully prepared with five layers of salad so that I'm getting my daily serving of vegetables, but then I wrap it back up because my appetite has died.

I'm about to get up and find a bin, because just having food near me is making my stomach churn, when Leo appears and plonks himself down right next to me.

'Are you going to eat that?'

I shrug and hand it to him. Maybe he'll go away now that he's got my lunch.

But no such luck. He opens the gladwrap and takes a bite.

'Yum. I've never had a packed lunch. I mean, one that my mum or dad made. I've always made my lunch myself. Even when I was in primary school.'

His chewing grates on my nerves.

'Mm... is that some kind of salad dressing? Or is it mayo?'

I ignore him and stare ahead. He's got to be bullshitting about the 'never had a packed lunch thing' because I can't imagine that his parents have never once made his lunch. I mean, what about kindy or pre-primary?

When he swallows, it's so loud I want to punch him in the throat. My shoulders bunch up. It's so hard not to react, to not tell him to get the fuck away from me, but I manage to resist and shift a couple of inches away from him instead.

'Yum,' he says, between noisy lip-smacks. 'Your mum is amazing. I hope you're grateful for what she does for you, Gabriel.'

I gnaw on my cuticles and keep telling myself that if I ignore him enough, he'll get bored and go away.

'So,' he says, taking a swig from his water bottle. 'I've noticed that Catelyn has been making eyes at you and trying to get your attention.'

I do nothing. Not even shrug. A bead of sweat travels down my spine. I don't know why I'm scared right now, but something about Leo's calm arrogance is freaking me out. It's almost like he thinks he holds some kind of power over me.

'I wonder if she wants to know more about Saturday night. About what happened to her,' he says.

'Maybe,' I say, breaking my silence. More so to see what he'll say. If he'll fess up to what I thought I saw.

'I think you need a friend right now, Gabriel,' Leo says, shifting a little closer to me. 'And I'm happy to be that friend.'

What is this guy on? I shuffle away from him. He's really starting to piss me off.

He takes out his phone.

'It would be awful if Catelyn saw these.'

My heart stops as I watch Leo swipe across several images which show me bent over Catelyn's half-naked body, me with the edge of the bed sheet in my hand... I was putting it over her body, covering her up, but of course the image makes it look like I was taking it off. Acid begins to bubble up inside my stomach.

'But I'm happy to forget these exist... and keep them away from Catelyn... and everyone at school for that matter. As long as you let me be a friend to you. Let me help you.'

I say nothing. I feel like one of those animals on a nature show, the prey innocently lapping at the edge of a waterhole, before they discover a predator in the midst. The one that viewers feel bad for and say, 'oh, he's a goner.'

'I found her like that and covered her up. You know that. And I saw you. I saw you–'

'You saw nothing,' he says, his voice cold and gravelly. 'I saw plenty though, and I have the pictures to prove exactly what I saw.' He slips his phone into the inside pocket of his blazer. A tiny device which wields the power to ruin me. 'I just wish you hadn't had all those shots, Gabriel. I mean, I tried to warn you. I tried to remind you that your mum said "no drinking" when she dropped us off.'

A rage bubbles in my stomach and threatens to rise up into my head and make me do things I'll regret. I don't care how many drinks I had, even though I know I only had three. I would never hurt Catelyn or any girl. I know this because I just wouldn't. It's not me.

'Why are you doing this?' I ask. 'I hardly know you.'

Leo sighs, like he's trying to be patient with me, like I'm the crazy one.

'It's because I care. Something's changed in you since Saturday night. You weren't yourself...' His voice trails off and he shakes his head. 'Do you even remember the pills Grayson gave you? I'm pretty sure you took one and then you gave one to Catelyn, or was it Brad? You and Catelyn were pretty chummy at the party. Everyone saw you guys sitting super close together.'

I don't respond. He's got to be bullshitting. I don't even remember seeing Catelyn until I saw her in that bedroom passed out. And I didn't even speak to Grayson.

'Yeah,' Leo continues, his voice animated like he's enjoying this. 'You had a conversation with her... something to do with your mum. How you guys have hot chocolates on Sundays together. How you two are close.'

I freeze. The hot chocolates on a Sunday thing is true – and nobody at school knows about it. But I can't imagine sharing that with Catelyn or anyone. Like, I'd die if anyone thought of me as a mummy's boy.

But how would Leo know this unless it's true?

Shit. Shit. Shit.

What if Leo's right? What if I did take something... whatever Grayson gave me. But I don't even know Grayson that well. And I felt completely straight when I found Catelyn. The three shots I'd had, had worn off by then.

'What else did I do?' I ask, wondering if it's possible to have felt straight on the night but acted in an entirely different fashion. It freaks me out. My heart races.

'Don't worry,' he says with a smile, while staring at me intently, his eyes extra pale in the daylight. 'I'm here for you.' He pulls his phone out, checks it and then slips it back in his pocket. 'So, I was thinking of coming over tomorrow after school. We can hang out... game or something. Or I could help your mum to cook dinner.'

I shuffle slightly away from him again. 'Why would you want to help my mum to cook dinner?'

'Aren't you close with your mum? Or did you lie about the hot chocolate Sundays?'

I feel heat rise to my cheeks. I hate that he knows things about me. And I hate that he's talking about my mum like he knows her. He knows nothing about her. And I want it to stay that way.

But that bloody phone and those photos. Maybe... maybe I'll have him over and then get him to cook with my mum – despite me not wanting him within an inch of her. But I'll have to bear it until I manage to get a hold of his phone and delete those photos. I'd have to think up a good reason to be on his phone though. Maybe make sure mine is flat and ask to borrow his to show him something on YouTube.

I'm going to have to put on a show, make him believe that I suddenly consider him a friend and don't mind him invading my life and hanging out with me and my mum. I'm not sure that I'll be able to pull it off. Just having him only inches away from me right now makes me want to shove him against the shed wall and press his pale face hard against the rough brickwork until it draws blood from his pasty skin.

I run my hands through my hair and lean forward, my eyes concentrating on an ant as it makes its way across the concrete carrying with it a gigantic-looking crumb.

'You alright there, buddy?' Leo asks, patting me on the back. I stiffen at his touch and nod.

'Yeah,' I say, and decide that I may as well start playing along with his shitty game. 'Thanks.' I continue to watch the ant. If that little guy can carry something probably ten times its weight, then I can at least pretend to be Leo's friend to get through the next twenty-four hours.

The siren goes, signalling the end of lunchtime. It's a sound I normally hate – except for when it announces home time – but today I welcome it. I don't have any classes with Leo for the rest of the day so I'm going to enjoy this small window of freedom and use the time to plan my next move.

As I nod goodbye to Leo and head back to my locker, I realise that I'm feeling hopeful. I still feel like crap after seeing those photos – not just because I'm in them but also because I hate seeing Catelyn like that. It makes me wish I'd done more to protect her... to help her.

I don't know why Leo wants to hang with me, or my mum. It's freaking weird. But I'm going to have to let him. I'm going to have to make him think I want him around. That I want and need him as a friend. Then after I get the photos and destroy them, I can tell him to piss off and leave me alone.

I grab what I need for my last two classes from my locker and slam it shut, feeling slightly better than how I've been feeling since Saturday night.

But then I walk into Home Economics and realise that the only empty space available is at the workstation Catelyn is standing at.

Her dark eyes follow me as I make my way through the classroom and come to stand at her bench, standing right at the end, as far away from her as possible.

She hands me an apron with a soft smile, and the sick feeling that I had at lunch returns with a vengeance.

8

I'm surprised on Friday morning when Gabriel informs me, before stepping out of the car at the school drop-off, that Leo is coming over after school and will be riding home with us this afternoon.

Before I can respond, he shuts the passenger door.

For a few seconds I sit there in the idling car, wondering if I'd gotten it wrong all along. That perhaps Gabriel does in fact consider Leo more of a friend than I'd initially thought. Perhaps this week, after whatever it was that occurred on the Saturday night, he's bonded with Leo somewhat.

Several horns honk and I realise I'm holding up the drop-off queue. Instead of the middle finger I want to give them, I wave a quick sorry to the driver behind me and start moving.

As I leave the school grounds, I wonder why I still have a heavy feeling in my stomach, like dread. Gabriel is moving forward from a difficult week and is having a friend over. He's starting to merge back into life. I should be happy really.

I mentally chide myself for being such a worrywart and decide to stop off for some groceries so that I can prepare a nice dinner tonight. I presume they'll game the afternoon away, so I also grab some snacky treats for the boys.

As I bag the groceries in the self-serve checkout, my mind wanders back to Leo. He texted me randomly last night, just a smiley. I didn't respond, in case it kick-started a long, drawn-out conversation where he tries to convince me to invite him over to spend time with Gabriel – of course, this was before I knew that Gabriel in fact wanted him to come over.

I felt completely guilty for not responding, especially considering that he's all alone in that great big house. But I'm cautious of his growing dependence on me, if I can call it that. I feel as though I'm overstepping some serious parent-student boundaries by having conversations with him via text. It doesn't sit well with me that I'm yet to meet his parents. If it were any other of Gabriel's friends or even someone new, it wouldn't bother me at all – you hardly get to know the parents of your children's friends once they are in high school. It's just the way that it is.

But I've never been personally texted by a kid before. That's what's strange about this.

Then again, maybe I'm overthinking things. Leo was worried about Gabriel, that's all. And now that Gabriel is having Leo over to hang out, I'm sure that I won't be hearing from Leo again via private messages. He'll text Gabriel himself from now onwards, one hundred percent. I was likely the go-between while Gabriel wasn't saying much and wasn't responding to texts. It makes sense really.

But I'm still hopeful that Gabriel will start interacting with his old friends and game with them again. I miss hearing his laughter filling up the house. I miss his smile, too, and that twinkle in his eyes. His joy is so infectious that you can't help but feel uplifted in Gabriel's presence. It saddens me that whatever happened at that party has dimmed his beautiful inner light.

The client I ran out on the other day has emailed me a couple of times, saying that he'd like to reschedule. Earlier this morning I informed him that I won't be taking on any new clients. Someone recognising me from my secret past is the last thing I want to deal with right now. I've got enough to worry about with Gabriel, though hopefully not for too much longer, and Joe acting stressed and those texts from N.F.

When I arrive home, I unpack my groceries, put them away and get comfortable on the couch with my laptop and a cup of tea. I've got quite a bit of work to catch up on from last week and I dive right into it. The distraction is a soothing balm to my frazzled soul.

At noon, as I shut down my laptop and start to mentally plan out what I need to get done, preparation-wise, for dinner, my phone lights up with a text from Joe.

Hey, you wanna meet for lunch? :-)

I stare at the message and smile at first, but then I frown. We haven't met for lunch since before we had Gabriel, back in the days we used to both work at the restaurant. I wonder if this is something to do with the messages he's been receiving from N.F.? I've heard countless stories of cheating husbands who begin to give attention to their wives out of guilt. Not that I have ever thought that Joe would cheat. Well, I'd never thought it physically possible seeing as he has impotence. But then again, there is such a thing as emotional cheating.

I take a sip of my tea and groan inwardly.

Oh God... what if it's me? What if he can't get it up for me, but he can for other women? Just like he can for porn?

My heart sinks but then I shake my head and text my husband back.

I'm overthinking again.

Sure. Where would you like to meet?

He replies a few minutes later.

> *The carpark at Woodies Point. I'll bring some fish and chips. You could bring some white wine if you like.*

Again, I frown. This is completely out of character.

> *But won't you have to go back to work?*

> *Nope. I've booked off the rest of the arvo. Thought we should spend some time together, you and me and also with Gabriel after school. I think we need this time as a family.*

I remember that Leo is coming over and curse him under my breath. Family time tonight would have been perfect and we could have shared a nice night with Gabriel and got him opening up. Damn.

> *His friend is coming over after school. Leo. I'll explain when I see you. See you soon.*

While I'm pulling a chilled bottle of white out of the fridge my phone pings.

> *WTH? Not that kid. You said he was weird and that you didn't like the look of him.*

> *He's just a kid, Joe. I think I was just worried for Gabriel that night. He's a nice enough kid and if it's going to help Gabriel return to his happy self then I'm pretty happy about it.*

> *Yeah. Okay.*

I grab some paper cups, serviettes, my sunglasses, and head out the door.

Not even Leo coming over can ruin the fact that Joe is making an effort and that my family has hope of being happy again.

But while Joe and I are sitting in his work van, our fish and chips steaming up the windows while the ocean roars in front of us and the seagulls screech and swoop nearby, my phone pings with an email.

'Leave it, please,' says Joe, who's in the middle of discussing plans for a family getaway down south that will have Gabriel smiling again.

I happily ignore my phone, and make some suggestions as to where we could stay for our getaway and Joe's face lights up and he starts making plans for what we three can do together. Kayaking, fishing, and some days of just soaking up the sun on the beach with a good book.

Joe and I chat and laugh and sip our wine, and it feels so good to be connecting like this after what has been such a strange week. We feel as one again and I can tell that Joe feels it too.

I can't wait to tell Gabriel all about our little getaway. It'll bring us closer together as a family.

My phone pings again.

Then again.

Joe stares at it.

'Okay, maybe you should check it. Sounds urgent.'

I shrug. 'It's only emails.' I'm hoping that it's not the prospective client that I ran out on yesterday. Why won't he leave me alone?

'Just check the bloody thing,' says Joe, his cheeks and neck flushed – from the wine or irritation, I can't be certain. It reminds me of how suspicious he seemed when I received Leo's texts the other night. I can already feel that oneness I'd felt only seconds ago, the binding fabric of our happy family, beginning to tear. Why is my husband so hot and cold?

'Okay, okay,' I say and swipe up, gulping down the last of my wine.

All three emails have no subject.

The first says, 'I KNOW YOU.'

'Is it work?' asks Joe.

I ignore him while my pulse thrums loudly in my ears.

The second email says, 'YOU CAN'T HIDE ANYMORE.'

The lingering taste of the wine in my mouth and throat turns sour.

The third and final email says, 'I KNOW WHO YOU ARE ANNA.'

My blood cools as I re-read the sentence over and over again, and I shiver.

'What's wrong?' Joe asks. 'What is it? Is it Gabriel?'

I force myself to breathe. To function. To look normal.

'No.' I wave a hand in the air and glance up from my phone. 'No, it's just a prospective client berating me. Taking their business elsewhere because I cancelled on him yesterday. Says I'm unprofessional.' I close my emails and drop my phone into my lap.

Joe holds my gaze for what seems like forever and I almost think he doesn't believe me, but then he visibly relaxes beside me and draws me into one of his soothing bear hugs over the gearstick.

'Oh, Daph,' he says. 'Everything is going to be okay. You've got me and that's all that matters.'

I relax into his warm embrace.

Maybe I've been overanalysing Joe too much. He has his own stresses about our relationship, about his work, and of course worrying about Gabriel. I need to cut him some slack. I slip my own arms around him. He laughs as my free hand slides from his waist to his back. Joe's always been ticklish. And I notice how much firmer he is. The softness of his belly has been replaced with taut muscle I'm unfamiliar with. How have I not noticed that he's lost weight and toned up?

I feel terrible. Like I've neglected him. I hug him extra tight and inwardly resolve to focus on my husband more than I have been lately.

He chuckles at my tightened squeeze and kisses the top of my head.

Inside this steamy van with my husband, my belly filled with fish and chips, and wine, I feel safe and I want to stay here forever.

But all I can think about are those three emails.

There's only one man who knows that I'm Anna, and I've been on the run from him for over twenty years. The very same man who threatened to take my life should he ever find me again.

'I'll ruin you first, then I'll kill you. Slowly.'

And now it seems he's finally found me.

9

Daphne

For the entire afternoon I've been obsessing and fretting about the emails. The sender, of course, is iknowyouAnna@gmail.com which gives nothing away except the fact that it gives everything away. It has got to be him. Nobody in my new life knows me as Anna. Not even Joe. And if it is my ex, then not only is my life in danger, but I'm also worried for Gabriel and Joe. Because I know what he's like. To make me suffer he'd hurt them first.

Despite the fact that my ex had found someone new while I was still living with him all those years ago, he still considered me his property. Just the mere suggestion of me wanting to leave around that time, even just for a weekend away to visit my foster grandmother's grave, sent him into a rage like I'd never witnessed before.

The day I left him was the worst day of my life – because of the horrific thing that happened that day – but it was also the best day of my life. Because it was the day that I finally said enough is enough and escaped.

Even now, after all these years, he certainly won't stand for me having a life and a family. He'll hate that I have a child with Joe. He'll hate that I've made a life without him – a better one.

Joe, who was supposed to return home with me after our fish and chips lunch by the beach but didn't, finally texts me.

> *Sorry, it seems I didn't get the afternoon off as I'd planned. Just work crap. Sorry.*

> *No worries. I'll see you tonight for dinner. Remember Leo will be here.*

> *Won't be home for dinner. After you told me the kid was coming over, I said yes to a client dinner. Sorry. But this is a biggie. Super important apartment complex getting built.*

> *Sounds exciting! See you after your dinner then :-)*

He texts me back a heart emoji and I can't help but wonder if this client is in fact the mysterious N.F., and if they're a client at all. The feel of his newly taut muscles beneath his shirt lingers on my fingers and only adds to my suspicions.

I recall that feeling, when my ex had started to become distracted and was on his phone every second and spending less and less time at our apartment, and I wonder if the same thing is happening. Except this is different. I needed to leave my controlling ex. It was a blessing for him to be distracted, even if I didn't fully comprehend that at the time. And I was only seventeen.

With Joe it's different.

I love Joe.

I love him so much and he represents everything that is fairy tale about a happily ever after. Sure, we could use some help in the bedroom, which, I'm hoping I'll eventually get Joe to open up to me about. But his love for me I've never questioned and thought I never would.

Until recently. Until the appearance of N.F.

But, N.F. or not, I soon realise that Joe not coming home for dinner gives me the entire evening free to do some private investigating.

I've never searched for my ex on the internet. I've always been frightened that he has some kind of computer software that will alert him to my whereabouts if I punched his name into a search engine.

Now, though. He's left me no choice but to look. I need to know if he's still on the other side of the country. I need to know that he isn't a true physical threat to me. That this is just something that was born out of a bout of boredom or perhaps an alcohol-fuelled moment of spite. Maybe he hasn't been actively looking for me. Maybe he happened to stumble across my name... I'm not sure how as I don't have any social media, not even for my home business. I only have business cards that I am careful to hand out to prospective clients only, and very sparingly at that.

My heart races and my stomach swirls, making me feel ill. To think that I might actually find him. To think I might learn what he's been up to since I escaped his clutches.

My stomach flutters, part anxious, part excited. It sickens me that he still has any effect at all on me.

I'll have to be careful though, to not let Gabriel see me searching for my ex when I'm home. My son is such a perceptive boy, he's an overthinker like me, and I don't want to give him anything extra to worry about, seeing as he's already got so much on his mind.

But he'll have Leo to occupy him, and as long as I supply them with plenty of snacks and a nice dinner later, they'll likely disappear into the gaming room and not emerge until Leo needs to go home.

I contemplate asking him to stay if his parents are still away, but then I never sleep properly when a guest sleeps in the house, it leaves me wired and tossing and turning all night. It's a side effect from having lived under too many different roofs with too many different people when I was growing up.

I like a stable home life without much change.

When it's just Joe, Gabriel and I, that's when it feels like a true home, that I'm safe and sound.

But in saying that, I bet it would be nice for Leo to wake up to a lively home with breakfast cooking and the bustle of a family. Not that we're a huge family or anything. But it's got to be better than him rattling around alone in that mansion for days on end.

I must remember to ask him for his mother's number so that I can make contact with her and introduce myself.

I leave the house ten minutes earlier for the school pick-up so that I can pick up a treat for the boys – some cheeseburgers and chocolate shakes from the local burger place near the school. Gabriel is going to love it, and I'm hoping Leo does too. I almost texted him earlier today to ask if he likes cheeseburgers, and which flavoured shake he likes best. But it felt too intimate and strange to text him that. Like I'm trying to play mum.

So, I left it and hope he likes chocolate.

Inside, the car is hot and stifling when I pull up at school and I wind down the window to allow a gentle afternoon breeze to sweep in and cool me down.

I sigh and take a sip of my own treat, a caramel latte. I haven't had a caramel latte since I was eighteen, when I first came to Western Australia, and I've missed the sweetness. I'll need the extra energy the sugar provides to survive an evening of detective work.

As I sit and sip my coffee, I wonder if the emails could potentially be from the client that I ran out on the other day. He has been pretty persistent in trying to get me to change my mind and take him on. He also thought he knew me.

I rest my head back against the car seat and exhale. Maybe the emails aren't from my ex. Maybe I'm not in any danger after all.

The siren goes. Students emerge from their classrooms and the peaceful grounds come alive with shrieks of laughter and chatter. The kids are all excited for the weekend and it shows on their smiling faces.

My heart sinks a little as Gabriel and Leo approach my car. I can tell that Gabriel is not happy just by the rigidity of his walk. His cheeks are flushed and his eyes downcast.

Leo, on the other hand is positively floating towards the car, his pale green eyes bright. He has a huge smile on his face.

'Hi, Daphne,' Leo says as he climbs into the back seat. He sits in the middle so that his head completely fills my rear-view mirror.

'Hello, Leo, how was school?'

'Great,' he says, smiling at my reflection in the mirror.

I smile back.

Gabriel sinks into the passenger seat, no greeting.

'Hi, Gabe, how was your day?'

I hand the brown paper bag of hamburgers to him and his mouth twitches, I'm going to tell myself that it was the beginnings of a smile and leave it at that. I'm not about to push him while he's feeling off.

'There's a cheeseburger in there for each of you and I got you both a shake,' I say, taking one of the chocolate shakes from the drink holder and passing it over my shoulder to Leo. 'I think they've warmed a bit though. It was so hot in the car.'

'Thank you so much.' Leo beams from the back seat. 'It's fine. Thanks, Daphne.'

Gabriel stiffens at Leo's use of my first name for the second time.

'Leo,' I say, as I pull out of the queue and slowly exit the school behind a long line of cars. 'Are your parents back from their business trips?'

Leo glances at me in the rear-view mirror and shakes his head. 'No, unfortunately. They're not back for another few days. So, I'll be alone tonight. Again.'

Gabriel stiffens up even more and I realise now that I should never have asked Leo this. There is no way that I can invite Leo to stay the night now. Not with the way Gabriel is behaving. Perhaps something happened today to make him regret inviting Leo over?

'Well, if there are any leftovers, I'll send them home with you tonight if you like,' I say, in an attempt at salvaging the awkwardness of not inviting him to stay.

Gabriel visibly relaxes. And my heart flutters with joy. We are two souls in tune with each other again and I can tell he's silently thanking me for knowing instinctively that he doesn't want Leo staying the night.

He picks up his shake and takes a long sip.

'Thanks, Mum,' he says so softly that I'm pretty sure Leo can't hear.

'You're welcome, love,' I say and smile softly as I navigate my way out of the school grounds.

'Leftovers. Great,' says Leo, unable to mask his disappointment. 'Sure, I'd love to take them home. I mean. I can cook pretty good but it'll be nice to have something made with love for me.'

Gabriel keeps sucking on his straw but I know that he silently agrees with me that what Leo's just said sounds a bit weird.

'I've got some work to do this evening, boys. So, I've brought lots of snacks and I've prepared a lasagne too, that you can have a slice of whenever you like. I'm assuming you guys will be gaming most of the time?' I say this with a wide grin.

Gabriel nods, his face blank, and keeps staring out the passenger window. Leo, however, beams back at me from the rear-view mirror.

'I'm happy to help in any way. I can wash the dishes or I can even help you with your work. I'm pretty good with numbers. I get As in maths all the time.'

With Leo around, I realise I'm going to have to search up my ex in the privacy of my bedroom.

The poor kid. He's simply starved of a bit of attention and love, that's all.

'I'll keep that in mind,' I say, beaming him my warmest smile. He seems content and smiles to himself before taking a sip of his shake and staring out the window as we finally turn onto the main road out of school and journey home.

* * *

Despite my reservations about how the afternoon would go for Gabriel, it hasn't exactly been the worst. Gabriel seemed to decide to put in a bit more of an effort with Leo once we arrived home, and now the two of them are in the front room, gaming together, and even shouting at the screen in triumph while I warm the lasagne in the oven.

I take a sip of a cold glass of delicious sauv blanc while I mentally thank Leo for bringing Gabriel back to life. While the boys are entertained, I open up my laptop on the kitchen bench and, with trembling fingers, punch my ex's name into the search engine and hit enter.

Nothing could have prepared me for seeing his face for the first time in twenty years.

And when I see it, I turn and vomit into the sink.

With shaky hands, I turn on the tap and wash my mess down the drain before the boys can see. I splash my face with cold water and gulp down several deep breaths.

Oh my God. Oh my God. Oh my God.

I don't know exactly what I feel. It's a combination of revulsion and fear... I think. But then adrenaline rushes through my veins. As much as it makes me sick to see his face, I'm almost excited. After over twenty years of hiding from him, of forcing myself not to look him up in case it somehow resulted in him finding me, or worse, if I succumbed to some kind of twisted regret for leaving him – here he is, right in front of me.

Justin Cooper Mallory.

Those frosty blue eyes stare back at me from the Facebook profile as I pat my face dry with a tea towel that smells like garlic and onions. It's a public account.

Of course. He'd want anybody and everybody to have access to him – as many women as possible.

That's so typical of him. And I feel a sudden onslaught of love for my sweet husband Joe.

Just seeing my ex's face again is enough to start the heart palpitations, the sweaty palms, the nausea.

I reach for my wine and take a long gulp.

Even from a digital screen he has the power to reduce me from a strong capable woman to a frightened girl.

I'm desperate to close the window and erase the search but I need to do just one thing.

I scroll below the profile pic and there it is.

Perth. WA.

I shut my laptop and slide it away from me, knocking my phone off the counter. The screen is likely cracked from bouncing against the tiles but right in this moment, I don't care.

My ex is in Perth. He's here.

My blood runs cold and I have to brace myself against the sink, my nails digging into the wooden benchtop.

He probably knows where I live and has been watching me, and Joe and Gabriel. Maybe that's why things have all gone south.

Maybe he's contacted Gabriel. He may well have emailed my son or contacted him via social media. Or Joe, because my son and my husband haven't been themselves of late.

Oh my God.

I take another sip of wine and realise that it might be time to tell Joe everything.

But how do I say it? How do I tell him about my past? Not just about the horrible video but about everything else. Everything.

I'm not that girl anymore, that sad lonely vulnerable girl who allowed herself to be treated so terribly.

Joe will be sickened when I tell him. Maybe he'll want to end the marriage.

How will we explain to Gabriel what's going on? My stomach heaves at the prospect of Gabriel knowing about the video, or worst still, watching it.

No. I can't tell Joe. Telling Joe would lead to Gabriel finding out. And that cannot happen.

I'll have to deal with this myself.

I'm not that frightened little girl anymore.

I'm a strong woman and I will protect my family like a lioness.

I'm as much a threat to him as him to me. I could expose him.

Justin would be locked away if the police ever found out what he'd done to me, a minor at the time, for the duration of our relationship. And I have the proof, thanks to the litany of pornography sites on the net.

From the brief glance I'd taken of his social media profile page before I slammed the laptop shut, I know that he has a partner – a wife or girlfriend, I can't be sure. But whoever she is, I'm one hundred percent certain he wouldn't appreciate her knowing about me and what he did to me.

I reach for my wine and take a large gulp before setting the glass down and reaching for my laptop.

Two can play at this game.

I open my emails and read over what he'd written.

I click reply.

> *No, you don't know me. You have never known the real me and you never will. Contact me again and I'll go to the police. I'm pretty sure you wouldn't want that, would you?*

I hit send and a ripple of satisfaction shoots through my veins, warming the cold feeling from earlier.

Take that.

Take that, you cruel, narcissistic bastard.

10

Daphne

However, a few seconds after I hit send, cold fear returns and ripples through my body, obliterating any sense of satisfaction.

I've just foolishly done the one thing that I promised myself I would never do if Justin ever attempted to contact me.

I responded. I've fed his ego. I've taken the bait.

And here I am using his name again, personalising him when he doesn't deserve to be.

Basically, I've allowed my ex to take control of my emotions again. I'm his little puppet, just like I was all those years ago.

I slam my laptop shut.

My stupidity leaves me breathless. Now he knows that it is really me at the other end of this email address. I've just given him confirmation. I could have simply ignored his emails. I could have deleted them without response and perhaps his interest would have dissipated.

My heart begins to race again and I drain my glass of wine just as Leo enters the room. I choke as I swallow and proceed to have a mini coughing fit before I signal, one palm up to a concerned-looking Leo, that I'm okay.

'I'm fine. Just drank too fast.'

He smiles at me and comes to stand on the other side of the kitchen bench. He has a strange, floaty kind of walk, where it appears that his arms and legs aren't moving and yet, somehow, he glides forward.

'Oh wow, dinner smells amazing,' he says, his pale green eyes wide.

'I hope you like it.' I beam my warmest smile and his face lights up. And I have to say, that after nearly a week of Gabriel desperately trying to avoid me at all costs, it feels pretty good to receive a positive response from a teenager.

'Well, I've only ever had frozen lasagne from the supermarket so I'm pretty sure I'm going to love it.'

I literally put a hand to my heart. I can't help it. He's so sweet and brimming with gratitude.

'Oh, well in that case, if you do end up loving it, I'll definitely be sending you some home. I've made plenty.'

His pale cheeks turn a slight pink.

'I would love that. Thanks so much.' He drums his long fingers against the faux-marble benchtop.

'What's Gabriel up to?' I ask, but as soon as I do, a huge laugh erupts and then a scream from the front room and we both share conspiratorial smiles.

'I'm sure you can guess,' says Leo, now leaning against the breakfast bench. He touches my empty wine glass and wipes away a strip of condensation. 'Can I share a wine with you?' he asks, his eyes downcast while he slides his fingers up and down the delicate stem of the glass.

'I'm sorry, Leo,' I say. 'It wouldn't be right. Especially without your parents to give permission and it just... it's just not right for us to consume alcohol together. You're a minor.'

He glances up sharply. 'Why? Why does age make it not appropriate for us to share a drink and a chat? I'm a mature boy. I think if you give me a chance, you'd find my conversation stimulating enough.'

I'm a little surprised by his outburst and by the simmering rage behind his pale eyes. He's a boy who's obviously had to grow up way too fast and live

66

independently from quite a young age, so much so that he sees himself as an adult.

But he's still a boy. Just a boy crying out for a little attention.

'How about I give you a wine glass filled with Coke?' I cringe inwardly a little, wondering if my suggestion will come off as patronising, but he smiles.

'Okay,' he says rolling his eyes but still smiling.

I fix him his drink and ask him to see if Gabriel wants a glass but Leo just waves a hand in the air.

'Let's just leave him to his game. It's pretty intense and I'd hate to break his concentration and cause him to lose.'

I laugh. 'Ah, very true. Spoken like an expert gamer.'

He takes a sip of his Coke and shrugs.

'I actually don't game that much. I tend to watch more YouTube than anything. I like nature documentaries.'

'Really? So do I! I'm obsessed.'

He lights up.

'Maybe I can come over one night. We could do a marathon and stay up all night watching.'

I picture Joe, who loves his night-time cuddles on the couch with me, coming home to finding Leo and I pulling an all-nighter. Joe who hates nature shows and loves watching classic cinema and horror.

But Leo is so excited and animated, and is already reeling off a huge list of documentaries we should watch together and what snacks he will bring.

I'm not quite sure how to burst his bubble, but I decide to take the easy way out and use Gabriel as an excuse.

'Sounds like fun, Leo. But let's give Gabriel a bit more time before we make any further arrangements as I think he still needs a bit of space while he processes whatever it is that he's going through.'

Leo's face falls and my heart dips.

'But gosh you've been so amazing, Leo. The fact that he's over there shouting at the television screen is a testament to your kindness and your efforts of being a good friend to him. Joe and I appreciate it so much.'

He takes a sip of his Coke and blushes again.

'Thanks... it's just... it's what anyone would do. I'm not really anyone special.'

I shake my head.

'Don't sell yourself so short, Leo. You're very kind-hearted and I bet your parents are super proud of you.' I beam up at him. 'In fact, do you think I could have your mother's phone number? I'd love to introduce myself to her and let her know how kind you've been to Gabriel.'

From the way he tightens his grip around the wine glass he's holding, I'm fairly certain Leo doesn't like my suggestion. But I'm not sure why. If his parents have managed to bring up such a thoughtful boy, they can't exactly be monsters. Busy with work perhaps, but that's the norm of today. I've just been blessed to be able to work from home. It's always worked so well for me, in that if Gabriel has needed me during the day for whatever reason, then I've been able to put my work aside and get back to it later on in the evening on the couch with my laptop balancing on my thighs and a huge mug of tea on the armrest.

'She'd be too busy to talk to you. I know her. Trust me. She'd be annoyed if you reached out to her. You'd become another thing to deal with, another to-do on her list.'

I try a different tact.

'Okay, but I'd still like her number for future arrangements. Perhaps if we invite you over another time... or, if I need to contact her in case of an emergency.'

He sets the glass down on the counter and pulls his phone out of the back pocket of his school uniform trousers and taps the screen.

A few seconds later I've got a text from him with his mother's name and number.

'Thank you, Leo. I really appreciate this. And I promise I won't bother her unless I have to.'

'It's fine,' he mumbles, before taking a long gulp of his cola.

An awkward silence ensues, during which my empty stomach rumbles embarrassingly loud.

Slipping my hands into a pair of well-used crocodile-shaped oven mitts that Joe brought home from a work trip to Darwin many years ago, I open the oven and crouch to check on the lasagne, making as much noise as I can while I do so.

A waft of deliciousness envelopes me, all rich tomato sauce, basil and bubbling cheese. Yum. My tummy rumbles again.

I stand and set the hefty tray on top of the oven with a clang.

'Would you like to call Gabriel, please, Leo?'

He stares in my general direction with his mouth open a little, his eyes unfocused, before he blinks rapidly and returns from wherever his mind has just taken him.

'Could you call Gabriel, please? And let him know that dinner is ready.'

Leo's gaze shifts to the left and he scans the various fridge magnets we've collected over the years.

'Oh, I'd better not. He actually sent me in here to eat because he wanted to concentrate on his game and told me he wasn't hungry.' Leo shrugs and finally meets my gaze. 'I think it's his way of getting rid of me so that he can connect with his friends. It's good for him though, to be gaming again, so I don't mind at all.'

'Okay then,' I say, tugging off my oven mitts and turning the oven dial to off. 'You and I can eat together if you like, and Gabriel can eat when he's ready.' I beam a smile at Leo even though I'm annoyed at Gabriel for ditching his guest and leaving me to entertain him. Then again, it'll likely do me good to have some company, a distraction, a break from berating myself over and over for replying to my ex's emails. I could perhaps ask if Leo has found out any more information behind what happened on that Saturday night at the party.

'Sounds great,' he says, his eyes crinkling up with genuine joy. 'I'd love to eat dinner with you.'

'You'll regret it soon,' I say, grinning. 'I'm going to grill you until I know every single thing about you.'

Leo pales a little, and his breath catches, but then he recovers and shakes his head and releases a nervous laugh.

'I'm pretty much a vault, so you can try to extract information, but I don't like your chances,' he says good-naturedly.

I laugh and cut Leo a large and extremely hot square of lasagne, the cheese still bubbling on top.

'I hope you're hungry,' I say. 'Oh, and please be careful as it's ridiculously hot. I wouldn't want you to burn your mouth.'

'I'm starving,' he says. 'And yes, I'll be careful, Mum.'

We lock eyes over the lasagne and he blushes and grins. 'Sorry, it's a joke. Because you're warning me to be careful with the food like I'm five or something. It's something mums do. Well, other people's mums.' He rolls his eyes and I relax and smile.

I cut myself a smaller piece because lasagne always manages to fill me up quickly and then I cover the rest of the tray with foil and the two of us take our plates and glasses to the table and slip into our seats.

'This is so good,' Leo says, dragon-like steam escaping his lips after he swallows the first mouthful. 'Oh my God! It's amazing.'

'Thank you,' I say, basking in his compliments. Joe and Gabriel are so used to my cooking that words of praise are few and far between. Not that they don't appreciate me or anything. It's just become such a mundane and regular thing that they expect it now just like one expects water to run out of a tap.

Joe used to cook such lovely meals, gorgeous, brightly coloured dishes he had learned to master from his days as a chef. I recall that I, too, became complacent and had started to expect his gourmet meals without so much as a quick thanks. That is, he used to cook until he suddenly announced that he was going to quit being a chef and train as an electrician, something that his father and grandfather had both done for a living.

Not that he needs to cook. I'm home all the time anyway so it makes sense that I do all the cooking. Plus, he still cooks a huge Sunday breakfast for us all and for that I'm super grateful.

I take a bite of the lasagne. The pasta melts in my mouth.

While Leo is telling me a bit about his childhood, what little he recalls of his grandparents, who have all since passed away, my phone pings from the arm of my favourite couch across the room. It's the special ring for an email notification. My body stiffens. I get a tonne of work emails but usually during the day. It's 6.30pm and I worry it's my ex. Again, I silently chastise myself for responding to his rubbish emails. I should have deleted and blocked him.

Leo pauses mid-sentence.

'You can go check that if you like,' he says, but I can see the disappointment on his face. The poor kid has been alone at home for who knows how long, so in that moment I decide to ignore my phone, psychotic ex and all.

Anyway, I'm actually enjoying myself with Leo. Hearing about his childhood is a wonderful distraction.

'My phone can wait. Please continue, Leo,' I say, waving my fork in the air. 'I love hearing about your life. I've always been fascinated by other people's childhoods.'

'Oh, do you like to chat with Gabriel's other friends too?' he asks, a look of mild disappointment on his face, as though he doesn't like the idea. 'I bet you're really close with them. Like, you're probably like their second mum after knowing them all for so many years.'

I think about Gabriel's friends. Some of them I've known since kindy and my heart warms. They are like sons and daughters. I have always loved having them over and have missed it since the Xbox became their virtual hangout.

'Yeah. Well, I mean, I'd like to think that I care for them like most mums care for their children's friends.'

He cuts into his lasagne and eats, chewing thoughtfully.

'Do your parents know your friends really well?' I ask.

After he swallows, he looks at me. The sun has gone down outside and the dimness in the room darkens his eyes and gives him a vulnerable appearance.

'Um... I've only just gotten to know Gabriel, so they haven't met him yet. But it would be nice if they get to know him.'

I can barely swallow the mouthful of lasagne I'm chewing. A wave of sadness hits me hard right in the chest. Gabriel is Leo's only friend? I find it extremely sad.

'I'm sure you've had other friends over the years that your parents have met?'

He shrugs.

'Maybe. I can't remember.'

'Oh,' I say, thinking that's a strange thing to say. Surely you remember if you had friends or not. But I do feel a sad for him. I've always felt for different kids, kids who don't fit in, because that was me as a kid, and especially as a teen. Of course it was, unfortunately, my loneliness and inability to fit in which led me to my ex. And that realisation makes me feel instinctively very protective of Leo. A great need to protect one of my own kind.

'Well, you're welcome here anytime, Leo. Gabriel could use a friend right now and you're already doing wonders for him. He hasn't been on the Xbox in so long.'

'Thanks,' Leo says, blushing and he puts his head down and eats.

I hear the grind and scrape of the automatic garage door go up. It desperately needs a service.

Joe's back earlier than I thought, seeing as he was supposed to be eating dinner with a client. I wonder what on earth is going on with him. I mentally note to ask him about N.F. later, after Leo's left.

The door to the kitchen opens up and when Joe bursts through, he glances at Leo, not even trying to hide his disappointment that the boy is here.

'Joe, this is Leo, Gabriel's friend. He's been looking out for Gabriel and listen,' I say, nodding towards the front room, grinning while Gabriel shouts from the other room. 'He's gaming again, can you believe it? After a week of nothing.'

Joe nods but he doesn't smile or come forward to shake Leo's hand. He's behaving rather rudely actually, and I widen my eyes at him to silently warn him to be nice.

But Joe ignores me and glares at Leo while he puts his sunglasses and hat on top of the fridge.

'Why isn't Gabriel at the table?' Joe asks me.

'He doesn't want to be disturbed,' says Leo.

Joe narrows his eyes at Leo's intrusion to the conversation, but then goes on to ignore him. My husband stares at me, brows raised.

'Gabriel asked Leo to come out and eat with me because he gets distracted while someone is watching him game.' I shrug. 'I'm just happy that he's our Gabriel again. Thanks to Leo.' I say those last words in hopes that they'll trigger some kind of gratitude or at least civility from Joe.

But no. Joe nods just once. This is so unlike him. He's behaving like a jealous baboon who's unhappy to discover a new male in his territory.

'I can give you a lift home when you're ready, mate,' Joe says, staring past me and directly at Leo. 'As soon as you finish your dinner.'

11

Gabriel

'So, what's your dad's deal?' Leo says, before he takes a bite out of the sandwich my mother made for me this morning. 'Mmm, it's turkey, isn't it? I wouldn't normally eat turkey, but this is nice – your mum makes everything nice. But yeah, your dad on the other hand, he couldn't get me out of the house quick enough. He seemed pretty angry.'

I shrug, feeling a pang of nostalgia when I see my old group playing basketball on the courts. We haven't played basketball since year eight. It makes me wonder if they're trying to get my attention.

I glance away, feeling like a jerk. But the last thing I want is any of my good buddies to find out about all this Leo crap I've got going on.

I remember what Leo said about my dad.

'My dad likes his privacy. I don't know.'

Leo chews and swallows so loudly it makes me want to punch him in the throat again.

'Well, anyway, let's forget about that.'

He whacks me on the arm when he notices me sneak another glance at my friends and raises his brows when I reluctantly look at him.

'You did well Friday night. All that shouting and laughing and carrying on while you were gaming.' He snorts. 'Your mum thinks I'm a saint for bringing you back to life.' He shakes his head. 'I swear she loves me.'

The siren wails.

Thank fuck.

I get up and fight every instinct to shove Leo out the way. He takes his sweet time and I need to pass him to get to class.

'Hey what's the rush. I thought we could wag the last classes and just... I don't know, go back to your house and hang out.'

I frown and take a deep breath in a bid to calm myself in Leo's presence.

'Look, I know you've got those pictures and think you can make me do anything, but I can't just wag school whenever I like. I'll get into trouble and then my mum will be on my back about it. She'll get suspicious. And anyway, she works from home so she'll be pissed off that we're there disturbing her.'

'I can't imagine your mum being pissed off,' Leo says, a far-off gleam in his eyes and a half-smile on his lips.

I want to twist and rip that smile off his face with my bare hands. Seriously... I want to smash him until he ceases to exist. I don't believe I've ever hated another human in my entire life. Until now.

Finally, he stands and balls up the plastic wrap from my sandwich and tosses it at my forehead before walking out from behind the sports shed. He strolls in the direction of his locker – which is thankfully nowhere near mine.

I breathe a sigh of relief but my relief doesn't last long. Catelyn waits at my locker and she looks relieved to see me.

Heat creeps up my neck, into my face, and my scalp tingles as I burn with shame. Even though I didn't have anything to do with her being naked – at least I'm ninety-nine percent sure I didn't – I hate that I saw her. I hate that she doesn't know that I saw her.

Or, that maybe she does.

'Hey, can we walk to Maths together?' she asks.

I shrug, my face must be as red as a stop sign right now. She must think I'm a freak.

The entire walk is silent, well, we're silent, unlike everyone around us who is noisily rushing between their lockers and classes.

Once inside the classroom, I make for the seat way at the back, in the far right corner. The seat beside it is already taken, which means I can escape Catelyn and her questioning eyes. But then the guy sitting there shifts over to the next seat to be with his friend and Catelyn quickly pounces on the chair and half smiles at me once she sets her laptop and water bottle on the desk.

I open my laptop and fire it up and open my maths digital textbook, swiping to the page the teacher has written on the whiteboard.

'Work from this page onwards. Whatever you can manage. If you complete the unit, great. If not, the rest can be done at home. But it needs to be completed by tomorrow's class,' says the teacher and most kids groan softly.

The school has fairly tight internet security and all social media is blocked. But I can't focus on maths, because idiot Leo is on my mind, so I decide to use my phone's hotspot so that I can log onto Instagram and see what he's been posting... just in case he's stupid enough to post something from the party.

Once I'm in, I'm disappointed to see that his account is private. But his profile shows zero photos so I breathe a sigh of relief.

'Why aren't you two following each other? If you're such good friends?' Catelyn asks.

I frown and move my laptop a fraction, just enough so that Catelyn can't see what I'm doing anymore but not enough to seem like I'm trying to hide something.

'We're not friends,' I say, trying to keep the outrage out of my voice. It's not her fault I've allowed that dickhead to manipulate me.

'Oh,' she says, frowning, deep in thought. 'Why did he go home with you the other day... Friday I think it was?' she asks.

She's been watching me. I'm not sure if I should be flattered or worried.

'Oh that. It was for something for school. An assignment,' I lie, hating that since that Saturday night I've become somewhat of a professional liar.

She shivers.

'Are you okay?' I ask.

'Leo just creeps me out.' She shudders and meets my gaze. 'We dated in year eight. For twenty-three hours, I kid you not, so not even a full day, and he acted like I'd ripped his heart out and stomped on it when I broke it off. Like twenty-three hours. We didn't even know each other that well and I was super shy back then so I hardly had much to say to him in those twenty-three hours. Anyway, he hasn't spoken to me since and whenever he sees me, he stiffens up and gives me this hostile glare, as though he still holds a grudge for some baby relationship when we were only thirteen.'

'Oh wow, really?'

'Yeah. I swear he thinks I owe him or something for "ruining" his life. It's so weird.'

'Yeah. That's insane,' I say, my heart beating like mad and my skin turning cold. That same psycho is now blackmailing me so that he can come to my house and eat dinner with my mother. I shudder.

Catelyn watches me for some time while I try to pretend that I'm getting stuck into my schoolwork, which of course I'm not.

'Do you mind if I ask you some questions? About that Saturday?' she asks, quickly glancing to see if the teacher, who's looking at her phone, is noticing our chat.

'No. I don't mind.'

'Okay, well, I can't remember much about the night. But... I'm getting flashbacks. Just weird, random... I don't know... moments. One of them is of your face, hovering over me and... I just um... I'm wondering...' She inhales and releases a shaky breath and spreads her hands across the keys of her laptop. 'Basically, I'm just wondering if you and I had s–'

'No!'

She shrinks away from me and a few kids turn to stare, brows raised at my outburst.

'Alright, alright, back to your work, people,' says the teacher, over her glasses. She resumes texting on her phone.

'Sorry,' I say, shrinking in my seat a little, my face on fire. 'But we didn't do anything. I don't think we spoke all night.'

'But I saw you,' she says, her head tilted in thought. 'You were definitely leaning over me. And I'm pretty sure I was naked at the time. Because that's how I woke up. Naked. And, well, I know that I slept with someone, I just don't know who.'

She blushes all the way to her hairline, and my face burns like it's on fire.

I'm not sure what to say. A huge part of me wants to confess exactly what happened – well, my version of events. Since that night, I've been dying to tell someone, to unburden myself of what I saw.

And I owe it to Catelyn to tell her about Leo. I owe it to every girl who has been ever taken advantage of. It's the right thing to do.

But those photos. Those shitty photos that Leo has on his phone. I know it'll be his word against mine and I would die if Catelyn thought that I had taken advantage of her, or if my mum thought that I had hurt a girl. It's not how she brought me up. It would ruin her.

Because no matter how much I profess my innocence, nobody would believe me after seeing those suspect-looking pics.

My life is over.

It's fucking over.

'Are you okay?' Catelyn reaches over and gently touches my arm.

I flinch and immediately regret it after she snatches her hand back and tucks it under the desk. It almost makes me want to cry, her kindness. I don't deserve it. Because I'm a gutless wonder for not telling her.

'Look, I know you're a good guy. I'm not accusing you of anything. I'm just trying to piece together what happened. Like, I know what everyone thinks of me. I know I've got a reputation. But I've changed. Or, at least I thought I had.' She frowns and shrugs. 'I guess, a part of me doesn't want to believe I just slipped back into my old ways so easily. Like, I can't even remember the night. And I pretty much went to the party intending to stay straight.' She shrugs again and stares down at her laptop. She looks so small and vulnerable.

I feel like the biggest arsehole. No. I am the world's biggest arsehole.

'I'll try to ask around, see if anyone else knows anything,' I say, feeling sick. I'm such a two-face. 'I'll tell you if I find anything out.'

'Thanks,' she says, her dark eyes so deep and so trusting.

Despite how rotten I feel right now, I realise that I've said more to Catelyn than I have to anyone since that party – which oddly feels good. I just wish that I could tell her the truth right now.

'I had to take the morning-after pill,' she says, staring into space. 'Even though I don't know who I did it with. I know it happened.'

My blood runs cold. So, Leo must have actually had sex with her.

Oh God. My stomach churns and I concentrate on my breathing because if I don't, I'm going to freak out any minute.

I'm a coward. I'm a gutless coward.

Tell her about Leo. Tell her now.

'Hey,' I say, my heart pounding and sweat trickling from my neck down my spine. Just say it. Just tell her the truth.

My phone buzzes in my blazer pocket. I glance at the teacher and discreetly take it out.

It's from Leo.

I swear beneath my breath and read his text.

Just a little reminder that I've got those photos of you, ready and waiting to share with the big wide world.

I inwardly curse him. It's like he can predict my every move, like he's watching me – which is impossible seeing as he's not in this class. Maybe he just has some kind of sixth sense.

Anger burns in my chest, in my throat, it radiates through my whole body.

'You've got all of twenty-one followers,' I text back. 'Hardly the big wide world.'

Looking me up on Insta, are we?

I don't respond.

You do realise that those twenty-one followers will share and share and share and share until everyone sees them. Even your mum will see them.

She doesn't have Insta.

I'll text them to her.

You don't have her number.

I, in fact, do.

My mum never gives out her number. Only her clients and close people.

Well, we're pretty close, your mum and I. We've been texting.

That can't be true. My mum would tell me if she received a text from Leo, because that would be weird, right?

STAY AWAY FROM MY MUM!

Temper, temper, Gabriel.

'Are you okay?' asks Catelyn.

Sweat continues to trickle down my back, dampening the thin shirt beneath my blazer. I nod.

'Just some family stuff,' I mutter as I stare at my phone, trying my best to control my breathing. I'm dying to get some fresh air, to just bust out of this classroom and run away from this place and everyone in it. Instead, I text Leo one final reply, my fingers angrily tapping at the screen.

> *Just stay the fuck away from my mum!*
> *I'll be your fake friend. But stay away*
> *from my mum!*

I slip my phone back into my blazer pocket and inwardly resolve to tell the truth as soon as possible – within a week, but earlier would be obviously better. Catelyn deserves the truth.

But how will I get around the fact that I'm being blackmailed?

Then it comes to me. A solution.

I'll have to act like I actually want to be Leo's friend. I'll have to invite him to a sleepover, or convince him to have me over for the night.

Then, while he sleeps, I'll get a hold of his phone and delete the photos. I didn't get the opportunity on Friday night when he was over as he had his phone on him the entire evening.

So, sleepover, get him nice and tired so he passes out with exhaustion – maybe with the help of a little of dad's whiskey, then bam, use his fingerprint to unlock his phone and bye-bye photos.

It's so simple.

I laugh to myself.

'Are you okay?' Catelyn asks, half smiling, but her eyes wide in reservation. 'You're acting kinda crazy.'

I smile at her and sigh with genuine relief.

She deserves to know. And I'm going to be there supporting her when she and everyone finds out. Hopefully it can make up for the cowardice until now.

'Yeah. I'm good. Thanks. Thanks for asking,' I say, feeling my cheeks warm again, but in a good way.

'No worries,' she says, and she slides her finger over the mouse pad of her laptop and gets to work on her maths.

I do the same, but I'm only pretending to do my maths.

In reality. I'm planning the downfall of Leo.

And when he leaves me and my family and Catelyn and all girls alone, then maybe, just maybe, I can get my life back.

12

Daphne

My phone buzzes on the bathroom benchtop, lighting up with incessant texts from Leo. I ignore them before stepping into the shower.

For a few minutes, I allow the warm water to wash away my cares and I try to be in the moment and just focus on shampooing my hair and getting myself ready for a fun night out with my book club girls.

We've scheduled drinks at the local pub this time, as opposed to the usual cheese-and-cracker affair at one of our houses or at best, a chat over coffee at a quiet cafe. At first, I was a little apprehensive about the pub idea that Kate had suggested at the last minute. Our original plan had been to meet at Lila's place. It's her turn to host book club. But Kate had insisted on the pub.

Public places, especially busy public places have always made me uncomfortable. Because the sheer volume of people increases the chances of being recognised from my past.

But I'm feeling rebellious today. Defiant. Unwilling to be held ransom by my past anymore.

I received another email today, taunting me to tell my husband the truth about my past, about Anna, before they do.

My ex is just trying to control me by using my own fear against me. The fear of losing my family and the fear of harm coming to them. He obviously has been doing some deep digging to have finally found me. I don't know how he managed it. I don't have social media and I have a new identity.

Perhaps he's bluffing. Perhaps he doesn't even know that I'm married and just wrote 'husband' to see if I react to confirm his guess.

But anyway, the email has triggered an outrage in me.

I escaped him all those years ago and I'm not going to just roll over and let him control me anymore. I'm not the docile, love-starved teenage girl he met all those years ago.

I'm a different girl now.

Woman.

I'm sick of being afraid.

But by the time I've conditioned my hair and shaved my legs and stepped out of the shower, I've managed to let my imagination go crazy – Justin lurking in the shadows of the carpark at the pub, waiting to pounce – and I'm a nervous wreck all over again.

Nothing's changed.

I want to be free of Justin. I want to be immune to fear. But the truth is, I'm still ruled by my ex, because no matter how much time passes, he still has my perfect life in the palm of his hands. One word, one call to my husband, my son, or even my clients... and I'm finished.

I hate him.

While water drips down my naked body and onto the spongy blue bathmat, I spend the next five minutes on my phone stalking his Instagram page, which I'd found this morning over my first coffee, shaking my head at the loved-up quotes about his 'queen'. The pics of him kneeling before her as he proposes. It's like watching a very convincing actor play an Oscar-winning role.

There is no way he is the kind, loving man in these photos.

But judging by all the 'she's so lucky', 'you're a softy', 'SIMP', everyone believes the role he's playing. They're all eating it up just like I did when I first met him and became enchanted by his charm. It's frustrating, to say the least.

The phone vibrates in my hand and when I see that it's Leo again, I'm torn between feeling pity for the kid but also slightly annoyed. Although Gabriel has seemed a lot better since Leo came over, something seems off about their friendship. I sometimes wonder if they even like each other.

And though I am grateful for the support Leo has provided Gabriel during this difficult time, Leo's texts are starting to drain me.

> *Sorry, Leo. I'm about to head out. I'll text you later on if I'm not home too late.*

I don't even bother reading all fifteen of the texts he'd sent, but I scan over them quickly and wince when I see that he'd been preparing dinner and had sent me step-by-step photos of the process. Like a kid wanting to impress his parents.

After he reads my text, the three dots appear and then disappear as he decides not to write back.

I sigh and push Leo to the back corner of my mind and concentrate on getting ready for tonight.

Within half an hour, my hair is dry and styled into soft, dark waves that frame my face. My natural-but-not-actually-natural makeup is done, and I'm wearing a cute shirt with ladybugs all over it and a pair of faded skinny jeans and my favourite orange, pop-of-colour heels.

Joe sends me a text and tells me that he can't wait to spend some one-on-one time with me tonight. I remind him that I'm going out with my book club girls and he doesn't reply despite reading my message.

Great.

Now I have to appease my husband later on tonight as well.

I think about how Joe hasn't been coming home at his usual time in the evening, but instead hours later. And of course, he keeps receiving texts from N.F.

But the strangest thing about Joe is that he has hardly spent time in his study this week. No more after-dinner porn. It either means that he's trying to give it up for the sake of our relationship and is staying back at work to distract himself, or – and this possibility scares me – he has found someone else. Someone with the initials N.F.

I shake my head and beam a smile at myself in the mirror. Overthinking again. I need to learn how to let things be. To stop trying to control the outcome of not only my life but that of my husband and son. What is, is. What will be, will be.

After one last glance in the mirror, I nod and leave the bathroom to find the novel we're to discuss tonight as well as my clutch purse. I grab the keys and head down the hallway to give Gabriel's bedroom door a gentle rap with my knuckles.

'Yeah.'

I carefully open his door and find him staring intently at his laptop screen. Instead of sitting in the dark he has his bedside lamp on and is sipping a mug of steaming coffee and has a plate filled with snacks beside him.

'You look so focussed, Gabe. What are you working on? Is it an assignment?' *And happy*, I want to say. *You look so happy!*

He thinks for a quick second, then nods, a spark of light shining in his dark eyes. My Gabriel is back.

'Fantastic! I guess I'll leave you to it then.'

'You look nice, Mum,' he says and I have to restrain myself from putting my hand on my heart and bawling happy tears.

Instead, I walk over and bend to plant a kiss on his forehead, enjoying the comfortingly sweet scent of his kids' apple shampoo – still his favourite after all these years. I stand and stroke the dark curls away from his forehead.

'I love you so very much, Gabriel.'

He flicks his hair back into place. 'Love you too, Mum.'

I smile. Gabriel is talking to me again.

'I'm off to the pub with the book club ladies.'

'Don't have too much fun,' says Gabriel, rolling his eyes.

I laugh, and when I leave his room, I must admit I have a bit of a spring in my step. All of a sudden, things don't seem so dark. Maybe I'll even build up the courage to tell Joe the truth about my dark past, to finally come clean and purge myself of my heavy secret. Maybe I should also out my ex about his shameful behaviour all those years ago. His fiancée has a right to know. This is the man she is planning on marrying. On starting a family with sometime in the future, according to her social media posts.

Still, the idea of telling Joe about my past almost kills my mood, despite how liberating I know doing it will actually make me feel. Once Joe knows, I have nothing to be afraid of anymore. Because my biggest fear would have been realised.

But I'm not quite ready yet, even though I need to do it sooner rather than later now that I'm receiving those threats via email.

And I don't want to think about it anymore. Tonight, I want to celebrate the fact that my Gabriel is back, smiling and rolling his eyes. And most important of all, talking to me. I still want to know what occurred on that Saturday night, but for now I'm just happy that he seems more like his happy, usual self.

* * *

By the time I arrive at the pub, my emotions are in check, and I feel somewhat excited at the prospect of a nice chat about books over a glass of wine with my book club girls.

The pub smells of spilled beer, steak, curries, and chicken parmigiana and the bar is sticky with the residue of someone's cocktail.

Lila, Sam and Kate wave at me from a corner table to my right, raising their glasses and indicating that I should order a drink before I join them.

I order a large glass of white wine.

While the barman pours my drink, I stiffen as I hear a gruff voice shouting my name from across the room, to my left.

'That'll be twelve dollars, love.'

I open my clutch purse with trembling fingers and take my credit card out, during which I sneak a glance at the man calling my name.

I sigh with both relief and frustration. It's the potential client I cancelled on, the one who said he thought he knew me from somewhere. Bloody heck. Can't he just go away? At least it's not my ex, though.

He raises his espresso martini and beams a smile my way.

I squint a little, as though I've forgotten to wear my glasses and quickly tap to pay for my wine and hurry to join my friends, pretending that I didn't see him or hear my name being called.

'Let's go over there where the couches are,' I suggest to all three, nodding towards the more dimly lit area.

'You mean where that couple are practically making babies?'

'Yeah,' I say, laughing when I spy the couple Kate's talking about. 'But look there's a whole couch for us in the corner. Quick. Let's snatch it up.'

'It's too dark where the couches are,' groans Kate. 'We need to be out here.' She throws her head back and squints at the bright light overhead. 'Under the spotlight so all the cute men can spot Lila.'

'But it does look cosy,' says Lila, who is going on two years single after her husband cheated on her, is still a little angry about it, and definitely does not want to be noticed by any men.

'Yes, it's comfy over there and maybe even bit quieter,' I say. 'Perfect for chatting about the book.' I wave the paperback I brought with me in the air and Kate and Lila share a glance and erupt into giggles. They proceed to laugh, until they are both in fits, each trying to explain why they are laughing so hard only to erupt into even more laughter.

I watch on amused, sipping my wine and shaking my head, my heart warm. These two are just the distraction I needed.

'Well, I absolutely loved it,' says Sam, a cosmo in her hand. 'And I'm completely in love with David,' she says touching my arm.

I feel bad now. I didn't even know there was a David in the book. This is the first time that I haven't completed a book before our catch-up and all it does is remind me of the reasons why I haven't been able to read.

Kate and Lila roll their eyes. 'Book? Who cares about the bloody book?' says Kate.

I grin. Kate and Lila are the biggest book-nerds in our club and are usually sticklers for following the strictest procedure at our meetings, which include reading from a long list of questions regarding characters, plot and setting – which usually takes two hours or longer to answer. But it's pretty fun to see them let loose for once.

'Kate won five thousand on a scratchie!' says Lila.

'Oh my gosh, really?' I ask.

Kate nods, her face serious.

'I honestly still cannot believe it. That's why we're celebrating. We are going to get good and wasted, Daphne. I'm going to order you a special drink to have after that wine. You only live once and all of that.'

'Yeah, and you only die once too, after you drink and drive,' says Sam.

Everyone grows quiet for a second, before Kate flicks an ash-blonde curl out of her eyes and smiles. 'I'll shout everyone an Uber. I mean, I can afford it,' she says, standing taller and raising her brows regally.

'I've got to start early in the morning,' says Sam with a shrug. 'Sorry for being a wet blanket.'

I don't exactly want to get so drunk that I need an Uber. Wait. What I mean to say is, I do want to get drunk, but tonight is not the best of nights for that, as I still haven't spoken to Joe, so I'll stick to my two drinks and then have a sparkling water or two afterwards. Lila and Kate are so drunk they won't even notice anyway.

I shepherd them over to the far corner of the room towards the one vacant couch and we settle in and despite Lila and Kate's earlier eyeroll, we discuss the book for at least an hour, forgetting our noisy surroundings for a moment. In typical fashion, our varying opinions clash, but we still manage to listen respectfully to each other so that everybody feels heard.

Sam is practically swooning as she discusses the protagonist, David, and we nod and agree with almost everything she says about him. It's probably the one thing we always agree on – swoon-worthy male characters. And even though I haven't read much of the novel yet, I instinctively know that I'd like David, just from Sam's observations of his character. Makes me want to read more as soon as I get home tonight. While Joe and I aren't having any sex, the romance in the books I read is the next best thing.

Lila elbows me and suddenly I'm not in medieval England anymore, but back at the bustling pub.

'Daphne,' she says. 'Don't look now, but there's a hot guy checking you out.' She glances somewhere behind me and I freeze a little. Firstly, I think of my ex, but then I remember that annoying almost-client that I saw earlier. I wish he'd just disappear. He's going to ruin my fun night.

I shrug. 'I don't need any hot guys in my life. Joe's the one for me.'

Kate cheers loudly and bangs her glass against mine a little too hard.

'Here, here,' says Lila. 'You're a good, loyal human. Joe's lucky to have you. At least he knows you're not going to run off with the first person who looks at you a certain way, or works for you.'

From the stiffness of her expression, and the way that her flute glass is trembling, I worry that she's going to burst into tears. It's been two years since her partner got his secretary pregnant and decided that Lila was merely something in his life that needed disposing of. Though she tells us repeatedly that she's over him, every time I see her, she can't help but bring him up.

'You know,' she says, after taking a lung gulp of her prosecco and draining the glass. 'I went on his Instagram. He's finally got an account now that he's with her. Because, you know, she's an influencer.' Lila makes air quotes.

'Anyway, his account is all photos of their new home by the ocean, paid for by his fiancée's family inheritance, and about a million photos of their little toddler who of course looks like one of those babies from a nappy commercial, all blue eyes and gummy smiles. And he's cute, the little kid. I wanted him to be born ugly. I hate myself for thinking that but I want my ex's kid to be hideous. And I want his fiancée to dump him and I want him to be depressed and living out of his car somewhere.' She looks at her empty glass and tips it to make sure that it's empty. Then she looks up at us each in turn. 'Does that make me a monster?' Tears pool in her eyes. 'I am a monster, aren't I? Because I want their pretty baby to be ugly. Who thinks like that?'

'Those Instagram babies are all photoshopped anyway. Honestly most of them look like freakish little dolls,' says Sam, shuddering. 'I personally think it's creepy. Anyway, I'm going to get you another drink.'

'Wait,' says Lila. 'Can you get me a cup of tea instead? If they sell tea here. I think I've had enough.'

We all murmur in agreement and soon Sam is winding her way through the beer and wine swilling crowd, back to the bar with an order of four cups of sweet, strong tea.

'So how are you and Joe?' asks Kate.

'We're pretty good,' I lie.

Kate sighs. 'Oh, you two are so cute. Honestly, I think you are the only one who has the perfect relationship. My husband gets on my bloody nerves. I love him, but he drives me insane sometimes. I have to keep finding him jobs around the house on the weekends just to keep him busy.'

So that I don't have to respond, I knock back the rest of my wine, which has gone warm and tastes slightly bitter. I need to go to the toilet, but I'm worried about running into that guy.

Sam returns and joins us on the couch. 'The teas are on their way,' she says, before gulping down the rest of her cosmopolitan.

I don't know why, maybe because tonight is the first time I've felt truly connected to the girls, but I'm so tempted to share my secret. Right here, right now. Just to see what they all think.

But I know I'll regret it once I do. Because once you release secrets into the wild, you can never gather them back up and keep them to yourself anymore. They cease to be your secrets anymore. The reason I want to keep it all a secret is because it gives me a sense of control. And I had that control for so many years, until my ex, the only other person who knows my true past, had to come back to screw it all up.

'I wish I had your life, Kate,' says Lila rather wistfully, her hazel eyes shiny with emotion. She blinks at the steaming cups of tea that a waitress sets down before us. 'You've got a hubby you've been with since you were teenagers. And you two still have sex. Actual sex. And lots of it. And you do weird stuff too... what was it? That thing on the lawnmower.' She puts a hand to her mouth and her eyes widen. 'Sorry. I'm not supposed to tell, am I?'

Sam frowns and giggles at the same time. 'Sounds bloody painful.'

'Forget I said it,' says Lila, who apologises to Kate again.

The usual Kate would blush and stutter, but this Kate, drunken Kate, merely shrugs. 'It's fine.'

Lila's eyes tear up again. 'It's something I miss so much. The intimacy. The being held after. That used to be my favourite part.'

Kate grins, obviously trying to lighten the mood, and elbows me. 'I bet you and Joe get up to some good and proper nasty stuff.' She winks exaggeratedly at the others. 'It's always the quiet ones.' And they all laugh.

I smile. She's partly correct. I do enjoy sex. I've always enjoyed it. Even after Justin nearly ruined it for me.

Joe is the one who actually killed my sex life. That's the sad fact. By preferring his hand on himself and his eyes on random women on-screen.

'Oh, she does have nasty sex. Look at that face, you little slag,' says Sam, leaning forward winking at me and spilling most of her tea onto the carpet in the process. 'Oops, look at me spilling my drink and I only had one cosmo,' she says, laughing.

I laugh, despite my dire sex life. Mainly because everyone is being so uninhibited tonight, so open and real. And I realise that I quite like it.

'We should ditch the tea and get a round of proper drinks again so Daphne will spill,' says Kate with a loaded wink.

I feel like the fun police when I announce, 'I'm driving actually, so it's only tea for me here on in.'

The girls pout and we all fall silent for a few seconds, before Sam's eyes widen and she leans forward. 'Oh my gosh, it's the hot guy. The one who was staring at you before. He's coming over!'

My heart lurches into a state of panic, as though it's frantically attempting to beat its way out of my chest. I want to run away with it.

But because we are seated with our backs to the dim corner there is no escaping him.

Oh gosh, what if he recognises me from that video? Surely, he won't mention what he's seen in front of my friends. Nobody would say something like that in public, surely?

He crouches down by the side of the couch and smiles at me, his teeth startlingly white in the dim, bluish lighting of the pub.

'Hey, I'm glad to see that you're feeling better,' he says with a devilish grin on his handsome face.

I blush, feeling mildly embarrassed that he'd guessed that I had faked my sudden illness that day.

'Thank you. Yes. I'm feeling much better and I'm sorry that I had to cancel any future appointments with you. I'm just so back-to-back with my current clients.'

He glances at my friends and back at me. 'I'm sure you are very sorry,' he says with a knowing grin.

I frown at him, completely perplexed at what he's implying. Heat begins to creep up my neck, flooding my face. Sweat gathers on my upper lip. I don't like where this is going.

'But hey, I realise where I know you from,' he says, brows raised.

My pulse throbs in my eardrums and I abruptly stand. He follows suit.

I feel the eyes of my friends burning my skin so I lead the man away from the couch and over towards the long corridor leading towards the toilets. People stream past us from both directions. A woman staggers into me and mumbles an apology when she spills a bit of her drink on my arm. Something cold and dark seeps into my cardigan and through my shirt. I shake my arm and sigh with irritation.

The man laughs and looks me up and down before he speaks.

'Sydney to Perth, 1999. Qantas flight. I was the dorky guy sitting next to you reading Ken Follett. Remember? Benjamin, the wannabe writer. I used to have glasses but I wear contacts now. We ended up reading together for most of the flight. Taking turns with the chapters. I kept critiquing Follett's writing style, like I had a clue,' he says, rolling his eyes.

For a moment everything stops, the chatter around me, the laughter, the music... even my heart. And then I remember. I remember him! The first kind person I spoke to after leaving Justin.

A ripple of happiness tickles my spine. It's a nice memory. Something I'd completely forgotten. I'd worked so hard to forget my past that I'd swept away some of the good memories too.

I can't help but smile, and then laugh. Yes. The young man I remember from that flight did harp on about character arcs and symbolism a bit.

I'm so happy that I impulsively stand on my tiptoes and give him a little hug.

'I do. I do remember you!' I take a step back now, embarrassed by my spontaneous embrace. 'Oh, my gosh! How are you?'

'I'm good. I'm good. You know,' he says. 'I'm so happy you're looking so well. I remember you tearing an entire packet of tissues up, one by one, into tiny little pieces. I knew you were going through something. You were shaking for the whole journey. I always wondered what became of you.' He leans in and I can smell his aftershave. It's so strong it makes me dizzy. 'To tell you the truth, I always wondered if you were on the run,' he says, his blue eyes, shiny with kindness, are fixed on mine. 'I remember your fingertips were all stained black, like you'd coloured your hair.' His gaze strays up to my hair and back to my face.

I let out a shaky laugh and wave away Kate, who is now standing behind Ben and gesturing to me with wild hands that she'll help if I want to escape him.

I wave her away and give her a thumbs up, smiling over Ben's shoulder.

'You were right,' I say, admitting the truth out loud for the first time in my life. 'I was escaping a bad relationship so, I guess, on the run in a sense. More so running towards a new life here in sunny Western Australia.'

We chat a little more and I agree to see him next week and take a look at his books because now I know that he poses no threat.

After promising to give him a call on Monday morning, I order a couple of plates of nibblies for the girls and I. Kate and Lila definitely need something in their stomachs to go with the tea and to soak up all the booze from earlier.

An hour later, the white serving plates are empty, the teacups are drained, and the girls are almost sober. We even manage to chat about the novel some more, which is nice and again, makes me all the more eager to get home, into my pyjamas and lose myself in a good story.

We kiss each other goodbye in the carpark, under a beautifully starry sky, while autumn leaves circle around our feet in the cool night breeze.

Once I'm in my car, I don't have longer than ten seconds or so to think about Ben and how amazing it is that we've crossed paths, when my phone rings.

I pull my phone out of my clutch purse and my heart panics for the second time in one night.

It's Leo. He usually texts. Something must be wrong.

I answer right away, trying my best to ignore the drunken group of young men who are taking turns to kick an empty beer can across the carpark in front of me.

'Hello? Leo?'

'Hi, Daphne,' he says, his breathing heavy.

'Is everything okay? Did something happen with Gabriel?'

'Gabriel? No. Why would I be calling about Gabriel?'

'Oh. I'm sorry. I just thought... well, anyway, is everything okay with you?'

'No. It's not.' His voice is tight with irritation. 'I think there's someone in my house. It's either a break-in, or... I've got a ghost.'

'Have you called the police?'

'No. I just thought you might... oh, don't worry about it.'

'Wait. Would you like me to send Joe around?' I look at the time on my car stereo. It's 10pm. I wonder if Joe's even home yet.

'Oh, you're still out?'

Why does that question make me feel like I'm being judged or interrogated?

'Yes. But I'm in my car about to go home.' I shake my head as I watch the can-kicking group of men gather at a bus stop along the main road. Now they are shaking a poor, defenceless rubbish bin. And why am I explaining myself to a teenage boy?

'Do you think you can come to my house and just walk through all the rooms with me? It's just, that's what my mum and I do together when we're home without my dad.'

I can hear the little boy in Leo's voice and my heart melts.

'Okay. I'll be there in five.'

13

Daphne

Leo is waiting for me in the driveway, wearing blue flannelette pyjama bottoms and a faded, grey Minecraft shirt. His hair flies around his pale face in the wind and he looks to be shivering, his eyes round with fear. I'm so glad I came. Imagine if I'd ignored him in such an obvious state of distress? I'd never forgive myself if something had happened to him.

He comes to my passenger door as soon as I kill the engine and opens it for me, a smile of relief relaxes his face.

'Do you still think there's someone inside?' I ask.

His brows raise, as though he's forgotten about the intruder already, and his smile recedes.

'I don't know. I've been waiting out here since I spoke to you. I'm not going in unless you come in with me,' he says, his pupils so dilated that the paleness in his eyes has been swallowed by the darkness of his fear. He looks so fragile and I'm puzzled as to why his parents don't coordinate their business trips so that one remains at home with Leo while the other is away. It seems a little inconsiderate.

'Of course,' I say, smiling softly. 'Let's do this together.'

It feels strange and illicit, stepping into this boy's home without his mother or father being here. But what else can I do? He needs an adult right now and I can hardly turn him down. And anyway, it feels good to be helping him out. Poor kid just seems so lonely.

There's an awkward shyness about him too, as though he's been rattling around in his huge house alone for way too long, and doesn't know how to be around people comfortably. I really must call his mother. Maybe I'll give her a buzz tomorrow morning. Just to let her know that Leo and Gabriel are friends and that Leo has spent a bit of time cheering Gabriel up of late, and that I just thought that she should know. But that sounds plain weird the more I think about it. But I do think reaching out to her will make me feel a little better about situations like this where he's reached out to me for help.

Leo closes the front door behind us. The sound of the locks clicking echo across the glossy, tiled entrance of the grand home, sending a cold shiver shooting down my spine.

'Is it wise to lock it?' I ask. 'If a murderer chases us, we'll have to waste time with locks now,' I say, and quickly grin, trying to ease the tension in the air.

He says nothing, but his face grows serious. Poor Leo. I don't think Gabriel has been scared in that kind of way since he was around nine years of age. But then Gabriel has never had to spend the night in his own home alone.

'My mum usually links her arm through mine,' Leo says, his face pale.

'Oh, okay,' I say, and link my arm through his, secretly wondering if there's some kind of surveillance camera inside the home. Houses like this usually do have it.

My stomach turns at the thought. Imagine the parents have one of those modern units that link up to their phones, and they are watching me, a strange woman, link her arm through that of their teenage son's before wandering through their home.

'Are you okay?' he asks, dragging his eyes away from the top of the staircase where the rooms are dark and ominous-looking, to check on me.

I release a sigh and shake my head. Who cares if the parents watch me? Leo will tell them that I'm Gabriel's mum and that he asked me for help after hearing a noise. I'll probably get a thank you text. Who knows, it might allow me to explain who I am and break the ice.

'Yes, I'm fine,' I say, just wanting to get this over with. 'Just a little apprehensive. It's so dark upstairs.'

He grins down at me and then rolls his eyes. 'Who's protecting who?' he says and tightens his grip on my arm. 'Let's go up there. It's where I heard the noise. Near my room.'

I draw a deep breath, wishing Joe was here. I don't know what's freaking me out more, Leo or the possibility of someone hiding in the shadows of this mansion.

'Okay.'

We take the stairs, slowly. Heat radiates from Leo's body. He's sweating, his shirt damp against my arm. He needs to take a shower.

Once at the top, he leads me towards a dimly lit room with glowing stars dotting the ceiling and a neatly made queen-sized bed in the centre with a navy doona on top. A wide-screen television, connected to what appears to be an Xbox, much like Gabriel's, sits directly across from the bed.

'Wow,' I say. 'Nice room. It's bigger than my master bedroom.'

'It's okay,' Leo says, shrugging, staring at the floor.

'Do you ever play with Gabriel?' I ask. 'On the Xbox?

Leo shakes his head.

'I friended him, but we haven't played yet. In fact, I don't think he friended me back.' The muscles in his forearm ripple and tighten against mine. 'It's probably with all the drama going on lately, since that party, you know? He probably forgot to add me.'

'Yes, for sure.' I think about how Gabriel seemed tense while Leo was over, almost like he didn't want him around. And yet it was Gabriel himself that invited Leo into our home. Something certainly doesn't add up.

Suddenly it seems sinister to be walking around in the dimly lit upstairs of a deadlocked home with a very tall teenage boy I hardly know. The Xbox has me thinking of Gabriel and how much I'd rather be home with him right now.

'Want me to send him a message? I could ask him to game with me while you're here. Then I can say, oh hey your mum is at my house. That would be pretty funny.'

Oh God no, I think, but hide my horror behind a gentle smile.

Not only would Gabriel think it weird that I'm here in Leo's house at this hour, I hardly want to sit and watch Leo game for hours on end. I just want to go home, get into my pyjamas and finish the novel that is waiting for me on the passenger seat of my car.

After having such a great night with the girls tonight, I can hardly wait for the next catch-up. It's so nice to have a group of girls I feel comfortable with. I've never experienced that before. Friends. Besties. I never stayed with a foster family long enough to stay at the same school and develop deep friendships.

Maybe, eventually, I'll be able to speak to them about my past.

And now that I have also visited a busy pub, and survived. I feel like I'm slowly starting to look my personal demons in the eye. Baby steps.

'Actually, I'm pretty tired, Leo. So that will have to wait. Plus, we don't allow Gabriel to be on after 10pm.' I draw a deep breath and rub my hands together. 'Okay, next room. Let's go kick some intruder butt.'

Leo smiles and leads me to the next room, then the next. Once all wardrobes are checked, under-beds, bathrooms and even the attic, we head downstairs and check the kitchen, the dining room, the living area, the lounge room, laundry and then finally, he leads me into the theatre room.

It's pitch-black until he turns on the light.

'Wow,' I say, putting a hand to my chest like Scarlett O'Hara.

'It's pretty good,' he says, blushing, as though he'd built the room himself.

I tug my arm free from his sweaty grasp and walk down the red-carpeted aisle between the two rows of gold-trimmed, red velvet seats.

'How wonderful,' I say, sitting down, facing the large white screen on the wall. I sigh with exhaustion. My feet throb in my heels from all this room-checking.

'Yeah,' he says, collapsing into a chair beside me. 'We can watch a movie if you like. Anything you want. I've got Netflix, Disney Plus.'

I stifle a yawn.

'Oh gosh, I'd absolutely love to, Leo, but I really can't. I've got work to finish tonight and then I need to get up early. I've got back-to-back client meetings tomorrow.'

Leo's face drops and he looks away. 'Okay. Maybe another time,' he mumbles – his voice quiet, his ears reddening.

'Okay,' I say, getting to my feet. 'I'd best be off and leave you to get some sleep.'

'Oh, I never sleep properly while my parents are away. I just game all night or read or...'

'Oh, what genre do you like to read? I'm a huge book lover too.'

He stands, a little taller and prouder it seems, his concave chest attempting to puff up.

'Sci-fi mainly, but sometimes I like fantasy, hard fantasy. You?'

'Thrillers mainly. Domestic and psychological. But I can pretty much read anything as long as I find the characters interesting. Some of the hard fantasy I've ready is pretty good.'

He shrugs and folds his arms across his chest and fixes me with his pale green eyes.

'So, what makes a character interesting to you?'

I pause for a moment and mull over his question.

'Flaws, I suppose. I like looking for imperfections in people. Not superficial flaws. I mean flaws on the inside. I think reading about other people, and the mistakes they make, helps you to feel better about who you are.'

He blushes a little and runs his hand along the back of the theatre seat he'd just been sitting in.

'I can't imagine you having any flaws.' He looks at me intently. 'It's almost like... you're perfect. Like you were just born completely flawless inside and out.'

Now it's my turn to blush. If only he knew about my past and about the video. He'd be disgusted by me.

I turn and exit the room, heading for the front door, the heels of my orange shoes click-clacking against the tiles. Leo shuffles behind me.

'Sorry. I made you uncomfortable just now, didn't I? When I said that you're perfect.' He slips his warm, sweaty hand around my arm. 'Is it because you think you're flawed? Or because you might have done something that makes you feel bad as a person? Something that makes you less than perfect?'

I flinch and slowly turn around, pulling away at the same time. His hand drops to his side.

My heart races and the sweat on the back of my neck feels cold all of a sudden. Why am I feeling this way? As though I'm scared of Leo? There is no way he could know about the video. He's just a boy. It'd be impossible for him to recognise me. I looked so different back then.

We lock eyes, but his unblinking gaze is too intense to hold. I stare at the brass doorknob instead.

'No... it's... it's flattering for you to think that I don't have any flaws.' I glance up and force a smile. 'But of course, I'm far from flawless. I don't believe there's a person alive who isn't.'

He smiles softly and reaches out towards me, but after I visibly stiffen, he tucks his hand behind his back.

'Hasn't your husband ever said that to you? That you're perfect?'

I look away and reach for the brass doorknob, but remember that he's locked it.

'It's locked,' I say, feeling short of breath all of a sudden. I step aside so that he can unlock it.

Making no move to let me out, he blushes slightly and shifts on the spot instead.

'Thank you so much for coming here tonight, Daphne. I really appreciate you caring enough to come out and check that I'm safe.'

And just like that Leo is an innocent, vulnerable boy again. I feel ridiculous now for getting so worked up and anxious to leave the house. It's not as though he's going to do me any harm. He's just a kid from Gabriel's school for crying out loud. I need to get a grip on my paranoia. It's all because of those stupid emails.

'You're welcome,' I say, my heart warming and no longer trying to jackhammer its way out of my chest. 'Joe and I are always just a phone call away.'

'Hug?' he asks, arms wide and eyes hopeful.

I hesitate and imagine his parents watching from a hotel room in Singapore via their security app. But how can I deny him? When I'm about to abandon him, leaving him all alone inside this mansion?

I lean forward for the briefest of hugs, then stand aside while he unlocks the door and opens it, letting in a swirl of leaves that have gathered on his doorstep.

A sigh of relief escapes my lips once I'm buckled into the driver's seat of my car.

The wind is picking up, whistling through the gaps in my car windows and it looks like that storm the news has been banging on about is finally coming. I cannot wait to get home to Joe and Gabriel.

As I back out the driveway I wave and motion for Leo, whose hair is flapping against his forehead in the wind, to go back inside the house.

He does and only when he is standing inside the home, waving from the front door, do I beep and drive away.

Once home, I check on Gabriel who is fast asleep, his breathing steady and his dark hair flopped over his forehead. After I gently stroke his hair back, I head to the master bedroom after doing an extra thorough door and window lock check of our own home. Being at Leo's has left me feeling jittery.

When I step into the bedroom I tiptoe around, not wanting to wake Joe who needs to get up early in the morning. Instead of showering I get straight into my pyjamas, set my phone on the bedside table and go into the ensuite bathroom to wash my face and take my contact lenses out.

Once I'm done, I creep back to my side of the bed and Joe rolls over to face me.

'Where were you?' he asks, not appearing sleepy at all. 'Tonight?'

I slip into bed beside him, the sheets warm from his body heat. Outside the wind batters against our windows and I shuffle a little closer to Joe.

'The book club meeting. At the pub. Remember?' I turn off my bedside lamp so that we're facing each other in the dark.

'Oh. Did you stop anywhere on the way home?'

I pause for a minute, thinking about what I'm going to say. It reminds me of my Anna days. Always having to think up the right answer, the answer that wouldn't set Justin off.

But with Joe, I've never had to lie. That's part of why I fell in love with him.

'I actually stopped in at Leo's place.'

Joe doesn't say a word.

My phone lights up and I quickly roll over to see four texts from Leo. I pull a face and turn back to Joe.

'Why did you go to that kid's place? It's a little weird, don't you think?'

'Yeah, I know, it is. But he called me just as I was leaving the pub and was really scared. He'd heard a noise and thought someone was in his house.'

'Where the heck are his parents?'

'In Singapore or somewhere. They're away on business.'

'Surely he can ring a grandparent or an aunt?'

I roll onto my back and stare up at the ceiling, irritation creeping under my skin.

'You don't think of that in the moment. I was genuinely concerned for the kid and couldn't say no. Imagine if Gabriel were on his own and needed help? I'd like to think his friends' parents would do the same.'

Joe grunts. 'True. But you should have called me. I would have come out and checked his house for him. We could have done it together.'

'I didn't know if you'd be in the mood. You seemed grumpy when I reminded you that I had book club tonight.'

'True.' He's silent for a few seconds. 'Work's been shitty lately, that's all.' He yawns. 'Anyway, I'm glad you're home. I missed you.'

Joe snuggles up from behind and spoons me, his strong, warm body setting me at ease. I've always felt safe in Joe's embrace. Loved. Cherished.

As my heart relaxes into a slow and steady rhythm, Joe begins to gently snore, and even though the sound normally irritates me, I nestle against the warmth of his body because I've missed him so much. I've missed having his body pressed up so closely against mine.

Then I feel it.

Hard and poking into my back.

I haven't felt it in so long, I wonder if I'm imagining it.

I reach around and run my fingers along his hard length through his pyjamas, feeling like I'm molesting my own husband. It sends a little thrill through me to know that he's reacting to my body brushing up against him. Maybe there's hope for us after all.

But then a thought terrifies me. What if he's been seeing someone and she is the reason behind it. He could be dreaming about her right now.

106

Wide awake, I stew over this for a while until my phone lights up.

It's Leo. Again.

He's left six messages. Mostly thanking me.

But it's the last one that makes me feel a little uncomfortable.

> *I liked it when you said that you wouldn't have been able to sleep until you knew that I was okay. It's really sweet to know that you care so much about me, Daphne. I like that a lot.*

After mulling it over for a good ten minutes, I decide to text Leo back. Because the boy is alone and I don't want him feeling abandoned while his parents are away. But I'm careful to not make it too personal.

> *You're welcome, Leo. And of course, we care about you. You're Gabriel's friend. All of Gabriel's friends are important to us. Goodnight.*

Without waiting for a response, I slide my phone back onto the bedside table and when it keeps lighting up, I put it on do not disturb.

But it's too late. I'm already disturbed.

14

Catelyn

I toss my unappetising and very warm cheese and salad sandwich into the nearest bin and take a deep breath before walking over to the back of the sports shed.

Today is my only opportunity to visit with Gabriel while he is alone at lunchtime.

Leo had to stay back in Science for watching YouTube during class time. I kind of felt bad for him when the teacher revealed the title of the video he'd been watching.

'How to get her attention, in a good way,' Mr Malobi had read out to the entire class, his voice light with repressed laughter.

Everyone had cracked up, except me. People are bastards. Leo turned every shade of red in the space of five seconds. And even though he's acted like a creep towards me in the past, I still felt bad for him.

But I have to admit, I was pretty happy when I heard Mr Malobi tell Leo that he had to stay in at lunch to finish his work. Because it meant that I could try to speak to Gabriel again, without worrying about Leo hanging around and listening in.

I still need to know more about what happened that night at that party. And also, I kind of enjoyed talking to him in class the other day. Gabriel is a good guy, and it makes for a nice change after spending time with so many assholes the past two years.

As I approach the back of the sports shed, my heart thunders in my rib cage and my palms begin to sweat. Great. Now I'm going to get nervous and clam up. This is so much harder than being forced to sit next to each other in class. This is voluntary contact. And I don't think I'm confident enough for it.

I think about the bottle of gin my mum has hidden in the pantry and know that it's the only way I can muster up the courage to talk to him again. Properly. And yeah, I know that it's a pretty stupid thing to do, considering I've been trying to be a better person and stop drinking and sleeping around and everything. But I can start fresh tomorrow. Tonight, I need the courage. Just one more time and then I'll start learning how to talk to people without alcohol running through my veins.

'Hey,' I say. Just thinking about the gin has already boosted my courage.

Gabriel is sitting with his back against the shed, but raises his head and glances at me, his head pulls back, as though he's shocked to see me, or frightened even. But he quickly puts his head down and stares at the grey bitumen in front of him.

The muscles along his forearms ripple with tension. Gabriel's vibe is screaming at me to back off. To not ask him any questions.

I have to tread carefully. Very carefully, or I'll lose him.

'Hey,' he says, eventually, raising his head to stare out across the fence line.

There's a long silence between us and for a second, I contemplate leaving, but then I think about my empty house and that bottle.

'Do you want to get drunk?' I blurt out. 'My mum's away at my aunt's for two nights down south, and there's a big bottle of gin at the bottom of our pantry.' I smile, even though he's not looking. 'She hides it all behind an enormous box of cornflakes and thinks I'm clueless.' I shrug and feel my face heating up. 'So, do you want to?'

109

Gabriel's lips curve into a gentle smile and then he turns to gaze up at me, a hand shielding his dark eyes from the sun.

'Yes,' he says quickly, as though he's as desperate as I to drink. 'When?' he asks.

'Straight after school,' I say. 'You can walk home with me. I just live up the street.' I nod over in the direction of my street over the fence. 'You can stay for tea if you like. I'm going to make coconut mango chicken curry.'

He nods and seems to retreat into his shell again. His handsome face strained.

'Meet me at the teachers' carpark,' I say and he nods and gets up just as the siren goes, almost like he sensed it, or because he wanted to get away from me suddenly.

He brushes past me. He smells nice. Clean. Not all sweaty and gross like most of the other boys.

I follow him, not because I'm a stalker, but because my locker is next to his.

But when we round the corner, Leo is walking towards us and he raises his thick brows when he sees me walking beside Gabriel.

'Gabe,' he says, nodding at Gabriel. I honestly had never been aware that they were so close. Their friendship, or whatever it is, is so confusing.

Gabriel nods and says nothing in reply and continues to walk until he gets to his locker.

Leo follows him and leans against the locker beside Gabriel's. My locker is only two away on the other side of Gabriel, so I can hear them converse.

'What'd you do at lunch?' asks Leo, who seems to be attempting to look calm and casual but is anything but. I can see the sweat at his temples, dampening his dark hair, and the way his pale eyes keep darting over Gabriel's hunched form to glare at me while Gabriel drags books out of his messy locker, makes me one hundred percent sure he wants me gone.

I turn my attentions to the books in my locker and pretend to be engrossed in an old history book, when from out the corner of my eye I spy Gabriel's usual bunch of friends walk past.

Gabriel stiffens and a couple of them look his way. One of the guys even slows down enough to playfully nudge him in the back with his elbow, but Gabriel just buries himself deeper into his locker instead of turning around to face his friend. After a few seconds, the friend gives up and moves on and joins the others who've already walked off, most of them shaking their heads. I wonder what that's all about. And how it's connected to that party, seeing as how none of them attended.

'Hello? Gabriel?' says Leo, banging on the locker like he's knocking on the front door to his house.

Gabriel pulls his head out of his locker, his jaw set and his dark eyes cold.

'What?'

'So... what did you do at lunch?'

Gabriel flickers his gaze my way for a fraction of a second. He seems very conscious of me standing there listening. And although I've already collected the books that I need and my laptop for my last two classes, I'm intrigued to see how these two interact. I've got a weird feeling something isn't right between them. Not genuine. But why? Why is Gabriel friends with Leo when he clearly seems physically repulsed by the guy?

Gabriel shrugs and flicks a glance at Leo. 'I don't know. Sat in the usual spot and ate.'

Leo shows no sign of noticing Gabriel's indifference or his extremely uninterested tone.

'Nice. Hey, you wanna come to mine after school? I've got a free house. My parents are still away.'

'Nah, I've got to be home early today. My mum wants me to start concentrating on my homework more. She's banning me from the Xbox too,' he adds with a poor attempt at a laugh. The lie rolled off his tongue so smoothly I'm not sure whether to be impressed or worried.

'Oh. Okay.' Leo raps on Gabriel's locker and pulls his phone out of his pocket, grinning almost like an evil villain from a superhero movie as he scrolls through whatever it is that he's looking at. He looks up from his phone, glances at me quickly and gives me a frosty glare, before he grins at Gabriel in a way that makes my skin turn cold and then turns and walks away.

Gabriel takes his laptop out and slams his locker shut and starts to walk away, then he abruptly stops and turns.

'See you after school,' he says, his dark eyes blazing with extra intensity – as though he's desperate for that gin. 'At the teachers' carpark.'

I nod. Blushing for some reason. 'Yep. See you then.'

I stand there for a bit, pretending I have more things to get from my locker, because I don't want him to think I'm stalking him. After half a minute passes, I start to make my way towards my second-last class.

As I watch Gabriel, who veers right to go to the Graphic Design building, I look around for Leo and realise that I've lost him. But when I glance towards Gabriel again, whose back I see disappearing into a crowd of kids, I notice Leo hiding behind a tree, clearly watching Gabriel.

I shiver.

I'll have to tell Gabriel about it today, when he's over. Maybe we can bond over Leo's weirdness. Not that I'm any less weird, watching Gabriel myself. But I have my reasons.

The second siren goes, to signal the start of class, and I quicken my pace and get to class just in time, the air-conditioned room a relief from all the warm sunshine outside.

'Sit down,' Miss Canter says, her eyebrows raised at Leo, who enters last.

His face falls when he sees that his usual seat at the back is taken and that the only available seat is next to me. Maybe if he hadn't wasted time spying on Gabriel he would have gotten here earlier and his usual seat would have been free.

Leo visibly shudders as he makes his way over to the seat beside me and sits.

Trying my best to forget he's there, I get out my laptop and start to record the notes from the whiteboard onto a new document. But no matter how hard I concentrate, a panicky feeling starts to form in my belly, just below my ribs. It's like a burning swirl of acid and I don't know why it's there. I wonder if it's because Gabriel is coming over today.

I picture us walking to my house together and to be honest, I feel part nervous about it, but also a little bit excited. Like I'm looking forward to not only potentially finding out what happened at the party, but maybe, just maybe, actually making a friend.

I guess the nerves present are because I don't want to screw it up. And I'm the queen of screwing things up.

Most people at school treat me like I'm a disease. All the girls ignore me, like I don't exist, or they assume I'm going to offer their boyfriends sex or something. And unless I'm at a party blind drunk and offering sex, guys don't want to know me either. And even then, I'm only popular for about twenty minutes, sometimes only five minutes depending on the guy, and then boom, back to being one of the most loathed girls at school.

Leo clears his throat and I notice that he's watching YouTube again.

I pretend that I'm reaching into my bag to better see what he's watching, and I manage to see the title.

How to keep the conversation going.

Hmmm. So, Leo has a crush on someone. Maybe that's why he's been acting so weird.

I wonder for a moment if it's Gabriel. I mean, he was spying on him from behind the tree.

It's only at the end of the day, when the siren wails, that the panicky, nervous feeling from second-last period disappears and I see Gabriel waiting in the bright afternoon sunshine at the teachers' carpark, the sunlight lighting up his brown hair, and, as I move closer, transforming his dark eyes into a warm chocolate brown.

'I've always wanted to coin this car,' I say, pointing to the principal's shiny red Mustang. 'But it's not the car's fault its owner is an idiot.'

Gabriel smiles and we fall into step beside each other. It's quiet, and neither of us is saying anything, but it's pretty nice and there's enough noise filling in the silence between us with the kids rushing past us and the buses and parents pulling up to pick them up.

Once inside my house, a bit of awkwardness creeps in between us. So as soon as I've dumped my school bag, I go straight for the large bottle hidden behind the cornflakes and Gabriel smiles nervously when he sees it. I get the feeling he's not a big drinker.

I jump when I stand, sure that I caught a flash of someone running from my yard.

'What is it?' he asks, coming to my side to stare out the kitchen window at my ugly backyard – a canvas of dead yellow grass.

'Nothing. I think I'm seeing things.'

'I see things all the time,' he says, his eyes staring at my yard but not at my yard. He looks pensive and I get the feeling he means something else. But the bottle weighs heavy in my hand and I feel like he won't tell me much unless he loosens up a little.

'How do you like it?' I ask.

He shrugs.

'I'm not sure. I've never had gin before.'

Honesty. It's so refreshing that I beam a smile at him and he blushes. He's actually really cute. Like really, really cute.

'Let's have it straight up,' I say, nodding, my heart pounding a little faster. 'Shots.'

He looks at me, the blush fading for a second, as though the suggestion of shots scares him a little. But then he blinks and sighs with what sounds like relief, his bunched-up shoulders dropping as though he's been holding them up his whole life.

'Hell yeah,' he says. 'The quicker it numbs me the better.'

15

Daphne

Steam rises from the coffee mug I'm cradling in both hands, and I take a moment to breathe and watch the dust particles dance about in the warm rays of afternoon sun that stream into our living room through the open back door.

Mid-afternoon is one of my favourite times of the day, along with the early mornings where I get to watch the morning sun rise and light up our eastern fence line in a golden slant.

The house is blissfully quiet and I'm enjoying the fact that life is slipping back into something akin to normality – well, Gabriel-life at least. I'm still not sure how things between Joe and I are.

Twenty minutes ago, while I was on my way home from a day of back-to-back client meetings at the cafe, I received a text from Gabriel informing me that he's going to a friend's house directly after school. When I texted back 'Which friend?', he replied that it was 'Catelyn' and that he'd be back later tonight, and to eat dinner without him.

The relief I feel, that it's someone other than Leo that Gabriel is hanging out with, is very real, coaxing my heart rate into an easier rhythm.

I still harbour some kind of motherly concern for Leo, though. His extreme loneliness does bother me... and the fact that he has to rattle around in that mansion all on his own most of the time – it can't be healthy for a teenage boy to be without company for such long stretches of time. But I soothe away my concern by telling myself that his parents will be home from their work trips soon and he won't be alone in that huge house anymore.

I take a sip of my sweet, milky coffee and push thoughts of Leo out of my mind and decide to check my dreaded emails. I had avoided looking at them for a few hours after I turned off the notifications but I'm going to have to check them again at some stage. My clients aren't going to wait forever for me to get back to them.

My stomach churns and I take another sip of coffee, hoping it'll calm my nerves, despite caffeine sometimes making me extra-jittery in uneasy situations.

Here goes.

I grab my phone and click on the white envelope and scroll through my inbox.

And finally, I can breathe again.

Nothing.

I place my phone face down on the couch and relax against the cushions.

Maybe he's gotten bored of taunting me. Hopefully he'll disappear and forget all about me altogether. Though I don't exactly like my chances, the fact that he hasn't written back to me is a pretty good sign at least – for now.

I glance at the clock on the kitchen wall. I'll need to hop in the shower soon and start getting ready for tonight. Joe and I are going out to dinner. We haven't spent any time together over the past two weeks, and despite the fact that we still hug and whisper 'I love you' to each other, I've been feeling a divide between us… and it's growing. Tonight, I aim to bridge that gap and get us talking again.

Early this morning Joe suggested that he's hoping to do the same. So at least we both want the same thing. Surely that gives us a good start.

In the shower, while I allow the warm water to wash away the honey-scented soap suds I've lathered all over my body, I think about the last email. How my ex threatened to tell Joe about my dark past if I didn't do it myself.

My stomach churns just thinking about Joe knowing. There's no way that I could tell him. Not tonight anyway. What if he is so disgusted that he gets up and leaves me at the table and walks out of the restaurant? Or worse, if Gabriel overhears us discussing it at home. How would I explain it to him? How would I explain to my son that I can be found on one of the most popular adult entertainment websites in the world, doing things that no one wants to know their mother has done?

No. Gabriel must never find out. His knowledge of what I've done in my past would fracture our relationship forever. He would never be able to look at me in the same way again. My heart feels uncomfortably tight in my chest just to think about it.

Joe, on the other hand. He needs to know. Just like I need him to come clean about what he gets up to each night after dinner in his study. Although I know already, I think he needs to know that it's okay... that I don't judge and that I want to help him get through this. That we need to be a team again and face everything together.

The restaurant is crowded and for a moment I worry we won't get a table because I've forgotten to book – which is unlike me, but I've had a lot on my mind of course. But Joe surprises me by giving his name to the maître d', who responds with a polite nod and escorts us to our table by the window in a little nook against the far corner of the restaurant.

'Honestly, I forget that you're still in touch with the boss.' I grin. 'Best seats in the house. Thank you,' I say, my heart brimming with warmth and love that I have for this man, a man who has given me my safe place to fall after the shitty first twenty years of my life. He's given me Gabriel too. My heart feels so full right now in this moment and I'm pretty sure Joe's does too, because he has a shine to his dark eyes that only comes when he's feeling emotional, in a good way. My old Joe.

He slides his hand across the table and our warm hands meet and entwine. It feels so strangely intimate. Like we're new lovers still getting to know each other.

Maybe that's how we should look at our relationship from this moment forward. Usher in a brand-new phase in our lives. This lovely, intimate dinner, in this charming restaurant where we first met, with its soft sparkling fairy lights and red-velvet chairs and waitstaff dressed in black.

'I've missed this,' says Joe, bending his head to plant a kiss on the back of my hand. 'When did we become strangers, Daph,' he adds, gazing at me with raised brows. He softly shakes his head. 'Let's never be strangers again. Let's always be open and honest with each other.'

I stiffen slightly and hope that he hasn't noticed. This is my opportunity to come clean, to tell him the truth about my dark past. But how can I do that here and now? While the romantic lighting casts a warm glow on my husband's loving face, while families and other couples laugh and enjoy their meals in the background, and the scent of delicious Italian food fills the air.

If I told him everything, Joe would release my hand. He'd pull back in horror. He would stare at me wordlessly and eventually get up, unable to believe what I've told him, and walk out, leaving me alone to be judged by the other diners, smug in the safety of their strong unions with their other halves. Nobody here would have a past like mine, I can guarantee it.

I sigh and instead of telling the truth of my past, I avoid it again.

'Let's never hide things from each other,' I say, and lower my voice to add, 'I love you,' before a waiter arrives at our table to share the wine list with us.

I order us a bottle of merlot, the same wine Joe ordered when he came in for a meal on his day off, twenty years ago, only a few weeks after we had started working together.

Joe grins.

'I'll never forget you that night. I was spellbound by you.'

I toss my head back and laugh, reliving the memory.

'You were drunk. All the other chefs kept laughing at you. The boss pretended he was going to throw you out.'

He laughs too, like he used to so long ago.

'They were jealous. They all wanted you too.'

'Um, most were married, so don't lie.'

He cocks a brow. 'I'm not lying.'

'Who comes into their workplace on their one night a week off?'

'I don't know, some sad loser who'd noticed the new waitress was not only gorgeous but smart and mysterious. But she wouldn't speak to him. So, he had to become a customer for that.'

'You forced me to speak to you. Unfair,' I say, narrowing my gaze playfully at him.

The waiter arrives and pours us both a glass after giving me a taster which I nod at.

'You know,' says Joe, staring after the waiter, 'we are the only two originals in this building right now, who used to work here twenty years ago. They've got a whole new team. I miss how it used to be.'

I gaze at the newly fitted kitchen with an open window for patrons to watch their food being prepared by young, dynamic cooks who relish their audience and put on a show flaming up pans and tossing pasta and brightly coloured vegetables in the air.

I raise my glass. 'To the originals!' I say, laughing.

'To us, the originals forever,' he says, winking before taking a sip.

My heart is full as we open our menus and discuss the new menu which is not as good as the one 'back in our day'. It's fun. But in reality, it still all looks so good and we can't decide what we'd like to try.

We joke about ordering a little bit of everything when Joe's phone, resting by the wine bottle, lights up.

N.F. strikes again.

I take a long gulp of my wine, downing half the glass.

'Who's N.F.?' I ask, playfully nudging his leg with my foot, trying not to let N.F. ruin my night.

Joe stiffens and draws his leg away, out of my reach, and tucks his phone away in his shirt pocket.

'Just a guy from work. He's probably just asking what time to start tomorrow. He always needs reminding.' Joe rolls his eyes then takes a sip of wine and keeps his eyes on the menu. Avoiding mine.

I smile, but I feel like crying.

I don't believe my husband. And it's a horrible realisation that makes me feel so heavy I could sink through the floor.

Years spent with a pathological liar either makes you lose all trust or hone your instincts. Joe has always been so honest in our relationship, so I've managed to build a healthy trust in what he tells me. But for the first time in over twenty years, I feel my bullshit detector pinging. Like I started to with Justin, once I got wise to his crap.

Justin.

The one who nearly ruined my life.

And now he has the audacity to send me an email out of the blue and remind me that he still holds a certain degree of power over me.

God, I hate him.

I skol the rest of my wine and Joe doesn't even notice when I pour myself another glass so full it spills over the rim. He's too busy being engrossed in the menu so that he can avoid the N.F. stuff. So that he can't reveal his lie.

Oh, it hurts. It hurts because although Joe doesn't sleep with me because of his sex issue, he's never been dishonest about things like texts.

I think of his excitement pressing against me in bed the other night and realise that it was likely N.F. he was thinking about, not me, his wife. He'd been asleep, probably entwined with her in his dreams.

I gulp down my wine and somehow order a meal with a big grin on my face while Joe avoids my gaze. To think the night was so magical only minutes ago.

N.F. I almost hate her as much as I hate my ex.

How dare she ruin this beautiful dinner.

We were connecting.

'Are you okay?' Joe finally asks, able to look me in the eye again after finishing his own glass of wine.

'Yes, are you?' I ask, challenging him right back.

He laughs and shrugs as though everything is fine and sips his refilled wine.

'Of course. I'm at a dinner with the most beautiful woman in the world who also happens to be my wife,' he says.

The booze is making me feel dizzy and I almost say, 'so why won't you have sex with me if I'm so beautiful?' but of course I don't. Because I'm desperate to bring the magic back, the sparkle of only a few minutes ago, even at the expense of my pride.

Over the next fifteen minutes, while we wait for the meal, we both make futile attempts to summon the ghosts of our earlier intimacy, but the silences between each joke and over-done laugh grow thick and fast, and while Joe excuses himself to go to the bathroom I finish the bottle of wine and sit alone feeling fuzzy and strange. I just want to go home.

I text Gabriel, remembering that he mentioned something about going to a friend's house. Catelyn. I ask him what time he'll be home. After a second text he still doesn't respond. The messages don't even deliver and I realise his phone must have gone flat. Great. I don't even know where this girl lives.

My stomach swirls with worry but I tell myself he's sixteen and I need to allow him some independence – especially since he's starting to come back to life since that cursed party. I stand, thinking it might be a good idea to splash some cool water on my face and straighten up.

That's when I see him.

Oh my God.

He's here.

Justin.

My knees wobble. I want to turn and flee the restaurant but I'm not sure I'm able to take a step without collapsing.

A waitress approaches me cautiously.

'Do you need some help?'

The distraction gives me the strength I need to function, and I shake my head and move as fast as I can on my unsteady legs, knowing that he is watching my every move, until I burst into the ladies' room.

I can't believe he's found me.

The bathroom is blessedly empty. I finally exhale and splash cold water onto my face and pat it dry with a paper towel.

I stand back and stare into my fake blue eyes and at my box-dye dark hair and realise that I've had to live a lie my entire life because of him.

And if he thinks he's going to make me run again. He's wrong.

I've got too much to lose.

I need to stop being the prey. The victim.

It's time I stood up to him.

Where the wine had given me wobbly knees only moments ago, it now bleeds courage into my veins. I storm out of the bathroom like a deranged woman on a mission.

A passing waiter widens his eyes as I swipe an iced water off his tray and march up to my ex's table, where he is dining with the gorgeous woman from his Facebook page.

Before he can pretend to recognise me, I upend the entire glass of icy water over his immaculately groomed head.

He gasps and jumps to his feet. His partner puts a hand to her mouth and then somebody grabs me from behind and starts to drag me away.

'What on earth, Daphne!?'

It's Joe, and he's leading me away from the table where Justin is shouting expletives at me, calling me 'that crazy woman', and his partner is standing with her hands on her hips glaring at me and then him, demanding to know who I am.

He shakes his head and stares at me like he doesn't know me. Like he didn't make my life a living hell, didn't force me to do things that I still have nightmares about. Like he isn't hassling me now by sending me threatening emails.

Everything I've ever wanted to say to him jams up in my throat and I choke, unable to speak.

The scenario played out so much better inside my head while I was in the bathroom. All that stuff about being stronger now that he can't hurt me anymore. I'm in shock. I'm in shock because I've forgotten how good of an actor he is – pretending that he doesn't know me. And I hate that I've forgotten. That I could forget how cunning he is.

A flurry of staff flutter around him, dabbing at his crisp white shirt with napkins. A waitress hands him a white towel to dry his hair with. They all cast judgemental glares my way. I want to tell them that I used to work here. That Joe still keeps in touch with the owner. That we have the best seats in the house. We are special.

But I'm still struck dumb and I watch, my face burning with shame, as Joe rips a couple of fifties out of his wallet and hands it to a passing waiter before taking my arm and leading me out of the restaurant and onto the busy street.

'Daphne! What the hell?' he says as he paces the front of the restaurant.

On the footpath I stand, trembling with adrenaline, unable to believe that I have just stared my abuser in the eye after so many years.

'Sorry,' I say, when Joe stops pacing and stands before me, the huge, unspoken question in his eyes.

Who is that man?

And what do I do?

I lie. I cannot tell Joe. I cannot allow him to know Anna. The weak young woman who had allowed that monster to control her. To abuse her.

'He's a client,' I say over the blaring horn of a disgruntled driver who just missed out on a parking spot in front of the restaurant. 'An ex-client. He's been harassing me. Sending me emails.'

'When? Why didn't you tell me?'

I shrug, because I hate lying to Joe and I don't want to lie anymore.

'Sweetheart,' he murmurs. His eyes glaze over in sympathy and he takes me into his arms and after a long hug, leads me to our car.

'You've seemed stressed lately,' I say, tears stinging my eyes as I think of N.F. 'It's like you're not plugged in to… into us anymore.'

Before Joe can respond, my phone rings.

I blink away my tears and pull it out, hoping it's Gabriel.

But it's Leo.

Joe stares at my phone.

'Not that creepy little fuck.'

'He's a kid, Joe. I have to answer it. It could be about Gabriel.'

'Hello?'

Joe glares at me, but his face softens when he sees how upset I am.

'Daphne, I've got Gabriel. He's so intoxicated he can't stand. I'll explain later. Come to 3 Torgay Way, Spearwood. Hurry.'

'Okay. Stay right there. Text me the address as well, so I don't forget. Please. Thank you, Leo. Thank you so much.'

'What is it?' Joe says.

'It's Gabriel. He's drunk and we need to go get him.'

The burning tears return. This night has gone from one disaster to the next.

Joe takes my hand and gives me a reassuring squeeze. One thing about Joe is that he's always so calm in these situations. Always dependable. And I'll die before I let N.F. take him away from me.

'Let's go get him, love. He'll be okay. All teenage boys get drunk one day. This is that day. Think of it as our boy growing up. His rite of passage.' Joe chuckles but I can see the worry darkening his gaze.

He squeezes my hand again and I feel some of the warmth and love I felt earlier. The sparkle.

I've still got Joe.

I've still got Gabriel.

And I will stop at nothing to keep and protect my family.

16

Daphne

Gabriel lies on a footpath, his head resting on Leo's lap, when we pull up at the address Leo had given me. I feel like we've driven onto a movie set, starring my son, starring us. It doesn't seem real.

I scramble out of the car, slightly wobbly still from the wine, but mentally alert enough to tend to my inebriated child.

Kneeling by his side, I take his limp hand in mine, shamefully grateful for a distraction from the restaurant drama with my ex.

'Gabriel?' I stroke his damp, dark hair away from his forehead, marvelling at how beautiful my son is, and close to becoming a man. 'It's Mum. We're here to take you home. Dad and I are here, love.'

Gabriel's shirt is soaking wet and as I bend down to get closer, the acrid combination of white spirit – vodka, or gin perhaps, and corn chips, fills my nostrils. I gag and draw back.

'Catelyn's,' says Leo, and though I'm not looking at his face I can hear the distaste in his voice. 'This is Catelyn's house. She did this to him.'

I glance over my shoulder at the house. It's old, but has its charm. A pretty row of rose bushes grow on the side of the pathway leading to the green front door.

'Is Catelyn okay?' I ask Leo. 'We should check on her too.'

'She's fine,' says Leo, dismissing my concerns. 'I've already tucked her into bed and she said that she'll be fine. Her mum called and told her that she was coming home a day early from her trip down south. She's probably an hour away. It's Gabriel I'm more worried about.'

Joe and I carry Gabriel to the car and I sit in the back with him so that I can support his drunken bobble-head.

'Why aren't you drunk?' I ask Leo, who's leaning against the open car door.

He shrugs. 'I was worried. I could tell that Gabriel was on a mission so I made sure that I stayed straight so that I could watch him. And Catelyn. She was in the same condition as Gabriel. Vomiting all over the place.'

'We can't leave her alone if she's in the same state as Gabe,' I say to Joe, my heart fluttering in panic. I can't leave a drunken girl in the company of Leo. I don't even know Leo that well. 'We'll have to wait until her mother gets home.'

Leo's eyes widen. 'No. No need for that. I've known Catelyn all my life. I'll stay out here and keep watch until her mum shows up. Then I'll walk home.'

'Tell you what,' says Joe, narrowing his gaze over his shoulder at Leo. 'I'll drop Gabriel and Daphne home and I'll be back to check on you and Catelyn. It'll take me two minutes to return. And if her mum's home by then I'll drop you home. If not, I'll wait with you both.'

Leo stares at me for a second, and I can tell he wants me to say that I can come back and get him. And I want to. Because I want to know more about tonight, about Gabriel and Catelyn, and why they were drinking tonight, a weeknight of all nights, but I've had too much wine to drink and I know that I won't be able to drive.

'Okay,' he says, nodding at Joe, but I can tell that he detests the idea.

Joe nods, no smiles, and we take off, Leo staring after us, the streetlight shining against his hair, making him look like some kind of fallen angel or... maybe even a demon rising.

I shake my head, feeling absurd and dramatic. Must be the wine and the events of the evening. I feel so strange. Like nothing about tonight is real.

Gabriel groans on my lap and I turn my attentions back to him. His wet shirt is soaking my dress but I don't care. He's here. Safe with Joe and me. I stroke his hair then lean my head back against the seat. No more wine. Not for a week – at least. I want a clear head. I need to focus on my family. Get us back on track.

I've got so much to do, but I know what needs to be done first. It's the biggest job. But it needs to be done if I want any sense of normality to return to our lives.

When we arrive home, I assist Joe in helping Gabriel, who has no control of his limbs, into his bedroom where he flops onto his bed face down. I try to roll him over but he complains noisily.

'I'll leave you to it,' says Joe and he rushes back out, no doubt to make sure that Catelyn is safe from Leo, the boy that Joe doesn't trust.

I get out my son's favourite T-shirt, it's so worn it's soft and thin. Somehow, I manage to wrangle him out of his wet shirt and into the dry T-shirt. His school shorts are the quick-dry sports ones, so I leave them on. His face is squished against the pillow and I leave him for a moment while I go and fetch a glass of water and some paracetamol should he need it in the middle of the night.

I set it all on the bedside table and sit on the bed, stroking his hair, and wonder if tonight was just a night of teenage fun or a cry for help. He's been pretty good of late. The other night, before I left for book club, he seemed his usual, motivated self. Old Gabriel. Pre-party Gabriel.

Surely going over a friend's house to drink, a girl's house, is hardly the worst thing a sixteen-year-old can do. Perhaps he has a crush on her, or her on him?

I was fifteen when I first drank. Shared a bottle of Grant's with a friend I had made at one of my foster homes and a random boy we met that afternoon. We drank it in a park, just passed the bottle around and took swigs, our throats burning and our eyes tearing up from the fumes until it was empty. When we decided to go for a stroll around the park, the footpath kept smacking us all in the face. We all laughed about it at the time, thought it was hilarious. And although adult me is horrified at the memory, it does help to remind me that teenagers do seek out these kinds of risky experiences, whether their parents or caretakers approve of them or not, and they do, for the most part, come out the other side unharmed.

Hopefully this is Gabriel just looking for a bit of teenage fun. I pray it's that.

I look at my watch, hoping that Joe is going easy on Leo. He's just a kid. And it's kind of sad that he has to look after himself while his own parents are away. That he has no family to stay with.

Speaking of which. His parents must be getting back tonight. Or was it tomorrow night? I make a mental note to message his mother tomorrow. Just a friendly text to let her know how wonderfully supportive her son has been to Gabriel.

Gabriel jolts awake, his dark eyes wide and hollow with fear. He shakes his head, violently, thrashing from side to side.

'No... nnno...'

I stop stroking Gabriel's hair, my hand raised above his head, my fingers trembling.

'Okay, I'll stop,' I say, setting my hand down on my lap. My son must be dreaming about something quite distressing. 'It's okay, Gabriel. You're safe. Everything is going to be okay.'

'Noooo... Leo... fuck off,' mutters Gabriel.

I freeze. Leo. He thinks Leo's here.

'Leo's home now, love,' I say, laying a gentle hand on his shoulder. His skin burns beneath his thin shirt. 'And you're home in bed. Safe and sound,' I say, bending to plant a kiss on his face and wrinkling my nose at the vomit stench that still lingers in his hair. I should really

130

have put him in the shower, but I think he'd die if he found out that I saw him naked.

I'd need Joe for that. But right now, Joe is at Catelyn's waiting on her mother and likely speaking to Leo. I cringe trying to imagine their stilted conversation.

'Video... he's got...'

I turn rigid at the mention of video.

'What video?' I ask Gabriel. My heart starts thumping in alarm.

'Leo... video... photos...'

'Wait, Gabriel. What are the photos and videos of?' I ask, my throat dry and my heart pounding in my ears. 'Please tell me, Gabriel.'

Gabriel's face twists and he lets out a groan, but his eyes remain closed.

'I hate him... fucking... hate him... Mum... Mum!'

'I'm here, love,' I say, stroking his sweaty forehead. 'Mum's here.'

'Love you... love you, Mum.' A lone tear rolls down his left temple and disappears into his damp, wavy hair. For a second, I panic when his breathing hitches, but all at once he releases a long, soft sigh, his entire body relaxing, and he begins to snore.

I stay for a few minutes, to make sure that he's breathing okay, just like I used to when he was a baby, then I tiptoe out of the room and check my phone.

I text Joe, asking if Catelyn's mum has showed up.

Then I click on Leo's name. With shaking fingers, I type out a text.

> *Gabriel mentioned some videos and photos you have. You need to tell me what they are.*

My fingers are trembling. My mind starts to race. Leo. Could Leo know my secret? Could he have been the one emailing me all this time?

But then why would my ex be visiting the first restaurant I worked at when I escaped him to begin a new life in Western Australia? It's the only place Joe and

I go to eat out. Surely Justin has been following me and knows this.

None of this makes sense.

I sit with my head in my hands for several minutes and then, when I still haven't received any texts, get up and fill a tall glass with water from the tap and take a long drink until it's empty.

I check on Gabriel again, who's sleeping soundly, and decide that I should probably text the school in the morning to say that he's coming down with a cold because he's not going to just sleep this one off. From the toxic fumes the pores of his skin are emitting, he's going to be feeling pretty hideous tomorrow. But I'm glad. Hopefully it will put him off doing it again any time soon.

Finally, my phone lights up.

I rush to it.

It's Joe.

Leaving the kid's house now.

Does he mean Catelyn's or Leo's? I decide to call him.

'Is Catelyn okay and did you drop Leo home?'

'Yeah. Catelyn's mum came home. She acted like I was some creep hanging around her house and wouldn't listen when I tried to explain what had happened. Anyway, see you soon.'

'Wait. So, how was Leo? Did he behave strangely in the car?'

'Quiet. Didn't say much. Was like pulling teeth.'

'Oh okay. His house is huge, isn't it?'

'Yeah. Funnily enough one of my apprentices lives on the same street. A much smaller house. Two houses down. I'm gonna ask him tomorrow what the family is like. I don't exactly want Gabriel hanging around just anyone. The first time he went out with that kid was when all this shit started.'

Joe is right. Though I've always appreciated Leo for being considerate of Gabriel this whole time, things haven't been the same since the night of the party, the same night that Leo came into our lives.

Joe and I say our goodbyes and I glance at my phone, willing Leo to text me back. It seems odd that he hasn't replied to my text.

When I check, it still says delivered. But I have no way of knowing if he's seen the actual message or not via notifications. Perhaps he's ignoring me for a very good reason.

I text again.

> *Answer me please. I need to know about the pics and videos.*

A few seconds later, those three dots appear in the text bubble. My stomach churns.

> *Sorry. My mum and dad just got back. I'm chatting with them.*

My face warms with shame. Here I am, like some demented woman texting a seventeen-year-old boy with my crazy demands. How terrible. What must his mother think of me? I wonder if she asked who was texting him and if he said 'oh my friend's mum'. I would just die of mortification.

He begins to type again.

> *Oh, he must have meant our assignment. We have an assignment due in media. I've got all the videos and pics and we were supposed to edit them tonight but I doubt Gabe is in the mood to edit. I'm happy to do them myself even though I know he really loves editing and wanted to do it. But it's due tomorrow. He'll still get credit though.*

I sigh with relief and quickly type out a message.

> *That's lovely of you, Leo. Thank you. Gabriel will appreciate it. Goodnight.*

Then I toss my phone aside and sit and stare into space, almost laughing and shaking my head, thinking about how I jump to conclusions so easily. Joe's always reminding me not to overthink things. But inevitably I always do.

The garage door creaks and groans and my heart warms. Joe's home.

I need Joe tonight. I need him more than ever.

Joe sweeps in and when our eyes meet, he smiles and I smile and then I allow him to sweep me up into one of his warm, squeezy, bear hugs.

'I love you,' he says, his lips brushing against my hair. 'Gabe and I are lucky to have you.'

And suddenly N.F. doesn't matter and my ex doesn't matter and Leo doesn't matter.

All that matters is that I have my little family of three under one roof.

We both stand at Gabriel's door and watch him sleep for a bit, our arms around each other, then Joe chuckles about how sick Gabriel is going to feel in the morning, and then we both get into our pyjamas and settle on the couch and snuggle while watching *Christine*. The main character, Arnie, reminds me of Leo.

While the movie plays, Joe falls asleep and I quickly grab my phone because I've neglected my work emails and there it is.

An email.

With a trembling finger I tap on it and read, my breath held.

> *Tonight... was very... interesting,*
> *Anna.*

Justin.

Oh God.

He's talking about the disaster at the restaurant.

And now I feel stupid for even considering Leo being behind the emails. And I'd texted him like a desperate madwoman about the pictures and videos that Gabriel had muttered about in his drunken sleep.

What must Leo think of me? What must his parents think of me? Here he was supporting Gabriel this evening, who could have ended up passed out on the road and run over by a car in his drunken state.

I should have thanked Leo, not written a nonsense text about videos and pics. Though I wish I could send him a text now and thank him, I don't want to run the risk of texting him while he's catching up with his parents, lest they think I'm some kind of lunatic – if they don't already think that, that is.

No. I'll have to wait until he messages me next.

Maybe he won't, though. Now that his parents are back, he won't have the need to message me. Which is for the best in truth.

Joe rolls onto his back and begins to snore.

I wish I could sleep. But I don't think I can rest until I've dealt with Justin once and for all.

I google Facebook, download the app, then create a profile – fake name of course – and find Justin's page. I click on the name of his partner, then friend-request her.

I close the window and put my phone on do not disturb.

If she accepts my request by morning, I'll write to her and tell her everything about my history with Justin. Then I'll go to the police and get a restraining order.

I'm no longer the timid mouse that Anna Trinovic was.

I'm Daphne Dubois.

And I'm tired of hiding.

17

Daphne

The next morning, I awaken to plenty of emails and calls due to the rescheduling of my clients' appointments and get stuck into it all after seeing a surprisingly healthy-looking Gabriel off to school – I didn't need to send that text to the school's admin after all.

Earlier, while Gabriel had been scoffing a bacon and egg sandwich between sips of a strong, sweet coffee, Joe had slapped him on the back and said, with pride in his deep voice, 'No hangover! This kid takes after me.'

And here I am, wishing that Gabriel had woken up rotten to remind him of what alcohol can do to you. Not that hangovers have ever really, in the history of mankind, deterred people from ever drinking again.

My morning seems surprisingly normal, previous-to-that-party normal, and I can't help but feel optimistic. The dark cloud that had descended upon our family has lifted and disappeared as quickly as it had arrived.

Everything looks better when the sun is beaming down from a bright baby blue sky.

I've got a full day with my clients and I look forward to catching up with them and losing myself in a world of numbers. I got up extra early this morning and baked a batch of muffins and wrapped them up individually in clear cellophane with golden ribbon to tie. A thank you to my clients for putting up with the recent cancellations and delays due to my 'family emergency' that kept cropping up.

After showering, I realise that I have forty-five minutes to kill before I need to leave for my first appointment of the day, so I slip on my bathrobe and make a second cup of coffee and sit out the back on our alfresco couch and enjoy watching the nesting doves disappear into the lush green foliage of our lime tree only to reappear and fly off again. The tree is blossoming, it blossoms twice a year, and white butterflies flutter obsessively around its shiny green leaves.

I sigh, and think about perhaps doing a little ten-minute meditation before I get dressed until I remember that I'd created a Facebook account and friend-requested Justin's fiancée last night.

I usually drink white wine these days and limit myself to two glasses, but last night I'd knocked back three and a half glasses of merlot in rapid succession and now I completely regret it. I mean, I managed to straighten up in time to look after Gabriel but... and although I'm proud of my efforts at putting up a strong front in the face of my ex threatening me, I'm not sure that I should involve myself in Justin or his fiancée's life.

Should I just ignore his emails and hope that he goes away?

My mind drifts back to the past, over twenty years ago, and I shudder at the memory of my time with Justin.

No, I won't ignore his emails. Absolutely not. Tipsy me on red wine was absolutely spot on. He will do this again and again to not only me, but to this woman he is about to marry, and many others.

It's my duty, not only as a woman, but as a decent human being. Justin's fiancée needs to be informed for her own safety. Then it will be up to her what she does with this information. But at least I will have done my best.

I highly doubt she would accept a friend request from a random woman she doesn't know, but with my coffee swirling around in my belly and my heart in my throat, I open the page and there it is staring back at me.

Jessica Riley accepted me.

We are friends on Facebook, Justin's fiancée and I.

I gaze at her profile pic and note the gentle smile and the love burning in her eyes and I know that this is not going to be easy. Judging by the pics she's posted of herself with Justin, and the comments left by her family and friends, they are all completely smitten by him.

Her sister, Jane Riley wrote:

> *Finally, you've found a good one. A*
> *guy you deserve. So happy for you sis,*
> *so happy for you both.*

Which leads me to believe that Jessica has a history of falling for arseholes.

I scroll further down and can see that she and her family are small-town celebrities of a sort – mingling with state bigwigs and even a few famous local actors.

The strange thing is that Justin is the type of guy who likes to be the big gun, the hero, the leading man who rescues a destitute girl and gives her the world on a platter. I swear he used to get a kick out of reminding me that I could be living in the gutter somewhere if it weren't for him.

But it seems that quite the opposite has happened here.

Jessica is no damsel in distress. She has a large family who love her and are obviously well known, seeing as they regularly attend large corporate functions with important people. Riley... Riley. I spy a logo on one of her posts and realise that she is the daughter of David Riley, the man behind Riley Constructions. They are a hugely successful industrial building company that has done so well that David is a regular contributor towards charity foundations.

Justin has certainly done well for himself this time.

He must love being associated with Jessica and her family. The son-in-law of David Riley. That would inflate his ego towards bursting point.

Interesting.

I wonder what David Riley thinks of him.

The curser blinks and I stare at it for a long while before I try and fail at crafting the perfect message.

I don't enjoy invading Jessica's perfectly crafted world. She and her family seem to believe that Justin is wonderful, but soon Jessica is going to open my message and have her fairy-tale romance turned upside down. Either that or she will simply regard me as Justin's bitter ex, a scorned woman stooping to low measures to exact her revenge on being discarded by Justin all those years ago. I can put money on that. Justin will paint me as somebody who is unhinged and dangerous and likely talk Jessica into blocking me.

But still, I must go ahead with it. She needs to know.

In the end I go for simple, frank information.

> *I used to date your fiancé, Justin. He was abusive and I escaped him only by changing my identity and fleeing to the other side of the country. The fact that he is here now, living in the same state, frightens me, and I, as a woman, am frightened for you. If you would like to meet to discuss what I know in more detail I'm happy to do so at a discreet and safe location.*
>
> *Again, I'm doing this because, as a fellow woman, I care. And also, because he has been contacting me, sending me emails, threatening emails.*
>
> *Please don't dismiss this. If you've ever had the slightest inkling that something is not right about him or that something from his past doesn't add up or if you've noticed a few lies...*

then trust your instinct. Please. Before
you go through what I did.
Yours truly...

I'm not sure how to sign it, I'm not entirely comfortable revealing either of my identities, so I decide to leave it at that.

'A concerned human being,' I type.

I click send and close the window, deciding that I won't look at it again until the end of the day. My clients need my full attention and I aim to give them just that.

I hurriedly slick my dark hair into a tight bun, dress, pack my laptop, notebook and muffins into my car and head out to the cafe for a long day of client meetings.

I feel good. I've done my bit. And even if Jessica doesn't reply or does not wish to meet me, I hope I've at least drawn her attention, sowed the seed... and hopefully she'll start to peer beneath the mask he has fixed upon his face.

For her own sake.

And maybe if she sees the real him and sends him packing, he'll run... back to the other side of the country and leave me alone for good.

At the end of a busy day with clients, I sit down with Gabriel who has offered to make me a cup of tea. He caught the bus home, because I couldn't pick him up today, and I look forward to having a little catch-up chat, a chat we usually have in the car on the way home from school.

We take our steaming mugs out into the alfresco area and enjoy the warm afternoon sunshine streaming across our out-stretched legs as we recline against the large, soft cushions on the outdoor sofa.

'So, I'm going to a sleepover at Leo's on Friday night,' he says.

I swallow down a mouthful of hot tea too quickly and scald my throat.

'Really?' I honestly didn't think their friendship would continue any longer now that Gabriel is back to his old self and Leo's parents have returned from their business trips, to my great relief.

He nods.

'Oh well, that's nice. He has a huge house,' I say, taking another sip of tea. Gabriel makes my tea extra sweet and I always enjoy it.

'Yeah,' says Gabriel nodding, but his eyes are fixed on a lone ant crossing the paver near his right foot and I'm not certain that he has even heard me.

'You'll have to let me know what his parents are like. I'm so curious,' I add.

Gabriel raises his eyes and meets my gaze. 'What? Oh, yeah. Will do.'

We continue chatting over our tea. Small talk about Gabriel's studies and who I saw today at work. When Gabriel drains his mug, he announces that he's going to take a shower and disappears inside the house.

After enjoying a few more minutes of the delicious sunshine, I drag my rather drained self, up and off the couch.

Once inside I wash my mug out in the sink and stack it on the dish rack to dry.

My phone pings.

It's Joe. He's having a late-night meeting with his workers.

Interesting.

I try to ignore my mind, which keeps whispering about the mysterious N.F., but it's rather difficult, so I decide to log back into Facebook and see if Jessica has read my message.

There it is. A message from Jessica.

My heart flutters up my throat as I pour myself a cold glass of sauv blanc and settle on the couch to read it.

> *Look, I'm sorry but my fiancé has never lived over East. He was born and raised here. I'm sorry that you were treated so terribly by your ex. But I think you have my fiancé mixed*

up with somebody else. He is such a kind and giving man, nothing like the person you've described and he's going to make a wonderful father.

So please leave us alone. As for the water in the restaurant. He didn't have a clue who you were and was very disturbed by it.

The next time you contact me I'll be calling the police. I think you need help moving on from your relationship. Please seek help.

This is the last time I'll write.

Goodbye.

Only a minute after I read her message, she unfriends me and blocks me so that I can't look at her page anymore from my profile. But a quick Google search – she's public – shows that I can still see what she posts.

A new post on her feed springs up.

A photo of Jessica with Justin, his arms wrapped around her tightly.

The caption reads, 'The love of my life'.

Oh God, I think. It's not like I didn't expect this reaction.

She's perfectly happy and oblivious to the real him beneath that mask.

Why would she suspect him? And why would she believe a random woman over the charming and handsome man she is about to marry?

Joe comes home after 8pm, looking tired and drawn, but he sweeps me up into his arms and hugs me for a long time. I relax into his embrace and breathe in his scent. I've always loved how he smells – like a hard-working man. Justin always smelled of aftershave, too much of it, so much that I never really knew his true natural scent. I'm so glad that Joe has never liked wearing aftershave and just prefers a hot shower followed by a spray of deodorant.

I watch Joe rinse out his coffee flask and upend it on the dish rack to dry.

'You know what my apprentice said when I asked about Leo?'

'What?' My heart immediately starts thumping.

'That he's a good kid from a good family. He doesn't personally know him. But he's seen the kid around. Teenager. Quiet but nice. Parents are loaded and they travel all the time.'

I sigh and my heart relaxes.

'Great. So, it's safe for Gabriel to go there tomorrow night for a sleepover. Phew,' I say and laugh.

Joe hugs me again and we watch as Gabriel enters the room, rolling his eyes at us. But he smiles to himself as he fixes himself his favourite snack, four slices of Nutella toast.

When he heads back to his gaming room, Joe and I smile at each other.

'Apart from the drunkenness of last night, he's been pretty good,' says Joe, his eyes a little brighter than when he walked in the door a few minutes ago, as though the sight of his son appearing happy has revived him somehow.

'So true. I think everything is finally going to be okay,' I say with a noisy sigh.

Joe nods, but when I look closely, there's a troubled look buried deep in his eyes and it makes my stomach swirl a little.

'Is everything okay, Joe?'

He nods, a sadness tugging at the lines around his eyes and mouth, and he strokes my hair.

'Everything is always okay when I'm with you,' he says and I wonder if those are the words of a guilty man.

'Same,' I say, because I can hardly speak, my head is too full of questions.

He pecks me on my forehead and breaks away.

'I'm going for a quick shower.'

'Would you like some dinner heated up?'

'Nah, I ate with the boys.'

'What did you eat?'

'Oh...' He pauses, needing to think, his face reddening. 'I can't remember the bloody name of the place. Indian, I think.' And then he disappears down the hallway towards the bedroom, leaving me wondering if I truly know my husband at all.

Though I'd love to have another wine, I remember my resolve to go easy on the alcohol and make myself another large mug of tea instead and go sit outside to admire the stars. I make the mistake of bringing my phone with me and when I look, I can't help but refresh Jessica's Facebook page.

I just about spill my tea when I see that she's deleted that post she put up earlier. Instead, she's posted a quote in white writing over a black background.

> 'We are so accustomed to disguise ourselves to others, that in the end, we become disguised to ourselves.'
> – François de la Rochefoucauld

My pulse throbs loudly in my ears.

What I said this morning... though it didn't reach her then, must have sunk in after a day of mulling over her time spent with him. Or perhaps she spoke to him and he gave her reasons to doubt him.

My seed has been planted.

I check my emails, waiting for a vicious message from him.

But there is nothing.

An elegant tabby cat slinks along the back fence and pauses to watch something in the distance, where darkness has swallowed up the other half of my yard, his green eyes alert and tail swishing. The neighbour's dog barks.

Justin's silence, or non-reaction, has me feeling afraid, much like prey waiting for a lion to pounce.

But I've started this, and I need to stand tall and finish it.

I think of all the women and men out there, who get manipulated, lied to and then abused both physically and mentally by their partners... and I know that I want to prevent that for as many people as possible.

A minute later, I sign into my Facebook page.

She's unblocked me and requested me as a friend again.

I accept it with trembling fingers and soon there is a message for me.

> *Let's meet. At Banning park. 9am.*
> *There'll be plenty of dog walkers and*
> *mothers with children so it'll be safe*
> *for the both of us.*

I don't have any client meetings for the first two hours of tomorrow morning so it works for me.

I reply with 'Yes, see you then', and close the window.

Already I feel a bond with this woman. An invisible ribbon tying us together, the knot tied by the same man.

Tomorrow I will meet Jessica face to face and tell her everything. She will be the first person I have ever confessed my past to.

The mere thought of it sends me stumbling to the bathroom to vomit into the toilet.

18

Daphne

I give Gabriel a hug in the car when I drop him off at school the following morning, which embarrasses him at first, but soon all the tension leaves his body and he leans into me. I bury my face in the crook of his neck, sure that I can still catch a hint of his baby scent. In reality all I get is Lynx.

'Are you okay, Mum?' he mumbles into my hair, still hugging me, forgetting about our surroundings for a few seconds. His peers dart in front of the car and weave between several vehicles, despite the duty teacher barking at them for being in a forbidden part of the school grounds.

When I don't answer, Gabriel draws away from me, his brow furrowing as he holds my gaze. He grips his school bag strap, ready to get out, but seems hesitant because of his concern for me.

'I'm fine,' I lie, smiling. I can hardly tell him that I'm meeting my abusive ex's fiancée.

'Okay. But you've been acting weird all morning,' he says, gnawing on his bottom lip, his eyes dark and watchful. 'Do you want me to take the day off? We can watch that new Netflix series you wanted to start. That true story one.'

I reach out and tuck a wayward curl behind his ear.

'Thank you, love, but there's no need. Plus,' I say, looking at his extra bag, the one with his bits and pieces for tonight, 'you've got your sleepover tonight.'

He nods and for a second I see something in his eyes. A fire. Something lighting him up from within. Aggressive almost. But his gaze softens when he smiles at me.

'Okay. But text me and let me know how you are at lunchtime.'

'I will,' I say, giving him an eyeroll despite melting inside at his thoughtfulness. 'But if I forget, please text me when you get to Leo's house. I want a reaction.'

'Umm, why? What do you mean?'

'The house, silly. You're honestly not going to believe how amazing it is. It's huge. Leo's family is loaded.'

Gabriel laughs.

Someone behind us beeps. We're holding up the kiss and drive lane but it's not like they can't go around me or anything. I purposely ignore a disgruntled woman who drives by us very slowly and puts up her middle finger.

Gabriel and I erupt into laughter.

It feels so good to have my son back.

'Okay, well, thank you, middle-finger-wielding woman, you've cheered up my mum,' Gabe says, grinning as he gets out of the car. He leans down and taps the passenger windowsill and then disappears into the throng of students heading towards their classes.

This is it.

I dragged out the dropping of Gabriel at school as long as I could but it's 8.35am now and I need to drive to the park and meet with Jessica.

I've started something big.

And I need to finish it.

My hands shake as I grip the steering wheel. Even though the park we're meeting at is beside a great big lake which has a popular bushwalking trail along it, and lots of children's playgrounds usually filled with kids, I'm still anxious.

But I'd say she's more frightened of me than I am of her. Who knows what stories Justin has filled her head with about me?

I could be a psychotic ex, a woman scorned, hell-bent on revenge. He will have painted me in a bad light, that's for certain.

But the fact that Jessica deleted her original post on Facebook and put up the quote about wearing metaphorical masks gives me hope.

Perhaps together we can fight against him. Who know what he's put the poor woman through already?

I arrive at my destination ten minutes early so I pull into a corner bay in the carpark and scan the park for Jessica. She told me she'd be wearing red so I eyeball all the ladies wearing red but don't see her anywhere. I am early, though.

I didn't say what I'd be wearing. And she has no profile pic of me to go by. So far, I've only posted a picture of a sunflower.

I wonder, after fifteen minutes pass by, as the digital clock in my car clicks over 9.05am, if she's chickened out already.

I decide to get out and wander around. This morning she asked to meet near the biggest Moreton Bay fig tree in the park, so I start walking, slightly away from the playground and nod and smile at the dog walkers who come my way.

It's a sunny autumn morning. Brightly coloured leaves crunch beneath my feet, but I don't get any enjoyment out of it whatsoever because I'm too tense and too busy looking for my ex's fiancée.

As fewer and fewer dog walkers pass me by and I move away from the chattering parents and noisy kids stationed at the playground, I shiver a little and wonder, as the treetops begin to obscure the sun, if I should just turn back.

Perhaps this is a bad idea.

She could be angry.

She could want revenge for me having ruined what she'd believed to be an ideal relationship with a perfect man. I wouldn't blame her for hating me for killing her dream.

But I'd rather she hates me forever if it means she'll escape what I went through at his hands.

I decide to wait beneath what I deem to be the largest tree and watch for her. That way I can build my courage to approach her in my own time.

Minutes tick by, and I'm just about ready to give up and return to my car when the sounds of leaves crunching behind me sets the hairs on the back of my neck on end.

I freeze. This must be her.

But before I can turn around, two strong arms wrap around me tight.

I want to shout but I'm in shock and the way I'm being squeezed is crushing my lungs. When the strong, pungent scent of aftershave fills my nostrils, I don't need to be told who has a hold of me. Because I'd recognise that scent no matter how many years have passed.

'Pretend like you know me and we're friends,' Justin says, his smooth voice slicing through me like a blade through old wounds which I now know have never truly healed.

A dog walker approaches from the distance and I mentally will him to move faster, to reach me before Justin hurts me.

'Don't say a word when he approaches, act happy, or I'm calling the police and reporting you for harassing my fiancée. My pregnant fiancée.'

'Okay,' I splutter, barely able to breathe in his grip.

He lets me go.

I sway on my feet, my head light as I stare up at him. He has deeper lines on his face of course, and more facial hair. But those icy blue eyes haven't changed a bit. They still have the power to freeze me from inside out.

He takes a step back and crosses his arms. His body language tells me he hates me. Is repulsed by me.

I take several rapid breaths in a row and try to remain as calm as possible.

'Look, Anna. Or should I say, Daphne. I'm happy now. I've moved on and I thought you had too. It's been twenty years.'

I take several steps back, shaking my head.

'No, it's the other way around. I've moved on. It's you that won't let me go.'

'Just stop it. You're doing it again, making things up and putting ideas in your head. We had a toxic relationship and you got very dependent on me and I had to cut ties,' he says, shaking his head.

My throat is so dry and so tight that I can barely speak. But I do. Because after twenty years he's still gaslighting me. Still trying to manipulate and control me.

'You... those men... you...' My voice is trembling and the words collide and get stuck in my throat.

'I've tried to put that behind me,' he says, his voice quiet and pensive. 'That devastated me.'

I look up at him, and almost laugh.

'It devastated you? You?' I do laugh this time, out loud, and the dog walker is now close enough to frown at me and move slightly away, glancing back over his shoulder before shaking his head, his black Labrador watching me curiously with large, shiny brown eyes.

That dog has more understanding and empathy than Justin will ever possess.

'Yes. Seeing your girlfriend with four other men is not exactly an easy thing to witness.'

'But you are the one who arranged it, you made me...' I shake my head, my words trapped beneath the ball of rage building at the base of my throat. This is just like him. Just like him to lie and to then believe his own lies.

'I'm trying to forget the past, Anna. You should too.'

I stare at him. He is unbelievable.

'You have not changed one bit. You're still the lying monster you were, Justin. And now you're harassing me. Sending me threatening emails, trying to frighten me and blackmail me. Well guess what? I'm not the same girl you–'

'Emails?' he interrupts, a deep furrow cutting into his brow. 'What are you talking about?' He shakes his head and glares at me, disgust curling his upper lip. 'You're just as crazy as you were back then. A crazy bitch. Always inventing stories. Always talking crap.' He leans in, his breath hot against my cheek. 'You still haven't learned to shut your mouth, have you?'

I rub at my wrists as though they're still bruised from his rough handling of me all those years ago and I cower. It's a default response ingrained in me.

Justin gets mad, I submit to quell his rage.

I glance around, my heart racing, and the closest walker is hundreds of meters away and moving in the opposite direction. He notices, too, that we are momentarily alone and steps forward, seizing me by my waist.

With a cruel glint in his eyes, he digs his fingers into my skin, enjoying my pain.

But something in me deep inside strengthens. I refuse to wince. I refuse to allow him that pleasure. Summoning up all my strength, I press my palms against his chest and shove him back.

His eyes widen in surprise as he stumbles back. A laugh erupts from his throat as he catches his breath.

'If you don't stay away from my fiancée and my unborn child, you'll regret it, Anna.' He spits at the ground near my feet, then turns and walks away.

Trembling all over, I stare at the back of his expensive suit as he walks away. It's only after he gets into his shiny black BMW that his fiancée must have paid for, that I take a deep breath and return to my car on wobbly legs.

19

Daphne

'Do you really have to go to book club tonight?' asks Joe, who'd agreed to meet me for a quick lunch by the beach. 'You only just had one.'

Somehow, after my encounter with my ex this morning, I'd managed to make turkey and salad sandwiches and filled a flask with hot coffee. I'd also swallowed down an anti-anxiety herbal pill containing calming properties just before I'd hopped into the car to meet with Joe.

The pill is already working. I feel strangely pleasant and relaxed.

'I can't cancel on the girls this late. It's never the same when one of us is missing.'

The truth is, the girls and I enjoyed our last catch-up at the pub so much that we agreed to meet again. 'For the benefit of our mental health', Kate had written in the group chat. Earlier this morning I considered cancelling, because I wasn't sure what emotional state I'd be in after meeting with 'Jessica'. But seeing as I ended up face to face with Justin instead, my worst nightmare, I realised that the worst is over. That he can't hurt me anymore because I'm not frightened to speak the truth.

Though I'm not going to rush out and announce who I am to the world or anything like that, I do aim to tell Joe and Gabriel and eventually go to the police to report Justin for what he did to me all those years ago.

Joe waves a hand in front of my face and I blink, back in the present.

'Sorry. I was away with the fairies.'

Joe smiles and shakes his head.

'Well okay, I suppose I can survive an evening on my own.' He rolls his eyes, grinning.

'There's leftover lasagne in the freezer from last weekend.'

'Oooh!' Joe rubs his hands together and I laugh.

I stare at the ocean through the window of Joe's van, steam blurring the churning waves, and enjoy the easy silence between us broken only by the sounds of our swallows and the shrieks of the random gulls being tossed about in the squally winds. The incoming storm has been predicted to finally hit our shores tonight. I'm glad Gabriel isn't one of those kids that needs to be out roaming the streets with his friends. I'm glad he enjoys the comforts of home.

'I almost wish Gabriel wasn't going straight to Leo's after school. I really want to meet Leo's parents.'

Joe screws up his sandwich wrap and takes a sip of coffee while staring out at the sea. 'Yeah.' He looks at me and laughs. 'I'm sure you'll get to meet them tomorrow morning when you pick him up.'

'True.' I sip my coffee and rest my head back against the seat, trying not to think about how Joe blushed last night when he couldn't remember what he'd eaten for his 'work' dinner.

'What are you thinking so seriously about? Gabriel's getting better and...' He drops his coffee cup into the cupholder and takes my hand in his, engulfing them in calloused warmth. 'And I reckon we are too.'

'I hope so,' I say, giving his phone a pointed look. If he has any secrets, about N.F. or otherwise, then this is the moment for him to tell me. 'I don't want to keep any secrets from each other anymore. Honesty only from now on.'

He glances at his phone then meets my gaze. 'And I hope that you can feel comfortable enough to tell me everything too.' His eyes soften. 'You've been so stressed lately. And... I don't know. I almost feel like you've been chatting more to that bloody kid Leo than to me. Seriously.' He shrugs. 'I feel like the biggest idiot being jealous of a teenage boy.'

I raise a hand and wave off Joe's words while shaking my head.

'Oh gosh, it's not like I confide in him or anything. He was just lonely while his parents were away and I guess he was concerned about Gabriel but didn't want Gabriel to think he was fussing.' I shrug. 'Since his parents have been back, he hasn't messaged so I think that'll be the end of it.'

Thank God. To be honest it was starting to get stressful. I'd get heart palpitations whenever I saw the phone light up with one of Leo's texts.

'Well, that's good.' He lets go of my hand and makes a sad face. 'Well, it's just a shame that the only night Gabriel is going to stay out you'll be discussing books with the girls at the pub.'

I raise my brows in mock judgement.

'You can talk. You've been coming home late, missing dinner...' I say it with a smile in my voice but I'm serious and I hope that my jokey probing elicits some kind of explanation for Joe's weirdness of late.

'That's work stuff, though,' he says easily. 'You've got to put in the effort to keep up the camaraderie with the boys, and Shelly of course.'

'How is Shelly going?' I ask, wondering why Joe has suddenly brought her up. He casually mentioned her in passing when she first started working for him last year, but hasn't since.

'She's good. Hard-worker. Better than the boys who are half her age, and she tries everything.'

'Okay you can stop there. I don't want to spend our entire lunchbreak listening to you singing praises of Shelly,' I joke, laughing for real now.

Joe chuckles and finishes his coffee.

I nurse mine, enjoying the cosiness of being in the car together. And the fact that we're talking easily again.

'I won't stay out late tonight. I'll just have one drink. I'm off wine lately. I think I just want to detox, go on a bit of a health kick. Get healthy.'

'You say that every three months.'

'I know. I mean it this time,' I say, hand on heart and a silly grin on my lips.

Joe shakes his head.

'Okay. You go off and enjoy your time with the ladies tonight. And then when you're done, come home and have your wicked way with me,' he says, with a devilish grin and twinkling eyes.

I stop breathing and then release a little laugh. He's joking. He's got to be joking. Or could this be the beginning of positive new changes for us? For the return of the physical intimacy between us that I've sorely missed. I can only hope.

'I'll make popcorn and you can cuddle me to death, how does that sound?'

I nod and smile, hiding my disappointment.

* * *

Three hours later, I'm stepping out of the shower when my phone buzzes.

> *You still coming tonight?*

It's a text from Kate.

> *I'm here early. Come now. I think I'm getting hit on, ha, ha! He's cute but this married lady is not interested.*

> *Yep. Just getting ready now. See you soon.*

I'm cheered by the idea of getting a one-on-one chat with Kate before the others arrive. We rarely get to do this and she's probably the one out of the girls I'm most comfortable with. Maybe I can open up to her about the intimacy issues in my marriage. Maybe it'll help to get another perspective on the situation.

I towel-dry my hair and then get to work with the blow-dryer.

Tonight feels like it's going to be good. The perfect antidote to a surprise meet-up with my ex.

I'm fully confident that the emails will stop now. A quick check while I brush my teeth confirms this.

I've scared Justin. Rattled him. It was clear by the way he was behaving at the park. He knows how easily I could cost him his relationship – if he manages to win Jessica back over that is. Hopefully she runs from him and never looks back.

I don't like that he used her account to set up the meeting though. It worries me that he has access to her social media passwords. Or worse, that she has decided to forgive him and has taken him back already.

If there's one thing Justin is good at, it is lying. He has a way of balancing the lies with so much charm that you don't hesitate to believe him. Because even if you know deep down that he is being dishonest, you just can't help but want to believe him.

All that money and status is too much to lose for Justin, so I suspect he has been loading up his lies with extra charm to win Jessica back.

But that's no longer my concern. Not for the moment, anyway.

Tonight is about having fun, a celebration.

Because I may have just defeated my nemesis. No more running. No more hiding.

Gabriel is at Leo's house and will hopefully dish on the parents tomorrow morning when he's home and, although Joe is not exactly ravishing me, he still wants to cuddle on the couch tonight and is being so loving... so all in all, life is not too bad.

Perhaps, now that we're communicating again, I can broach the subject of our lack of physical intimacy with Joe. He hasn't been spending any private time after dinner in his study anymore, which is good. But then again, he hasn't been home much either.

Still, tonight, I will celebrate.

I select a gorgeous red dress from my wardrobe that I've been dying to wear and some nude heels. I sweep my hair into an updo, spraying root touch-up to cover my now skunk-like blonde roots, making sure no smudges have been rubbed onto my forehead or temples, and then I grab my clutch purse, toss my credit card, phone and paracetamol, and I'm good to go.

'I love how you girls never take your books with you to book club,' Joe says, with raised brows and a tiny grin at the corner of his lips.

I roll my eyes at him and tap my temple. 'Because we carry our books in here,' I say. 'And anyway, I did bring it last time but it was a waste of time. We were having too much fun drinking to read,' I add with a wink.

He pecks me on the lips and watches me as I reverse out the driveway, a gentle smile on his face.

As I pull out onto the road, the last spectacular rays of sunshine beam through the clouds as the burning sun sets. The world looks brighter and much more joyful than it did earlier this morning, when it was all grey clouds with my ex at the park.

Those hopeful rays of light beaming out of the darkness remind me that life can be amazing. I just need to give it a chance.

I shake away the depressing images of my childhood that always seem to pounce out of the shadows of my mind whenever my mood lifts.

Yes. Life is very good.

My phone buzzes and I know it's Kate hurrying me up and I smile.

But when I pull up at the pub, I see that it's a text from Gabriel.

> *Hey Mum, just wanting to check that you're okay. I'm sorry I forgot to text you today like I said. Oh, and I love you. And I hope you never ever stop*

loving me, that you'll love me no matter what happens.

20

Catelyn

It's weird.

I'm getting more flashbacks from the night of the party. But it's not Gabriel I'm seeing. I mean, I still have those flashes of him looking down at me. But I have other images flickering through my brain.

Mental snapshots of a sweaty body, of dark hair... I'd had sex with someone that night, there's no mistaking it, but it wasn't Gabriel.

And yet, I distinctly recall Gabriel's presence. I don't understand it.

Someone was calling me names, the mystery dark-haired guy. Horrible things. He swore at me too. Kept swearing the entire time he was on top of me. But because my memory of the night is hazy, the voice isn't distinguishable. I can't even be certain that I even know the guy.

The only thing I truly know about the night was that I did not like what was happening to me. I can vaguely recall being repulsed by the guy.

And yet, I'd had sex with him. What does this mean? How did I get so intoxicated on a night I'd resolved not to get drunk? And did I actually give consent or not? This is what I really want to know.

When Gabriel was at my house the other night, I tried talking to him about what had happened at the party but he got so spooked when I asked him if we'd had sex – this was before the flashbacks had started coming – that he started chugging the gin way too hard and fast, which resulted in him getting so wasted he wasn't helpful to me anymore.

Not that I'm worried that Gabriel took advantage of me. I just instinctively know that he didn't. I actually get virgin vibes from Gabriel. Innocence and sweetness. And I can tell he's a good guy. Not once did he try to touch me or even flirt with me while drunk on gin. If anything, he kept asking, even when the gin hit him so hard that he was slurring his words, if I was okay, if I needed water, or food or anything at all. Which I found hysterical given that I was only a bit tipsy but he was absolutely gone.

I still haven't found out why he was in that room at the party, and who the other guy was, so my plans of loosening his tongue with booze kind of backfired.

And then Leo had showed up at my house, like he'd been following us or something and he started yelling and screaming at me.

He started ranting and raving at me like a lunatic.

'How am I going to explain this to Daphne?' he'd screamed like a lunatic, spit flying everywhere. It was truly strange.

Then when I asked who Daphne was, he glared at me as though revolted, his top lip curled with disgust.

'A true friend would know the name of their friend's mum.'

Okaay.

Leo has been acting so strange lately. Like, he's always been a weird kid. Since the day I first saw him, when we all started high school, he's always watched me. I've lost count of the times I'd glance over my shoulder in class to find him staring directly at me. And yet whenever I do catch him out or we do make eye contact, he scrunches up his face and turns away like he's just witnessed something absolutely disgusting.

And now he's practically shadowing Gabriel. I know Gabriel is staying over at Leo's tonight, so they must be friendly enough to be comfortable to stay at each other's houses, but I swear I have never seen them hang out before the party.

Weird. Weird. Weird.

That's the only word for it.

My stomach churns with sudden nausea. Could it have been Leo that I slept with at the party? The dark hair fits.

My head feels light. Because I know that there is no way I would have consented to that. No matter how intoxicated I was.

It must have been someone else. Surely.

I think of all the other boys who were at the party – practically all the guys from our year. It could have been any one of them. They're always flooding my phone with messages whenever I post a pic. But in public, at school, not one of them will so much as glance at me let alone speak to me.

Screw them. Actually, no, not screw them. That's not going to happen anymore. I'm not screwing anyone anymore unless it's somebody that I actually like and who actually cares for me too.

I'm sick of seeking the approval of people who don't regard me as their equal. And I'm not putting the blame on them, no matter how much of a jerk a lot of them are.

It's me that has to take ownership of this strange need, this sickness. This desperate want to be liked.

But I'm working on myself, and I'm getting there.

Every time I feel like I'm invisible and the urge to get some guy's attention grows, I shut it down. I put on my meditation music and remind myself that I'm better than that. That sex should be fun, beautiful even, something to be willingly shared with another, and not a means to have my existence be acknowledged by others.

It's hard though.

Because sometimes I don't think I have anything else to offer. Nobody has ever told me that I'm smart or funny or just cool. Nothing.

They don't care. Girls or guys.

But Gabriel... he's actually given me hope that there may be good humans out there.

My heart warms when I think of him. Even though he was so wiped out by the gin, and could hardly speak, he managed to shut Leo down for being harsh and for yelling at me. He also mumbled, as he started to fall asleep on the pavement, that I'm 'a kind soul'.

That's the nicest compliment I've ever gotten from a boy and I like it. Kind. I'm a kind soul.

It makes me feel like I'm worth it. That I have something to offer this world.

Maybe I can make a difference.

I text Gabriel spontaneously, because he's a good guy and I feel so happy about our newfound friendship.

> *Hey, let's catch up again soon. No gin allowed, lol.*

Gabriel reads my message right away and texts me back.

> *Actually, yes. Don't even type that word (vomit emoji) it's making me sick, lol. I'd love to go to the movies with you, if you'd like. My parents have unfortunately gifted me with a love of retro horror and they're playing some in Fremantle at the Luna SX if you want to come. They've got these amazing red velvet chairs and the best popcorn.*

> *Yes! When?*

I hope I don't sound too enthusiastic.

He takes a while to write back and now I'm paranoid, but I breathe a sigh of relief when my phone lights up.

It's a message, but it's not from Gabriel. It's from an unknown number.

> *You'd better stay away from Gabriel or I'll release the video I've got of you.*

My blood runs cold. I've never allowed a guy to film me. Ever.

But Saturday night... maybe because I blacked out... oh God.

Who is this?

You give it to anyone, don't you? Just whore around for the guys like you're nothing. Where's your fucking self-respect? Passing out and letting guys have their way with you. This video of you disgusts me.

My heart is beating so hard my chest actually hurts and the whooshing of my pulse is so loud in my ears I drop my phone and cover them with my hands.

I'm. On. Video.

I try to calm myself with steady, even breaths. This person could be bluffing. They could have just heard that I'd passed out and are now trying to make my life hell just for the sake of it.

I wonder if Gabriel has spoken to anyone about what happened. Would he tell Leo? Surely not. I know he went to Leo's this arvo... and Leo is potentially the type of guy to do something like this. I mean, I could be wrong, but... he does look at me like dirt half the time.

Or could this message be from who I actually slept with.

I'm confused now. Because why sleep with me if they think it's so wrong and they're so disgusted by me?

Another message pops up. This time from Gabriel.

Great! Tomorrow night?

He's not acting like he knows about the messages I just received so I reply with a big thumbs up, but I'm confused as to who the mystery person could be.

None of this adds up.

The fact that a guy like Gabriel is friends with a creep like Leo, that's the biggest thing that doesn't add up here.

I know where Leo lives and just thinking about his house makes me shiver with disgust. My own place isn't the most amazing house and yeah, we have weeds growing out the front beneath Mum's beloved rose bushes, but Leo's house would have to be the worst I've seen. It's downright spooky-looking. Creepy as hell. I always walk quickly whenever I pass it.

It's the last of the acreages that's managed to escape housing development in the suburban area and there is so much junk stored at the front and spilling around the sides from the back of the house, it's a wonder the neighbours haven't complained or the council hasn't done something about it already.

I just can't imagine a strait-laced guy like Gabriel, whose mother packs turkey and salad sandwiches for him that belong on a bread advertisement, visiting Leo's house, let alone sleeping there.

Something about this whole thing just doesn't add up.

I decide to ride my bike down to Leo's street. He doesn't live far from me, and hey, he's been around to my house uninvited so fair's fair.

I get there in a few minutes and lean my bike against the rusty front gate which is hanging off a single hinge. It squeaks when I push past it and I step over the piles of motorbike parts and random old junk as I make my way to the front door.

I rap my knuckles against the flywire door.

I try to think of what I'm going to say, but then decide that I'm going to say that I swung by to speak to Gabriel about movie session times for tomorrow.

A woman comes to the door. Leo's mum for sure. Those pale green eyes. She sways and clutches at the door handle and frowns at me, putting a hand up to shield her eyes from the glare of the setting sun. I try not to focus on the sores which cover her pale skin, sores that she's been clearly picking at.

'What?'

'Is Leo home? I actually want to see Gabriel. He's sleeping over.'

The lady laughs and shakes her head.

A waft of stale booze, and something else, meets my nostrils and I hold my breath.

'Leo hasn't lived here for over a month. Jason kicked him out.' She shrugs. 'I don't know where he lives and I don't care.'

I don't bother asking who Jason is.

A wave of sadness washes over me. Leo may be strange, but I feel terrible knowing that he doesn't have a roof over his head. How has he been surviving?

Now I'm even more worried.

Because how can Gabriel be sleeping over at Leo's when Leo doesn't even have a home anymore?

21

Daphne

The pub's carpark is packed and it takes me a good couple of laps before I swoop in and secure a spot. Before I get out, I give Gabriel a quick call, just to check on him, during which he downplays the slightly emotional text he sent me earlier – it wasn't a cry for help he assures me. He's really happy to be spending time with Leo. Apparently 'it's all good, Mum'.

Still, before he hangs up, he tells me he loves me, just like in the text, and there's a wistfulness to his voice that almost brings me to tears.

As I sweep my index finger along the dampness of my bottom lashes, I tell him that should he wish to come home at any time during the night that I'll happily come and pick him up. It gives me an excuse to not have any more than two drinks with the girls. Right now, I need my wits about me more than ever.

I tell him, in a ridiculously whispery voice, that I love him to the moon and back and hang up before I get too choked up. All this business with my ex has been getting to me. Making me feel as though I need to clutch my family tighter and keep them within arm's reach always.

The air-conditioning inside the pub is unnecessarily cold and I shiver as I glance around for Kate.

'I'm outside, too bloody cold in there,' she texts, and I excuse my way through several groups of merry strangers until I find her sitting at a bench table beneath an umbrella which is no longer necessary now that the sun has gone down.

The warm air feels lovely and tingly on my skin and the clinking of glasses and the golden hues in the darkening sky give off a summery vibe.

I give her a quick peck on the cheek and sit down across from her and smile.

'What are you drinking?' I ask, nodding at her empty flute.

'Prosecco of course. I'll go get you one. The man that's been flirting with me is the bartender. But it's good now, he's not bothering me anymore. And bonus is, he knows I'm married but said I can still have all the free prosecco I like.' She flashes me a huge white smile and gets up and disappears through the beer garden crowd before I can respond.

When she returns with two tall flutes filled with golden bubbles, we chink glasses and toast to the fact that our book club gatherings are now more so an excuse to get together and have a drink and a chat.

'I'm so glad we changed the venue to the pub. It's so refreshing,' says Kate, her blue eyes sparkling.

'I know. It's been fun. I've really enjoyed our chats.' It's true. Before last time our conversations merely skimmed the surface of our personal lives. Purely superficial talk.

Kate is the first woman I've felt comfortable opening up to. Well, perhaps not quite opening up, but at least willing to go deeper and to listen. To cross the lines of acquaintance to actual friend. It's a huge step for me as I normally don't let anyone in for fear of revealing too much about my past.

But now that I've allowed myself to wedge a hand through an opening, a crack in my wall so to speak, I want more. It feels nice to have a friend. To have another woman's face light up to see me. To feel that warmth of sisterhood. Of belonging.

'Well, it might be the free proseccos talking, Daphne, but I realise that it's always you doing the listening and you're such a great friend to me. But I realise that I don't know a thing about you.' She shrugs her slim shoulders so that they touch the ends of her blonde bob haircut.

'I don't know if you have a perfect life with no problems or if you just keep things to yourself.' She narrows her gaze playfully. 'Now I'm guessing it's the latter, but I just want to say, before the girls get here, that I'm here for you.' Her eyes soften and she leans in slightly. 'I know something is going on with you. You've been sad and a little faraway lately, so I just want you to know that I'm here. Seriously. And I'm a vault so nothing you tell me will get shared with the others.'

My heart warms and despite only having had a single sip of prosecco I reach forward and give her warm hand a squeeze. I almost don't want to let go. But I do.

'Thank you. That means a lot.' I shrug, feeling awkward and vulnerable all of a sudden, and although my heart speeds up and my palms start to sweat, I decide to see how I go with this thing called sharing.

'Okay, well. I guess, my son has had a rough patch lately. He went to this party a couple of weeks ago and after it, he wouldn't talk to me for a while. He was ignoring his friends too.' I hide my fidgety hands beneath the bench and continue. 'He's a gamer and he's hardly touched his Xbox.' I gnaw on my bottom lip before taking a large gulp of prosecco, enjoying the sharp fizz of the bubbles against the roof of my mouth and my tongue. 'But I think he's okay now. He's sleeping over at a new friend's house, and, although this kid has parents who are never home, like away for weeks at a time, and he has messaged me a few too many times and asked me to meet him for coffee one night, he's okay now because his mum and dad are home… but anyway, Joe's been working late and he got a text from this person called N.F., who he says is a work colleague… and the other night he'd forgotten that he'd had Indian for dinner…' I stop, mid-ramble, and sigh, apologising profusely for my word vomit, before taking a long sip of my drink, draining the glass.

'Don't apologise,' says Kate, waving her prosecco at me. 'But wow... that's a lot you've been carrying around alone. Have you told no one?'

I shake my head, blushing. Embarrassed. I feel dirty now that I've told someone my private business. I've always prided myself on keeping the details of my personal life to myself.

'Well then, I feel privileged that you chose to share it with me. Really. Thank you,' says Kate, reaching over to give my hand a squeeze.

'I haven't even told you the half of it,' I say, staring up at the stars which have started to stud the now lilac sky. But I know I'm not ready to share the Justin stuff. Because maybe I'm so ashamed that I ever allowed myself to be treated in such a way. Maybe I'm not ready for Kate to know this.

'Hey, it's okay. We'll work through everything together and tackle one thing at a time. Now, first of all–'

'Hey girls!'

Sam and Lila approach our table, arms out ready for hugs.

Kate leans forward to whisper as she gets up. 'We'll continue this another time. Just you and me.' She pats my hand and then hugs both women.

I do the same and after some brief superficial chit-chat about our jobs and what we've been up to, we're soon chatting over the top of each other about the main characters of our current book, which I've still only managed to read a little of.

When Kate announces she's off to get us all free prosecco, I follow to help her carry them and nearly jump when I catch a glimpse of a man who looks like Justin at the other end of the bar. I turn rigid beside Kate, who notices and follows my gaze.

'What's wrong?' she asks.

The wine I've already consumed fizzes inside my empty stomach, and suddenly I feel light-headed. Maybe I'm imagining things.

'I just thought I saw someone that I used to know,' I say with a dramatic sigh that helps to loosen my shoulders.

'Someone from your past? That you'd rather not see?'

I nod, feeling fresh sweat break out at the back of my neck.

'We really need to schedule that private catch-up quick smart. You can come to mine tomorrow arvo. Jake is going to play golf,' say Kate.

'Okay,' I say, absentmindedly, as I leave her side and weave my way through the crowded room to the other side of the bar.

But when I get there, there's no sign of the man I saw. Whoever it was, he's gone.

I glance around the room and then at the nearby exit, through the entry to the carpark and shiver.

'Okay, I need that second glass of bubbly I think,' I announce to Kate when I return.

She grins and waves over the busy, handsome bartender, who is at least ten years younger than her.

'He's into milfs, apparently,' she whispers into my ear and I giggle.

The drinks appear in front of us. The way I'm feeling right now I could down them all, but of course I wouldn't because I have to drive.

We both thank him profusely and return to our seats.

'You've got several texts,' says Sam, her eyes wide and her mouth a grimace while she points to my phone, which lights up each time a new text rolls in.

Thinking of Gabriel, I immediately reach for the phone and sigh with disappointment when I see that it's Leo. He's sent me four texts.

But then I remember that Gabriel is with him and quickly open them.

Gabriel's gone.

She texted him and now he's gone.

He's left me and I think they might be drinking again.

I need you to come asap.

I sigh. So, Catelyn has texted Gabriel and he's left Leo. Not the worst offense to commit. But still, I suppose Leo has a right to be disappointed that he's been discarded just like that.

The ladies ask what's wrong, but I decide to do what I do best. Hide my troubles.

I stand and tuck my clutch purse beneath my arm.

Kate gives me a knowing look.

'Sorry ladies, family emergency. Teenage son has forgotten something for his sleepover and it's essential apparently.' I laugh and swipe at the air, as though this is all so comical and typical.

They all laugh and nod, but Kate eyes me knowingly and says, 'I'll walk you out.'

I embrace Sam and Lila, promising to stay later at the next catch-up, and then I'm alone with Kate, both of us resting against the boot of my car and staring across the packed carpark at the distant, twinkling lights of the suburbs surrounding us.

'Text me as soon as you know that he's okay.'

'Thanks,' I say. Touched that she understands without me needing to explain. 'For knowing me enough to see through my fake excuse.'

'It's not anything bad, is it?'

I sigh and glance up at the sky. 'It can't be too bad. He's ditched his friend for a girl.'

'It happens,' says Kate with a shrug and a knowing look.

'It's his friend that has issue with it, of course. I'm sure Gabriel is fine.'

'Wasn't that Gabriel who texted you?'

I meet Kate's eye. She looks rightfully confused. 'No. It was his friend actually. Leo. Strange boy. I kind of feel bad for him.'

171

'Oh, that's right. The kid who's been texting you. He sounds a bit needy, to be honest. Wouldn't most guys be happy for their mates to be getting a girl?'

I shrug and try to convince myself that Leo's not that weird.

My car keys jangle as I remove them from my clutch purse.

'Anyway, he wants me to come to his house. He's worried sick about Gabriel. I'm off to calm him down.'

'Hasn't he got parents for that?' I can tell that Kate thinks it's strange that Leo messages me. And she's right. It is strange.

'They're away most of the time. But actually, I thought they were going to be home tonight.' Interesting, I think. And a cold chill creeps up my spine as my imagination goes into overdrive. What if Leo has murdered his parents and their bodies are stuffed into the freezer?

I break out into a full body shiver and then laugh when I catch Kate's confused frown.

'Look, you march straight back in there and get another freebie from your flirty bartender. I'm okay.'

'You sure? I can come with and suss this Leo out.'

'Nah, he's just a kid. A kid who's crying out for a little attention I suppose. That's all. Just a boy.'

'Aww. You're a sweetheart to go out to him when you could be with your friends having fun.' She leans in to give me a peck on the cheek. 'Text me when you're home tonight.'

'Will do.'

She walks towards the entry of the pub but spins around, a wide grin to show me that she's being playful.

'If you don't text me later tonight, I'm going to get my bartender friend to take me for a drive to Leo's and search his basement for your body.'

I laugh and watch her disappear into the busy cram of bodies hovering near the entry of the pub and then get into my car.

Her words send another shiver down my spine, making my skin prickle, but I tell myself I'm being silly. That I'm just overthinking things. Poor Leo is just hurt that Gabriel ditched him. That's all. Teenage angst and stuff.

I smile but my smile vanishes as soon as I start my car.

I picture Gabriel out of his mind drunk again like last time and I curse myself for thinking that everything was great earlier. That's what I get for wishful thinking. What if he and Catelyn got drunk again? Without Leo there to let me know?

I try dialling Gabriel's number, but get nothing, so I send a text telling him that I know he's not at Leo's and could he please text or call me asap so that I know that he's safe.

I sigh and drive over to Leo's. I don't know what he expects me to do once I'm there, seeing that his parents are supposed to be home this weekend, but I decide it's a good excuse to finally meet the parents.

But when I pull up, it's only Leo who greets me at the front door and our conversation bounces along the clean white walls of the expansive entryway.

The house feels decidedly empty.

'My parents are at an overnight stay in Perth. Conference.'

'Oh,' I say. 'Did Gabriel take his things with him? Perhaps I can gather them up and take home now.' I'm eager to get out of this house.

'Oh. I thought you might like to stay for dinner as I've made enough for two and now that Gabriel has ditched me for Catelyn...' He shrugs, his cheeks flushing pink. 'You know what, I'll just chuck it all in the bin.'

I feel awful for him. And he's done so much for Gabriel these past couple of weeks, only to be ditched for a girl. And all I know about Catelyn is that she plies Gabriel with alcohol. Maybe if I eat and stay a little with Leo, he'll give me some more information about what's been going on with my son, that party and even Catelyn.

'It smells great,' I say with a smile, 'and I suppose while I'm waiting for Gabriel to call me, I can sit down with you to have a quick bite.'

22

Daphne

'You're not just saying that, are you? You actually want to stay and have dinner with me?' His green eyes widen and he gnaws on his bottom lip, his cheeks still flushed.

'Of course, of course,' I reassure him. 'I was in such a rush tonight that I left the pub without even eating. Just a glass of prosecco. I'm actually starving.'

'Oh,' he says, his face falling. 'I don't have prosecco. At least I don't think I do. I'm not sure what my parents have here but I know that they have a tonne of wine in a room downstairs. Let me go get a bottle.'

Before I can tell him no, that I don't want any alcohol, he disappears around the bend and I'm left standing alone in the echoing hallway.

The food smells delicious and I follow my nose down the corridor and I notice that although there are plenty of watercolour paintings decorating the walls, there are no family pictures to be seen. I was hoping to at least get a look at Leo's family. A glimpse into his private life.

My nose leads me into a huge kitchen, the kind you only see on television or read about in novels. I feel bad for Leo's parents for not being home enough to enjoy this kitchen. What a shame they don't get to enjoy the spoils of their hard work.

I would spend every minute in here. If Joe had access to a kitchen like this, I'd like to think that even he'd be inspired again, and his natural creative flair for cooking might return.

Oh, how the other half live, I think, half smiling. Then I remember that Gabriel hasn't responded to my texts and he could be passed out somewhere in the middle of a street.

And to think that I was only thinking a couple of weeks ago, when he went off to that party, that I was glad he wasn't sitting around at home gaming with his friends, and instead going out and being sociable. I wish I could turn back time and keep him safe under our roof for just a little longer.

This morning was nice though, the way he'd showed concern for me before he got out of the car. But there was that fire in his eyes, that grew and blazed when I mentioned the sleepover at Leo's house.

I suddenly want to get out of this mansion and just find Gabriel so I can see for myself that he's okay. If he doesn't message me back in half an hour, I'm going to drive over to Catelyn's to check on him.

I feel better already, knowing that I have a plan of action. I consider texting Joe or calling him to let him know what I'm doing, but I just want this night over with and the quicker I can get back home, hopefully with Gabriel in tow, the better. If I call Joe, I'll only scare him and he'll come rushing out to look for me.

'Do you like merlot?'

'Yeah, it's my favourite, actually. Well, it was my favourite. But then I switched to white.'

'What about prosecco?'

'That's just for when I'm with the ladies.' I shrug. 'I don't know why but it seems more like a fun, celebratory drink.'

Leo mutters something under his breath.

'I can go back and look for some. I mean... geez, they must have it somewhere in this monster house.'

'Merlot is fine,' I say, bristling a little at Leo's tone. I rethink that half an hour and decide to only stay for ten minutes and not a minute longer.

Leo's fingers tremble as he opens the wine and when he eventually unscrews the cap it falls to the ground and rolls under the stove. He swears under his breath and pours the red wine into my glass.

I wave a hand before it reaches the halfway mark.

'No more, please. I've already had a glass. Two is my limit but since I'm mixing drinks, I just want to drink half a glass.'

'Oh, well I was thinking that you could maybe sleep here if you like, while you wait for Gabriel. We could stay up and game or just talk. Whatever you like.'

I stare at him. He stares back at me hopefully, his brows raised, a half-smile on his lips, as though I'd actually sleep at his house.

'No thank you, Leo. I prefer to sleep in my own home.' I clear my throat. 'Plus, it would be highly inappropriate for me to stay here with you while your parents are away. You shouldn't really ever ask an adult to come and stay with you, Leo. I'm sure your parents wouldn't approve.'

He stiffens and pours himself some wine.

I want to ask him if he has permission from his parents to drink alcohol, but I feel as though I've chastised him enough already.

Leo's cheeks are now red and his lips a thin line. I've offended him by implying that it was wrong of him to ask me to stay.

'I'm sorry, Leo. I didn't mean to offend you. I think it's very kind of you to have offered me to stay. It's very sweet and for that I thank you.' I pause and choose my words carefully. 'But you're alone a lot, and I worry about you. And I know if Gabriel were alone at home, I wouldn't want him inviting an adult to sleep over. I'm sure your parents would agree with me.'

He takes a sip of his wine and grimaces.

I try mine. It's delicious. I hazard a guess that Leo isn't much of a wine drinker. He doesn't strike me as the type of teen to drink at all.

'Why don't you have something else to drink? Like a Coke?' I suggest.

Leo sets his wine glass down and stares at it for a while, frowning, deep in thought.

'Just because we have an age difference doesn't mean we can't be friends, you know,' he says, finally meeting my gaze, his green eyes blazing. 'We shouldn't give in to societal pressures. We should do what we like.'

'You have a point,' I say, because I can tell that my saying no to the sleepover has come across as a rejection. 'And I do enjoy our conversations. But, as an adult, I need to put your wellbeing and your safety first.'

Leo rolls his eyes before getting up, taking his wine glass with him and splashing the red merlot into the sink. He retrieves a can of Pepsi from the fridge and places it on the table to the right of his empty place.

I exhale, glad he's no longer drinking. The last thing I need is another intoxicated teenager to fret over.

Hopefully Gabriel has learned his lesson and isn't drinking again tonight.

I keep sneaking glances at my phone, willing my son to text or call me, while Leo busies himself in the kitchen and begins removing the lids from various saucepans. He returns to the table for my plate and loads it up before setting it before me.

The steam rising from the dish is fragrant and delicious.

'This looks amazing!' I say, looking down at my plate. It's way too much food for me but I'm very impressed. It looks like something that belongs in a restaurant.

'It's chicken Marsala. It's the first time I've made it. I found some Marsala in the pantry and looked up the recipe.'

'Wow. I can't believe this is the first time you've made this.' I beam a smile at him as he sits down across from me with his own plate of steaming food. 'Did Gabriel tell you that Joe used to be a chef?'

Leo's smile vanishes at the mention of Joe.

'No. No he didn't. But Gabriel doesn't tell me much. We hang out, but he doesn't open up to me as much as I'd like him to.'

I reflect back to the conversation I'd had with Kate at the pub earlier on. It had taken so much courage to share my troubles about Gabriel with her. Because it's just not something I grew up doing. Maybe Gabriel has subconsciously adopted my habit of not sharing too much of his private life with friends.

'Just give him time,' I say.

Leo nods at that then eyes the food in front of me and throws me a nervous glance.

I take the hint and cut a small piece of chicken and take a bite. Flavour explodes inside my mouth.

'This is so good, Leo,' I say. And I'm not lying. It's delicious.

Leo's eyes widen.

'So, you love it?'

I nod.

'And you're proud of me?' he asks and then blushes and quickly puts his head down and starts cutting into his own food.

'Of course, I am,' I say. 'I don't know any teenage boy who cooks like this. And I bet your parents are super proud of your efforts.'

'I wouldn't know,' he says. 'But, if you're proud of me, then I'm happy. That's all that matters.'

I nearly choke on my chicken. Poor Leo. He's becoming way too attached to me. It's sweet. But it also makes me feel uncomfortable. As though I'm encouraging his attachment just by being here.

'Are you cold?' he asks, after seeing me shiver. 'I can get you one of my hoodies. You could wear it and take it home. I wouldn't mind.'

'No. No. I'm good,' I say, swallowing down a forkful of mashed potato. 'No need for a hoodie.' I can only imagine Joe's reaction if I turned up tonight wearing a teenage boy's hoodie.

'Do I cook better than Gabriel?' Leo asks, taking a long gulp from his Pepsi.

'Yes. One hundred percent,' I say, taking a sip of my wine. 'Just don't tell him I said that.'

Leo smiles and stares back down at his food.

'Thank you,' he says, a rosy blush colouring his cheeks.

My phone lights up.

Halleluiah.

But it's not Gabriel, it's Kate.

Still, I eagerly check what the message says and write back to her.

Leo raises his brows, silently demanding an explanation.

'Oh, it's my friend. She wants me to come back and pick her up in a few minutes, so unfortunately I can't stay for much longer.' I quickly take another gulp of wine and shovel a forkful of food into my mouth.

Kate didn't actually write that at all. She asked if everything was okay and I texted back, 'Not in basement, so all good'. But now I have an excuse to leave and go look for Gabriel.

Leo's face drops.

'Oh, but you'll come back, right? I've made dessert,' he adds hopefully. And I feel awful letting him down. But I just can't see myself returning for dessert, not with Gabriel still out and with Joe waiting for me.

'I'm so sorry, Leo. But I'll probably go find Gabriel after dropping my friend off, so I just don't think I'll get back here. But I promise I'll text you and let you know when I've found Gabriel. I'm so sorry he ran out on you. That's a really mean thing to do.'

'It's okay,' says Leo getting up to dump his half-eaten dinner into the sink.

'I've never really had friends. Whenever I meet someone new, they spend an hour or two with me and then just dump and run.'

He stares into the sink, his shoulders bunched, and I come to stand behind him and watch as a pea rolls its way down the drain.

'I'm so sorry. If it helps, I was alone a lot as a child too.'

Leo turns around.

'I knew from the moment I laid eyes on you that you'd understand me,' he says, his green eyes intense. 'I just knew that we shared a connection.'

My heart humps erratically. I feel awful for Leo, so awful that a teenage boy is so alone that he finds solace in the company of a middle-aged woman. He needs kids his own age. Healthy relationships.

'Have you spoken to your mum or dad about this? About feeling alone? I bet they'd try to help.'

He laughs.

'No. They don't care... my mum, she...' He pauses and then shakes his head. 'I think she's always known that I'm abnormal. Sometimes I think she–' He shakes his head again.

'What were you just going to say? About your mum?' I pry.

He sighs and turns to face me.

'Nothing. You should go now. Just leave me alone to listen to my own voice echo off the walls.'

His face is red now and there are tears in his eyes.

My heart aches for him.

I reach up and put a hand on his shoulder.

'It'll get better, Leo. Trust me. Life gets better. I know this for a fact.'

He stiffens at my touch and then in a sudden movement that actually makes me jump in fright, he grabs me and hugs me, holds on to me for dear life and I hear him gulp huge breaths as he tries to fight back tears.

We sway, he's too tall to lean on me for support and we stagger against the kitchen cupboards.

'I'm sorry,' he says, letting me go. 'Are you hurt?'

My tailbone throbs but I shake my head.

'I'm more worried about you, Leo. You should never feel alone. And if you ever need to talk about anything at all, Gabriel and I, we're here for you.'

'Do you really mean that? You being there for me?'

'Yes. Of course.'

Sure, he is a little strange, but then he can't help it, being a loner. It's very sad. I bet his parents would love to know, though. I make a mental note to finally call his mum on Monday. Reach out.

'Thank you, Daphne, that means so much to me.'

My phone vibrates in my clutch purse.

'Right. I'd better go and get my friend,' I lie.

'Okay. If you have to,' he says, hanging his head down and pretending to sook.

'Oh, you big baby. I'll call you later and let you know how everything goes with Gabriel, okay?'

He smiles and follows me out to the door.

'Goodbye hug?' he asks. 'I promise I won't topple you over again.'

'Just a quick one.'

His shirt is damp with sweat and I pull away as quickly as possible without seeming impolite.

'Okay, well thank you for that amazing dinner.'

'Which you only took two bites of,' he says.

'Yes, but it was enough for me to know that you're a brilliant cook.'

'Sure, sure. But thanks for saying so anyway. I appreciate it.'

'It's okay. Bye.'

I walk to my car, the cool night breeze refreshing.

Leo comes out and stands by the mailbox to watch me reverse out the driveway, a single, pale hand raised in the darkness.

As I drive up the street, I swear I see a BMW, just like Justin's, drive past me. But the tinted windows are up and I can't see the driver.

I shiver and tell myself I'm being silly.

Deciding to head straight to Catelyn's to see if Gabriel is at her house, I turn left, when my phone vibrates.

I pull over and when I see who's messaged me, sigh with relief.

It's Gabriel, thank God.

Come to Catelyn's. Quickly please.

My fingers punch out a reply within seconds.

I'll be there in five.

Although I know that he can't be passed out drunk like last time because he's able to function enough to text, something in my gut, the heaviness there, warns me that something bad has happened and that the cloud that has hung over my family since that party Gabriel attended is still not ready to dissipate.

23

Daphne

Catelyn lives very close to Leo and I arrive at her home in less than three minutes.

I get out of the car and force myself not to race to the front door of the house and walk, as calmly as my weakened knees will allow.

After three knocks, a dark-haired woman around my age answers it. She sighs in a tired way that matches the deep lines in her forehead and on either side of her mouth.

'They're in the living room,' she says, her hazel eyes holding mine for a second longer than is comfortable.

I follow her into a cosy room filled with a large-screen television and a corner-piece brown couch covered in blankets and pillows. A lemongrass scent wafts from an illuminated oil diffuser that sits atop a DVD cabinet which is crammed with likely neglected movies seeing as the television is currently on the Netflix home page.

Catelyn is sitting on the far end of the couch, by the window, gnawing on her fingertips while Gabriel sits beside her. He glances at me, then quickly at Catelyn, concern softening his features while he watches her, before looking back at me and raising his brows in a silent plea for help.

It's such a relief to see him safe and well but I don't allow myself a smile because I can tell by the look on Catelyn's face that something is very wrong.

'I'm glad you're okay,' I say softly to Gabriel as I move to stand a little closer to him. I want to bend down and sweep him up into a hug but I sense I'll embarrass him if I do so right now.

'Thanks for coming, Mum,' he says and Catelyn looks at me briefly and I see a flicker of something in her eyes... something I often see in my own reflection. I gently smile at her and her lips twitch a little but the haunted look in her dark eyes remains.

My stomach twists.

Her mum motions for me to come into the kitchen.

'I found them sitting here on the couch, your boy rubbing my girl's back while she was crying. He's nice, your kid. Not like some of the other boys she's been involved with. I'm Linda by the way.'

'Thank you, Linda. I'm Daphne,' I say, reaching out to brush my fingers across her forearm in a show of solidarity. 'Is Catelyn okay?'

Linda sighs and her shoulders drop as she moves to put the kettle on and takes out two green mugs and sets them on the counter.

'Someone has sent her messages. They say they have a video of her. A sex video from that bloody party a couple of weeks ago.'

I think back to Gabriel and his strange behaviour that night and I wonder now if he'd seen something perhaps, something that he'd been frightened of. It certainly makes sense.

'Does she know who it is?'

Linda looks at me for a long time.

'The funny thing is, she remembers your son on the night. He's her first memory.'

My heart squeezes in alarm.

'Oh... I...'

'No, no, I don't mean that he did anything wrong. Catelyn said he didn't hurt her.'

I sigh with relief, but it doesn't last long because it still doesn't take away the sad fact that somebody hurt this woman's daughter.

'I'm so sorry,' I say, understanding what she must be going through. Knowing. 'Poor Catelyn.'

'Since she's started getting these messages, she's started to have flashbacks. She remembers one of the footy boys, from the school football academy, she recalls him giving her a drink and trying to get her to come into a room alone with him.' She pauses to drop two teabags into the mugs and to pour boiling water over them. 'Milk and sugar?'

I nod. 'Yes, one sugar please.'

'She remembers protesting that she didn't want to go in the room with him, that she wanted to stay around the pool area with everyone else. Then her head went all fuzzy and she can't remember much else.'

'That's awful,' I say, my heart breaking for Catelyn, and for Linda.

'But she does remember his hair and someone on top of her. She knows, from that night, that somebody had slept with her. She did initially think it may have been Gabriel but because she has only known him to be polite at school, she didn't think he would take advantage of her so she wondered if she'd had too much to drink and simply slept with him consensually.'

My mouth is so dry I can hardly speak. I keep picturing the look of horror on Gabriel's face when he rushed into the house that night. The tears he'd shed later in his bedroom.

'Did they?'

'God no.' She adds milk and a spoon of sugar into each mug of tea and stirs before setting them on the table between us. We both sit down.

'According to my daughter, your son is still a virgin, so don't worry.' She raises her brows. 'I'm not quite sure how she knows this but I'm going to take her word for it.'

I take Catelyn's word for it too. Though Gabriel is very interested in the opposite sex, he is definitely a late bloomer, and didn't really begin to show much interest in girls until earlier this year. But still, you never know. Do any parents ever truly know what their teenagers get up to?

'My poor baby,' says Linda, shaking her head and taking a gulp of hot tea. She blinks, her eyes filling with tears. 'She's a good girl. Got such a good heart. She doesn't deserve this. Nobody deserves this.'

Tears prickle my eyes. I cradle my mug of tea in my hands as I think about Catelyn, and what she must be feeling inside.

My own memories of the worst time in my life flood my mind. I know what it's like, to protest, to say no, and for it to all fall onto deaf ears. For the perpetrators to take what they want from you anyway, using their brute force.

'Are you going to go to the police?' I ask Linda.

'I want to but talking Catelyn into it is another story.'

I take a sip of my tea and think.

I wonder if this is the moment. I wonder if this, helping a vulnerable young girl who has gone through a similar ordeal as me, is the moment I decide to toss aside my private shame and actually accept that what was done to me wasn't my fault. That somebody, that a group of individuals, did me wrong. And maybe it's time for those individuals to be held accountable for it. Just like the guy who hurt Catelyn.

Catelyn should not have to hide away in shame for something that was done to her, against her will.

Maybe it's up to me to set an example for Catelyn.

To show her that enough is enough.

That we will not stay quiet anymore.

'May I talk to your daughter? If she will allow it?'

Linda glances up from her tea, brows raised.

'I've been through something like this. A long time ago,' I say, the mug of tea trembling in my hands. I set it down on the table. It's going to leave a ring of spilled tea on the surface, so I wipe at it with the sleeve of my jumper. I busy myself with this, unable to meet Linda's gaze. And I'm so mad at myself for allowing the shame to creep back in.

Linda sets her tea down next to mine and places a warm hand over mine. A lump grows in my throat.

'I'm sorry to hear that, Daphne. I'm really sorry. Yes, you can try.'

I meet her gaze. 'Thank you. I'll try.'

I stand, take a deep breath and enter the lounge room just as Linda summons Gabriel into the kitchen to help her to 'clean up'.

He frowns at me, puzzled, on the way out the room and I nod and smile at him, letting him know that it's okay, that I know what I'm doing – or at least I hope that I do.

Catelyn and I are alone together on the couch, the Netflix home screen beaming a plethora of movie and TV show selections at us from the television.

Catelyn seems as rigid and as tense as I feel. She doesn't know me apart from my being Gabriel's mum. And I don't know her.

But here I am, in the hopes I can help her, wringing my hands because I'm about to tell a story I've told no one.

I take a deep breath, sit on my restless hands, and send my mind back to 1999.

24

Anna, 1999

'Anna, I'm feeling pretty fucking bored. You're boring me,' Justin says, while I'm serving up the buttered green beans that I've prepared, along with steak and potatoes, for dinner.

He hasn't even noticed that I've tried out a new mushroom sauce recipe on the steak. Something that he mentioned he ate in France while away on business last year. It seems the more special attention I give to his needs and wants, the less he cares for mine, or for me.

It makes me sad. And the fact that I'm boring him worries me even more.

But a tiny part of me, buried deep inside, wonders if this is for the best.

Sometimes, while he's at work, I make a cup of tea and sit by the apartment window and watch the teenagers, seventeen-year-olds like me, as they make their way to school beneath the morning sunshine, giggling, huddling, playfully shoving each other, flirting. I wonder if any of the girls have to go home at night and cook their boyfriends a hot meal from scratch? I highly doubt it.

I want friends. I want to go to school. I want a family to come home to – or at the very least, someone who loves me to come home to.

But if I leave him… I'll have nothing. I don't have a home to go to and the last foster family were okay – my foster mum was kind enough, the brother weird but okay; he mostly kept to himself. My foster father however, I still get chills thinking of the many times I woke up to find him watching me sleep through a crack in my bedroom door.

I'm glad I got out when I did. And I think I'll be forever grateful that Justin noticed me working in the cafe that day last year. That the rain prevented him from leaving when we closed and that I kept providing him with free coffees while I helped the manager clean up and close for the evening.

I suppose I should be grateful. I live in a stylish apartment. If not for him I'd be living on the streets and there'd likely be no school for me anyway because I'm done with foster homes; so being one of those giggling schoolgirls is just a silly dream, really.

And it's not so bad here. Not really. He just needs to be less stressed and maybe if I make life easier for him at home he won't be as mean to me.

I don't tell him, but sometimes it feels like that when he gets mad at me, raises his voice and gets a little rough with me. It reminds me of one of my old foster dads, the one who used to beat me with a rolled-up newspaper whenever I wet the bed. He used to hit me so hard that it left red marks across my arms and back. I was only four, but I still remember crunching myself up into a ball in the corner of my room for protection from his blows.

But if I told him that, he'd get mad and then I'd have more bruises so it's just better if I be quiet about it. Life is easier that way.

'I'm having some friends over tonight. And do you promise me you'll do as I say?'

I nearly drop the saucepan. He never has friends over and I've certainly never met any of them. He always leaves the house to go meet with them. The idea of other men even so much as looking at me used to drive him mad with rage. Not anymore, I guess.

'Would you like me to make some food? Some snacks for you and your friends?'

He gives me a cold, dark stare that can make even his handsome face look a little ugly and shakes his head.

'No. Forget the food.' He slides his plate away from him, as though merely speaking to me has turned him off his food.

'Look. I've been offered a lot of money. These men are very creative and they are in the movie industry. You know, you could go very far if you listen to my instructions tonight and if you do what these men tell you to do. My friends.'

My skin prickles. The way he emphasised the word 'friends' makes me think they are anything but.

The old Justin, the one who would never have ignored me for whoever makes him smile at his phone now, would never have even entertained the idea of letting any men get near me.

He once wouldn't talk to me for twenty-four hours because I smiled at a pimply-faced checkout boy at our local grocery store. I had only smiled because he was a trainee and his hands were shaking while he was trying to pack our groceries. I was trying to put the guy at ease, but to Justin, I was flirting.

But now, since he's found someone else to text and smile about, I'm nothing to him. A way to get money.

It's strange. Part of me is relieved I'm not watched every second. But the other part of me wants his attention back, craves his approval.

'So will you do it? Will you listen tonight and do as I say?'

I nod. Maybe he'll stop smiling into his phone and be nice to me again.

I miss the old Justin. The one who used to romance me with beautiful words and bring home the prettiest flowers.

'Good girl,' he says and he smiles at me. It's only for a second, and doesn't quite reach his eyes, but I blush and lap it up.

'Okay. Now go and have a shower. You need to be clean for them.'

I stand there, with the saucepan still in my hand, saying nothing.

I want to know why I need to be clean and I'm scared he's going to let them be with me, but I remember the checkout guy and the jealous rage he'd flown into. He wouldn't let anyone touch me. Surely not.

Maybe they are, in fact, in the movie industry and maybe he wants to help me out and maybe even make us famous. He's always told me I'm beautiful. Maybe I really am. Maybe I've got a chance in this grey horrible world.

'Thank you, J,' I say, smiling at him. He doesn't look up from his phone.

Instead, he ignores me, and the carefully prepared meal, and smiles at whatever his new love interest wrote.

For some reason I stay there, waiting, hoping he'll look up and meet my gaze, soften his eyes at me.

But he sighs and waves me away with his hands, his gaze never straying from his phone.

25

Daphne

'I'm so sorry,' Catelyn says, her eyes wide and shiny after I tell her what happened that night. 'That must have been horrible for you. It must still be horrible.'

I'm as stiff as a board after finally telling someone my story, but when I suck in some air and finally breathe out, my shoulders relax and I can honestly say that for the first time in years, I feel a little lighter.

'It's okay,' I say, actually believing myself for once. 'It's in the past now. But I've been running from it. Hiding.' I lick my finger and rub at the root cover spray on my hairline until it comes away. 'See this blonde? I'm not really a brunette. And see my eyes?' I slide the contact lens across my eyeball then let it slide back into place. 'I don't have blue eyes either.'

Catelyn thinks for a moment and then she widens her eyes and sits straighter.

'Have you been hiding from him all this time? Did he threaten you?'

I nod. 'He threatened to kill me if I ever ran away.' I shiver from the memory, but also think about the Justin who I met in the park, the man desperate not to lose his fiancée, his meal ticket. I'm not afraid of him anymore. He's pathetic. A parasite that latches onto women to feed his ego.

I clear my throat.

'I've also been hiding out of fear of being recognised. The video footage of what occurred that night with those men... what they did to me, it's on every porn site on the net.' I meet Catelyn's gaze and grimace. 'I live in fear of the day that Gabriel will see it.'

Catelyn sucks in a sharp breath. 'Oh God. Oh God that's horrible.'

'It is. But hiding from it is even more horrible. It's consumed me. My whole life. And I'm sick of hiding. I really am. The only reason I didn't go to the police to report my ex and those men is that I didn't want a huge investigation alerting the press to that video's existence. I just wanted it to all go away.' I suck in a deep breath and straighten my back. 'But I've since realised that it never goes away. And it's still going to keep happening. To other girls, to women. To vulnerable boys and men too. It's time to speak up. It's time I held Justin and those men accountable.'

'But if you go to the police, the news reporters will probably mention the video and everyone will look it up.' Catelyn shudders. 'I'll die if anyone sees my video. I don't even know what's on it, but I'll die if it's released.' She sighs and looks at me from out the corner of her eye. 'Are you really going to go through with it? Report what happened to you?'

I look her in the eye.

'Yes, I am. I really am,' I say, surprised at the strength and determination in my voice.

'But then Gabriel will see the video.' Catelyn's eyes widen, clearly horrified at the idea.

Though I'm feeling strong and determined, I still shudder at the thought of Gabriel watching me in the video.

'Does your family know? Your parents?'

I stare at the screen, at the suggestions presented by Netflix. Catelyn or her mother must be a horror movie buff. Maybe the both of them are. I trace the seams of my trousers with my fingers.

'My parents passed away a long time ago. I never knew them actually.'

Catelyn bows her head and says nothing.

'Does your husband know?' she asks after a while.

'No,' I say. 'You're the first person I've ever told what happened to me. Nobody knows aside from you, me, my ex and those horrible men.'

Catelyn sniffs and wipes at her eyes.

'Thank you,' she says, her eyes red and shiny. 'For trusting me. I won't say anything to Gabriel.'

'Thank you. I will tell him... when I'm ready. Which is soon.'

She nods and thinks for a long moment. Our silence is comfortable now. Our experiences creating an unbreakable, invisible bond, a bond stronger and thicker than blood and water and anything on this earth. It's a spiritual bond.

'Gabriel is such a great guy. I've never known a guy like him,' says Catelyn, her eyes lighting up.

A warmth spreads throughout my chest at Catelyn's words.

'He's pretty special,' I say with a smile. But my smile fades when I remember what Catelyn has been through.

'Sorry to bring it up again, but... your experience. The assault. Do you think you'll report him? The guy who you think did this to you?'

She nods. 'The problem is, I'm not one hundred percent sure that it's who I think it is. There are two guys who may have done it. I remember Leo's face too,' she says, her voice trailing off.

My blood runs cold. Leo. Gabriel's underlying dislike of him. It makes sense.

'Perhaps you can explain what you remember to the police and let them sort out the rest. They will question the two boys.'

'Maybe. But I've slept with lots of guys from school before. Everyone knows it. They're just going to say that I'm a slut and that I wanted it.' She brushes her long fringe aside with trembling fingers. 'And what if I'm confused? What if my mind is imagining the stuff I'm remembering?' She shakes her head, second-guessing herself.

'Okay, well, how about you spend the next couple of days going easy on yourself and clearing you mind. Maybe something new comes to you? Then when you have more information, you may feel a bit more confident in what you have to say to the police. That's if you're ready to report it.'

'Okay, that sounds good,' she says, sounding relieved to have a bit more time on her hands.

I sit up straight and press my palms against my thighs.

'Also, do you know who sent you those texts?'

She shakes her head.

'I can show you the number. I was going to send it to Gabriel to see if it's any of the guys he knows but never got around to it.'

She taps her phone several times and holds it out in front of me and I freeze when I recognise the last three digits.

'This is the number?' I ask.

She nods.

I get my phone out and my heart starts racing when I look up the number and my fears are confirmed.

I stand, my blood draining from my head to my feet.

'Sorry, a friend of mine just texted. It's an emergency I'm afraid.'

Catelyn frowns slightly but lets me lie.

'Thank you for sharing this with me, Catelyn. It means a lot to me. And I hope together we can work towards a safer world for women like us.'

She smiles and tucks her fringe behind her ear.

'Can Gabriel stay the night? I feel safe when he's around. And we were going to watch some movies.'

Gabriel returns to the lounge room and he smiles softly at Catelyn and then at me.

'Sure. Of course, you can stay,' I say to Gabriel. 'As long as Linda approves.' It's actually convenient that he stays. Because it gives me time to confront the person who has been harassing Catelyn.

I have a quick word to Linda, expressing my availability for ongoing support for them both. Then I say my goodbyes to them while Gabriel walks me to my car.

Gabriel gives me a long hug.

'Why did you leave Leo's tonight?' I ask.

'We had an argument.'

'Oh?'

'I don't actually like him, Mum. I just went to his because I wanted to sort something out, get something from him. From that night at the party. He's been blackmailing me with it. I can't tell you what it is now, but I will eventually.' He glances back at the house. 'Well, you probably know a bit about it, but not everything. Anyway. My plans didn't work out and so I left Leo's. Plus, Catelyn wanted me to come over. She doesn't want me to be around Leo anymore. She doesn't trust him and neither do I.'

The thought of Leo blackmailing Gabriel sends a chill through me. What could Leo possibly be holding over Gabriel. Surely Gabriel isn't involved in what happened to Catelyn. Surely, he's not a part of that video.

I shiver, wishing that Gabriel had never offered to give Leo a lift to the party. Ever since Leo came onto the scene I feel as though our world has been tipped upside down. But wishing for something that can't be isn't going to help. We need to think about what we can do today to turn things around.

'Okay. So perhaps staying away from Leo for the time being would be wise,' I say.

'Yeah. Don't worry. I won't go near him,' says Gabriel. 'And I don't want you to have anything to do with him either, Mum. I mean it. You need to stay away from him.'

I'm touched by Gabriel's concern for me and reach out and squeeze his hand.

'Don't worry. I will.' I give his hand one more squeeze and let go. 'Love you.'

'Love you too,' he mouths as I reverse out of the driveway.

My phone starts to ring before I hit the road. It's Joe.

I pull over and answer it.

'Are you still at book club?' he asks.

'No, I'm in my car.'

'Have you heard from Gabriel? I don't want to alarm you but he may be in danger.'

My heart thuds in panic, despite knowing that Gabriel is away from Leo and safe and sound at Catelyn's.

'I just saw Gabriel. He's having a sleepover at Catelyn's house. He decided to leave Leo's earlier. He's safe.'

'Good.'

I wave at Gabe, to indicate he should go inside and after frowning and throwing up his hands in confusion, he does.

'Wait. Why would he be in danger?'

'You know my apprentice? Well, I told him that Gabriel was staying at the mansion with Leo and guess what? He said that the family are away in Europe, that he can't be sleeping there. That they are in Croatia and have been gone for a month already. They do this every year to go see family.'

I turn cold.

'Wait. So that's not Leo's home?'

I watch a skinny black cat sprint across the driveway in front of my car, my headlights illuminating its vivid green eyes. 'But I saw his bedroom with the Xbox set-up and stars on his ceiling. What the hell?'

'What? Why did you see his bedroom?'

'It doesn't matter now. It was that time he called and heard a noise. Anyway. It's definitely his home. He was cooking there tonight when I popped in after he'd told me that Gabriel fled.'

'You went there again? Alone? I'm telling you, Daphne, it's not his house. That kid is a fucking psycho.'

A cold chill travels from the back of my neck down to my toes. My heart flutters with fear.

'There must be some kind of explanation.'

My earlier gut feeling that something wasn't right, the first time that I met him in my car when we gave him a lift to the party, comes back in full force.

'There's something not right about that kid,' rants Joe. 'I knew it and I know it now. Do not let Gabriel go there again. God knows where this kid actually lives.'

'But he goes to school with Gabe, he must live somewhere nearby.' I recall now collecting him from the cafe instead of his house.

'Yeah, well, he obviously lives somewhere he doesn't want Gabe or you or anyone to know. He could be an escaped mental patient for all we know. Who knows? We should go to the police with this.'

'Okay, okay.' My phone vibrates in my hand. It's Kate. She must be checking in to see if everything is okay with Gabriel.

'I've got to go. Kate's calling me,' I say to Joe. 'I'll be home soon.'

'Okay. I'll wait up. Love you, Daph.'

'Love you too, Joe.'

I immediately call Kate and she asks me, her words slurred, if I can come pick her up from the pub.

'Thank you!' she says when I agree. 'Oh, my goodness, there was a guy asking after you. He was handsome too. Then he left and you wouldn't believe it, this woman asked after you. She said she really wanted to talk to you. She's still inside if you want to go speak with her.'

* * *

I pull up at the pub and watch people coming and going. I think about my ex and his partner, wondering if it could possibly be them that asked Kate about me.

Maybe it was Justin that I saw at the other end of the bar earlier this evening.

I take a deep breath, exhale, then lock my car and enter the pub, scanning the room for Kate.

But it's not Kate that approaches me.

It's her.

The fiancée.

Jessica.

'I'm sorry,' she says. 'But Justin and I were here tonight for an engagement party. He said that he saw you and that you were stalking him.'

I shake my head.

'I was here with book club friends.'

She nods and smiles. There's an awkward air between us.

'Would you like to sit down?' she asks, indicating a small table right by us, and I remember that she's pregnant with Justin's child.

I soften inside.

'So, I take it that you're still together?' I ask.

She nods, a blush darkening her cheeks.

'Well, for now we are. I've decided to give him another chance because of the baby.' She sighs. 'Justin said that he's a changed man. He explained that he had issues when he was younger but he's different now. He cried his heart out when I said I was leaving him. He begged for another chance, said he'd prove himself by being the best father and husband.'

My stomach knots. This woman is not only beautiful, but I can tell that she is a kind soul. Her dark eyes radiate love and forgiveness. Justin chose well.

'But I'm still unsure. And I want to ask you, face to face, woman to woman. Can I trust him? And are we safe?' She shows her stomach, a small mound of developing life. 'I need to know if my baby and I are safe with him.'

I feel goosebumps prickle my skin. If there was ever a time to be honest it's now.

'No. No you aren't safe. I hate to tell you this. But you look like you have a good strong family. Turn to them.

Ask them to protect you and shut him out of your life. You'll regret it otherwise. Trust me please, Jessica.'

She nods and sits back, her hands moving to cradle her small belly.

'Can I order you a drink? A lemonade? Or a cup of tea?'

Jessica nods, tears forming in her eyes.

At the bar I run into Kate. She tells me that she called her husband too, by mistake, and that he's coming to pick her up.

Jessica and I end up spending an hour together, over our tea. She doesn't ask me what exactly Justin did to me, but I gather she's already experienced enough of his dark side to understand.

We hug when we say goodbye, with Jessica promising to involve her family so that they can protect her, and to let me know how she's getting on.

Though I had planned earlier, after Catelyn showing me the phone number of the individual who has been threatening her with the video, to pay another visit to Leo, I've decided against it after what Joe told me.

I wouldn't feel safe with Leo in that big house now that I know he's been lying about living there this whole time. What else is he lying about?

I shiver. Glad Gabriel is going to keep his distance from now on.

When I pull up in the garage at home, I check my Facebook account out of curiosity, to see if anything has changed on Jessica's account.

There's a message waiting for me.

Has Jessica left Justin already?

My pulse throbs in my ears and my heart constricts with fear. What if my encouragement for her to break it off with Justin has put her in danger?

But when I open the message, it's clear that Jessica did not write it.

Bitch. I warned you.

The message comes with a link to an Instagram page.

'I don't have Instagram,' I write back, my heart pounding its way up my throat.

My phone pings.

Well, you'd better fucking get it.

26

Leo

That man who pulled into my driveway after Daphne left... the one in the fancy BMW, surprised me when he asked me who Daphne was.

I would never admit it to anyone, but I was shitting myself when he pulled up and called to me over the smooth hum of the car engine.

At first, I thought he was a cop coming to ask questions. Thought someone was finally onto me.

But then he said, 'The woman who just drove off, is she your mother?'

I was about to say no and explain that she's my friend's mum, or maybe even that she's my friend, but decided I wasn't just going to give out private information about Daphne like that. He could be a hitman for all I know.

After I shrugged, the man grinned.

'It's going to be like that, is it?' he said, with brows raised and a shake of his head.

Then he opened his wallet, which was fat and green with one-hundred-dollar notes. I'm not gonna lie, I moved a little closer to the car window after that.

'Oh, so you're interested in talking now?' The man laughed. He was cocky and self-assured and I decided right then and there that I hate his guts.

'I'll give you a twenty if you'll answer my question. I want to know if she's your mother and if this is her house.'

'The contents of your wallet or I'm going to go inside and lock my doors and send my Alsatian after you. He'll bite your pretty tires. I don't think you'd like that.'

The man had raised his brows at that. Typical bastard that gets everything his way. Just like those footy guys at school. God, I hate them.

Anyway, the guy looked at me for a while. It got pretty uncomfortable and I started shivering from the cold breeze blowing right through me.

But all of a sudden, he dug his hand into his wallet, took the thick wad of notes out and just handed them over to me just like that. Like the money meant nothing to him.

Geez. The rich are so careless with their cash. He could easily have kept three families fed for a month with this.

I took the money. It felt so solid and so strange in my hands and I couldn't help the fluttery feeling of excitement growing in my stomach.

I imagined how many girls from school I could impress with this cash. Catelyn wouldn't stare down her nose at me anymore. But then again, I don't necessarily want the approval of those girls anymore. There's only one female's approval that matters to me.

'Yes, she is my mother,' I lied to the guy. 'And this is my dad's house, so no. She doesn't live here. They're divorced.'

The man raised his brows at that. I wondered then who he was, and to tell you the truth I started to panic, my heart beating like crazy. I couldn't wait to get inside and lock all the doors and call Daphne to warn her.

'What's her address?' the guy asked.

'I'm not about to tell you that. She's my mother and I love her.' My heart sang when I said that. It felt so good. My mother.

'What will it take for you to tell me, kid. I can tell you're an astute businessman. Tell you what. Ask me for something. Anything.'

Well of course my eyes went straight to his watch, his Rolex.

'Give me the watch and I'll tell you.'

The man flung it at me without a second thought.

Of course, I dropped it and had to scramble around the driveway in the dark to find it and when I stood back up, I could tell the man saw me as an inferior – a beta to his alpha.

But the joke was on him, because I'm smarter. I wasn't about to hand him over Daphne's address and put her in danger.

So, I gave him my mother's address. Hopefully her new arsehole of a boyfriend answers the door. And hopefully this guy shoots him in the face.

I used to love my mother, until she started making all her boyfriends her priority instead of me. I especially started hating her after she let her recent dickhead boyfriend knock me around. The first time he hurt me, a swift punch to the guts, was because I got up to make toast in the middle of the night and woke him up. Mum responded by telling me I should have stayed hungry and let her boyfriend sleep. Then she went into the bedroom with the jerk and had horribly loud sex with him.

I lost all respect for her after that.

Daphne. Daphne is the perfect mother for me.

Beautiful, innocent. I bet she wouldn't behave like a slut. I bet she is the perfect, loving wife – dutiful to her husband but not slutty about it. Like a woman should be. Not like Catelyn. That whore.

I get hard thinking about the video I filmed. I hate seeing that dickhead in it, but I can easily turn down the sound and put my thumb in the way of his head and imagine that it's me having sex with Catelyn. That's what I do whenever I watch it. Which is quite a lot. The whore. Girls like that, in those kinds of videos, they don't deserve any respect.

Anyway, the man in the BMW, he said nothing more to me. He punched in my mum's address and then reversed out the driveway, his tyres squealing – which I thought was dramatic and highly unnecessary – before he sped away.

I almost felt bad for my mum but then I remembered how much of a whore she is, letting herself drink until she's passed out and letting her boyfriend do God knows what to her in the bedroom.

I went back inside and texted Daphne as soon as I locked the front door. She didn't respond so I texted her again and again.

That was two hours ago.

I need her.

And I hate that she's not replying.

I almost feel like she doesn't care about me.

But then I need to remember that she has a son and a husband and she can't help that they demand all of her spare time.

And the last thing I want to do is come off as even more needy than they are.

I want her to see me as a friend. Someone she can turn to if she needs support.

I hope Catelyn is true to her word and that she doesn't tell Gabriel the truth of where I really live.

She knows I'll send that video of her to everyone if she tells.

She's such a slut.

The fact that she had to ask me who the guy in the video was – I haven't let her see it yet – just confirms to me what kind of person she is. Does this mean she slept with more than one that night? Is that the usual with her?

And if so, then why didn't she go on a date with me when I asked her? Am I that repulsive? I would have treated her better than those football arseholes.

She's brought all of this on herself.

Stupid. She's stupid to not have chosen me.

But I'm not a jerk.

If she doesn't tell Gabriel the truth about where I really live, then I won't share the video. I'm not a monster.

I'm just a guy that has been denied the affection that he deserves.

It's not too much to ask.

Is it?

27

Daphne

Joe is still awake when I arrive home and as soon as I enter, he embraces me and I cling to him, resting my head against his chest and revelling in the comforting sound of his steady heartbeat.

So much has happened, and I have so much to tell him, but that Instagram link keeps playing on my mind and I need to tend to that first. But I promise myself that immediately after I'll tell Joe everything.

My phone keeps lighting up with texts from Leo, but I lay my phone face down. I know that I need to address what he's done to Catelyn, the threats and the video, but right now, I just want to focus on Joe, on our marriage, and the fact that these are the last precious hours I have with my husband before he learns about my past and everything changes.

Joe puts on a movie and makes us mugs of tea and I try to concentrate on the television screen and block out the chaos of my life right now, but it's hard. Luckily Joe is so tired that half an hour in, he's snoring softly beside me.

After helping him to bed, I return to the living room and sit on the couch and get started on creating my first Instagram account. While most people join social media to connect to other people or to share some creative part of themselves and their lives, I'm creating my account to see what kind of sick threat my psychotic ex-boyfriend is trying to blackmail me with.

Once it's created, I go back to the Facebook post and I notice that all of Jessica's pictures, including her profile, have been taken down. Though I know that Justin has taken over her account, a sick feeling still swirls in my lower belly and I resolve to call Jessica's family's business to make sure that she is okay.

I hover my finger over the link he sent me and my stomach feels sick, my heart racing.

But I have to find out.

I click on the link and it opens to a private account simply titled 'Daphne'.

I click follow – the account has no followers yet and only a single post. I'm soon accepted and I get a follow back right away which I accept.

The post is the video.

My blood runs cold.

I have not seen this footage in over twenty years. Even then I couldn't bring myself to watch the full length of it.

He's captioned the post.

> *This is Daphne, when she was known*
> *as Anna... her porn name.*

My blood boils. There are no likes and it's a private account, but he's obviously threatening me to go public with it.

When I finally figure out a way to communicate privately, I send him a direct message.

> *You know I was never a porn star. You*
> *know this was done without consent.*

> *Over two million viewers on Pornhub*
> *would disagree, bitch. Even they can*
> *tell you're enjoying it. Have you read*
> *some of the comments? You should :-)*

> *Take this down or I'm going to the police.*

> *No. You need to tell my fiancée, Jess, that you've made everything up about me and convince her to take me back or else this account will become public and everyone will see you for the whore that you are.*

I receive a notification. My new account has been tagged in a photo.

My stomach turns when I see his second post.

It's a dim and grainy picture of me smiling with Kate at the pub. He must have taken it earlier this evening.

The caption makes my blood run cold.

> *This is me now – I'm still the same slut deep down inside. My friend too. DM for sex. Groups welcome.*

I quickly send another message.

> *Take this down. Now.*

I get no response.

> *Forget it. I'm going to the police anyway.*

> *You'll be fucking sorry, Anna. Mess with my family. I'll mess with yours.*

He sends a knife emoji and I shiver.

I take screen shots of his posts, of the messages, and then delete my Instagram account. I will not engage with him.

After I tell Joe tomorrow, I'll go straight to the police. I can't bear to think of Justin lurking around and threatening my family.

For a long time, I sit on the couch, phone in hand, staring into space, thinking about how I'll feel when

Gabriel finds out about the video. How he'll feel. I realise that I'm trembling, not with cold, but with fear.

But then I think about Catelyn, and all the other girls who have gone through similar experiences, and a quiet rage grows inside of me, burying the fear.

It's time.

* * *

The next morning, I call Catelyn's mother to let her know that I know who has been threatening Catelyn with the videos and that I have his details.

Linda thanks me, and asks if we can meet for a coffee to discuss it all next weekend because Catelyn has decided to hold off going to the police until exam week at school is over. Linda explains that Catelyn doesn't want the added stress of police visits while she's trying to study.

As soon as I end the call, I put Leo's texts on mute. I cannot understand how he could threaten Catelyn like that. Or how he could have filmed her in the first place. I'm utterly disgusted. And the fact that he lied about where he lives just leaves me feeling cold.

But it still bothers me that he has had some kind of hold over Gabriel since that party, which makes me question what exactly.

I make myself a coffee and curl up on the couch. Being alone in the house on a weekend morning is so strange. But when I woke up, Joe had left a note on the kitchen bench, saying that he'd been called into a work emergency and wouldn't be home until the late afternoon.

I'm secretly relieved, glad that I don't have to tell Joe everything right away even though I know it needs to happen. But every time I picture myself telling Joe everything I begin to tremble and I break out in a sweat.

Gabriel shouldn't have to live with the knowledge that his mother is on Pornhub. No child should. The trauma of the kids at school finding out and teasing him about it.

But there is no other way.

I need to put a stop to Justin's threats. And I need to hold him accountable for what he did to me all those years ago, even if it means that everyone will find out about the video and know that it is me in it.

I close my eyes as flashes of the video from the Instagram post flicker inside my mind. Tears sting my eyes as I recall the face of that innocent, beautiful young girl in the video, the terror reflecting in her eyes.

It's about time I stopped shaming her.

Because she is me.

I'm Anna.

And Anna needs to be heard.

After I finish my coffee, I call Jessica's father's business and leave a message on the answering machine. It's an anonymous message. But I ask if somebody could please check on Jessica's wellbeing as I have reasons to believe that Justin is a dangerous man. Hopefully it's enough for the family to keep a close eye on her.

My phone rings and it's Gabriel. He's going to stay at Catelyn's for a few more hours so that they can revise for exams together. He sounds so happy, his voice light on the phone and I'm smiling by the time I put my phone down.

There are still several hours until Joe gets home so I decide to bake. It'll help take my mind off things and Gabriel is going to be so happy when he sees his favourite chocolate chip cookies in the biscuit tin.

I'm mixing the butter and sugar when my phone pings.

It's an email and I wipe my hands on my apron and open it.

My blood runs cold.

The anonymous emailer is back.

> *Please tell your husband or I will tell him for you.*

It's odd. If Justin is indeed the one behind the emails as I'd always thought, then why is he writing this when we only just spoke on Instagram? He certainly sounded more worried about getting me to speak to Jessica and saving his marriage than me telling Joe.

It doesn't make sense and I'm beginning to wonder if he was telling the truth that day in the park when he acted like he didn't know anything about the anonymous emails.

My mind immediately thinks about Leo.

Could Leo be the one who has known all along?

He does seem to have a strange fixation on me.

Could he be behind this?

Abandoning the cookie dough, I decide to call Joe. I need him by my side while I face this.

But when I begin to tell him about the threatening emails and that I think that Leo is responsible, before I even get to tell him about the video and my past, he begins to shout down the phone.

'Daphne. Stop. Please! It's not Leo sending those emails. Do not speak to or go anywhere near that kid. He's not right in the head.'

I take a breath and digest what he just said.

'Wait. So how do you know that it's not Leo sending them?'

'I just know. Because it's...' His voice trails off.

My pulse throbs hotly in my ears and my head feels light.

Surely not.

Surely not the one person I trust more than anyone in the entire world.

'Because it's me. I'm the one sending the emails.' He goes quiet for a long time and I can hear traffic speeding past him. 'I'm sorry, Daphne.'

28

Daphne

'So, all this time it's been you who's been frightening me? Threatening me? Not my ex?'

Joe rushed straight home after his confession and I'm grateful that Gabriel decided to stay on at Catelyn's to study for exams.

'Yes,' says Joe, his voice breaking. I've never heard his voice catch like that before. Not even when his father died. 'But I didn't mean to frighten you. And you've never mentioned this ex before, so how could I have known this would have scared you so much?' He meets my gaze, his face lined with misery.

I can't look at him. I stare out the living room window and watch a bird land on next door's oversized and very illegal satellite dish – I've always hated that big ugly thing. It eats up our entire view.

Now Justin's anger makes sense.

He wasn't trying to contact me. He probably hasn't given me a single thought since the day I left. His threats of finding me and hunting me down were likely a result of his ego being bruised. And maybe if he had caught me in the act of running away, he would have gone through with it. But he likely moved on with his new lover at the time and forgot that I existed.

And now, I've stirred the hornet's nest that is Justin's rage. He'd found a new victim and I've come along and ruined it for him.

Well, I'm not sorry about that at all.

That's probably the one positive that has come from this.

I've helped Jessica and her unborn child escape a psychopath's clutches.

'I don't understand. Why would you do this, Joe?'

He cradles his head in his hands. It's like staring at a stranger.

'You know the group chat I used to be on with the boys at work? The WhatsApp chat?'

'What's that got to do with this? You deleted WhatsApp years ago.'

He nods and sighs.

'Yes, well, you know how some of the boys used to send some rude memes and generally inappropriate stuff?'

'Yes... I know what guys can be like.' I swallow. My throat feels dry all of a sudden. 'Women do it too.' I think of the GIF Sam had once sent to the book club chat, to cheer up Lila after she found out that her husband had been cheating on her. 'But what's this got to do with anything?' I ask, even though I'm starting to guess where this is going.

'Well, one night, one of my apprentices sent a link to a Pornhub video. You were out on a book club night and I was feeling horny...' He looks at me and blushes. 'Sorry. I know we haven't had sex in ages. But this was back when we were doing it and we didn't have any issues. I was just bored. So, I opened the link.' Joe pauses and rubs his face. He sucks in air and blows it back out.

I start shifting away from him on the couch and he reaches out and grabs my hand.

'No. You need to hear this. You need to hear this right now, Daphne.'

I stay. Because I do love Joe and because I know the time has come to face the truth of my past head-on.

'I clicked on the link.' Joe pauses and swallows thickly. Tears pool in his eyes. 'And it was a video called *Anna likes to party*.'

He sucks in a lungful of air and continues, his hand holding tightly to mine.

'And I see this young girl. A teenager. And honestly... I wanted to turn it off because I could tell that these men were much older than her, and...' His voice breaks. 'And I could tell that she wasn't into it.'

Tears start to stream down Joe's cheeks. But he doesn't wipe them away. He just grips my hand tighter and continues.

'But just before I close the window, there was a closeup of her face. And as soon as I saw it, even though she was blonde, I knew it was you. She had your birthmark too. And then I thought about how you dye your hair and how you wear contacts and how you never liked discussing why you do it and I realised that... that it was you in that video.'

I let go of Joe's hand and cross my arms over my chest. My heart feels like it's on fire and my head feels tight, like its being squeezed in a vice. I hate that Joe saw me like that. I hate that he knows.

'I knew that it was you. As soon as I heard your sweet voice protesting.' Joe is bawling now, his head in his hands. I want to comfort him but I'm frozen.

Joe knows.

Joe sucks in a few more deep breaths and continues.

I stare at the floor and listen.

'So, I tried to forget I saw it and for a while I brushed it off as my imagination. I kept coming home and seeing you and thinking, no it can't be you. And every time I thought to bring it up, I felt stupid. And I felt stupid to even think it was you. So, I tried to forget. But of course, the boys kept bringing Anna up during work. And I got pretty pissed off one day. It was the week after the video was put up. One of the boys kept miming sex moves against a client's table and said he was "screwing Anna" and I lost it. I threw him across the room and he landed against the client's credenza. We damaged a whole heap of crystal. They claimed it all back on insurance but vowed to never use our services again.' Joe sighs. 'The boys never mentioned the video again. I deleted WhatsApp, and tried to forget I ever saw it.'

'But you didn't really. Because you stopped having sex with me around then.'

A blush blooms beneath Joe's olive skin.

'Yeah. I tried to forget. But whenever we got intimate, I saw those men and your frightened face and I just couldn't go through with it. Things stopped working down there.'

'But every night I'd see you in your study and a few times I saw that your laptop was open on Pornhub, so I just assumed that you were... getting your needs met that way.' It hits me then, what he's been up to. I cover my face with my hands.

Joe nods. We've always had an unspoken communication between us our entire marriage. That's what I've always loved about Joe. That he gets me.

'I've been spending these past years trying to get that video taken down. It's become an obsession. But for every one I get taken down, five more pop up.' He rubs his face and I notice the grey hair peppering his dark curls and the receding hairline and now I understand the stress he must have gone through doing this.

'Oh God, Joe. I'm so sorry. I should have told you about the video, about my past.'

'No. There's nothing for you to be sorry about. None of this is your fault, okay? None of it.' He takes my hands in his. 'I'm the sorry one. The gutless husband who tried to scare his wife into telling him the truth.' He shakes his head. 'I shouldn't have listened to him. I knew it was a bad idea.'

'Who? What do you mean?'

'I opened up to a college of mine, Nathan Foley. He's the one I grew up with. He's got a business like mine. The opposition really. But we both worked on the same contract a couple of months ago and we had a beer together one arvo and started to open up about our lives. He'd just gone through a divorce and after he told me about that he asked how my marriage was doing. So I told him about the video, and how I couldn't make love to you anymore... and he suggested that I email you anonymously, to get you to start talking to me about it, and that maybe after it was out in the open we could begin to repair our intimacy issue.'

'Why wouldn't you just come out and tell me that you saw it?'

'I don't know why. I'm stupid. An idiot. I thought, because you took such great pains to hide your hair and eyes, that you'd get upset if I told you I knew. I didn't want to hurt you, or scare you with a confrontation.' Joe shrugs. 'I thought that this might be a good way to allow you to come forward with it.'

'And scare me in the process,' I say, still shocked. Then it hits me.

'What's your friend's name again?'

'Nathan Foley. He's a good bloke. You'd like him. He was just trying to help.'

So that's who N.F. is.

A giggle erupts in my throat.

Joe's frowns in alarm. It makes me laugh even more.

'What's funny about this?'

I giggle some more then shake my head, my entire body convulsing.

'Oh gosh, Joe. I thought N.F. was a woman and that you were having an affair!'

Joe's eyes widen and then he smiles, his eyes crinkling up at the corners.

'Geez, Daphne. How could you even think that? Never, ever would I cheat on you.' He pulls me into a hug and presses his lips to my cheek.

'I love you and only you. There's no one else for me.'

I wrap my arms around him and snuggle against him.

Joe knows.

And it's okay.

I'm okay.

We're okay.
Maybe everything will be okay after all.

29

Anna, 1999

The lace of the lingerie I'm wearing scrapes roughly against my skin as I walk into the room. My heart flutters in panic when I see four men dressed in suits gathered around our cleared dining table with a huge stage light beaming over it, and a camera resting on a tripod.

Goosebumps prickle my skin and my stomach churns so much I'm worried I'll have an accident right here in front of these men.

'Justin?'

He doesn't even glance my way but continues speaking to the tallest man in the room. The other three men nudge each other and mutter things beneath their breath while their eyes linger over my exposed body. One of the men though, a younger one, isn't smiling much and seems nervous. His fingers keep twitching and he won't meet my gaze.

I look at Justin again and my heart sinks. I'd foolishly tried to believe that maybe I'd gotten it wrong. That he wouldn't ever allow another man to touch me. So foolish that I still got dressed in what he'd asked me to wear, thinking that once he saw me in it, he would never allow any man to come near me.

But he hasn't even bothered to look at me yet.

'Justin? Can we talk please?'

When Justin finally looks at me, he rakes his eyes up and down my body and smirks.

That's when full-blown panic hits me, making my heart race and my chest tight.

'Justin,' I say, my voice trembling. 'Please don't make me do this. I'll be so good. I'll be the perfect girlfriend. Please don't let them touch me.'

I back away from the men and bang into another camera that I didn't see.

The tall man swears and bends down to pick it up.

'Shit, if you've fucked up my camera, you're paying for this,' he says to me.

Justin shrugs.

'I'm sure it's fine. Just set it up again and shoot the damn video.' He glances at me, not meeting my gaze. 'I've got somewhere to be tonight. A date.'

My heart caves in as though he's just shot at it with an arrow.

A date.

I want to cry but I want out of this apartment and away from these men more than anything.

'Don't let them do this to me, Justin,' I plead. 'Please. You love me.'

'When did I say that?' he asks from the apartment door, brows raised, his lips in a smirk.

And I realise then, that it's only ever been me professing my love. He's never actually said it.

Justin disappears behind the door and locks it from the other side.

I run to the door and pound my fists against it, calling his name.

But soon my arms are pulled back and a hand covers my mouth as I'm dragged back into the dining room and held against the table.

'If you cry, we will hurt you,' says the tall guy, bending down to look me in the eye. 'We might even kill you,' he says, his expression stony.

I swallow back my tears and nod. And then for the next forty-five minutes I'm no longer inside my body.

I take deep breaths and focus on the ceiling, then I penetrate that ceiling and the ten floors above this apartment until I shoot through the night and reach the stars.

The velvet black sky is like a soft blanket of comfort to my soul and it is there that I stay until the terrible thing done to my body is over.

30

Daphne

On Monday morning, Joe promises to be home early so that we can both go to the police and report Justin and those men for what they did to me.

It feels so good to have his support and I have forgiven him for taking his friend Nathan's well-meaning but disastrous advice and emailing me anonymously about it. But that's in the past and we will be presenting a united front when we go to the police.

We haven't told Gabriel yet, as he has exams to complete this week. But come Friday, we have agreed to sit him down and tell him everything. It makes my physically ill to think about doing just that. But it must be done before it potentially gets reported in newspapers and on the internet.

I'm yet to have received a call back from Jessica or her family after I left my message on her family's business's answering machine. So, I go onto the company website and see that they've taken down the photo of Justin from their 'meet the team' page. They must know. Perhaps they've gone to the police themselves and have had to put their daughter into hiding to keep her safe. Who knows what Justin has been threatening her with to make her stay?

My phone lights up with a message from Gabriel.

Catelyn wants to go to the police on Friday afternoon after exams. She wants me to go with her. Can I?

He begins to text again.

She wants you to come too.

I smile, touched that Catelyn trusts me enough to support her and text Gabriel back.

It would be an honour to support her. As long as Linda is okay with it.

A few minutes later he texts back.

She said she'll talk to her mum about it tonight.

Okay. Please tell her that I'm so proud of her.

I will. Exam about to start. We're handing in our phones so you won't hear from me for a while. I might go out with Catelyn straight after school.

Okay, good luck with the exam and have fun. Love you.

He doesn't reply but I know that he's in the exam now and I sigh with relief that he'll be preoccupied with school and then Catelyn, while I get to the business of going to the police with Joe.

My shoulders actually feel lighter now that Joe knows, and I wonder how much lighter I'll feel after visiting with the police.

I open my laptop and try to get stuck into work, but my mind is elsewhere so I shut it down and toss it aside on the couch.

Despite what he's done to Catelyn, threatening her with that video – whatever that's of – and also lying to us about where he lives, I worry about Leo. He's just a seventeen-year-old boy. Where are his parents? What will become of him when Catelyn goes to the police about his threats?

He will feel betrayed when he knows that I am the one who revealed to Catelyn who was behind the anonymous texts. But I don't feel sorry that I did. For that he should be held responsible.

For the rest of the day I do try to force myself to complete some work, at least answer some emails and do some digital filing to tidy up, but I can't focus on anything more than that and when at 2pm Joe texts that he'll be home by 4pm, I put away my laptop for the day and take a shower, my stomach churning with dread for what's to come.

At 3.30pm I text Gabriel and ask how the exam went. He doesn't reply, but he probably forgot to turn his phone back on after he received it back from the supervising teacher.

Sick of pacing the living room, I go out to sit in my backyard, and try to calm my nerves by watching the willy wagtails flit along the lawn beneath our overgrown lime tree.

That's when my phone rings with a call from an unknown number.

I answer it, my heart thudding in my chest.

'Hello, bitch.'

'How did you get my number?'

'You think I'm stupid? You think I didn't have a key to the office?' He laughs like a demented person, which he is. 'Well, I did have the keys on the weekend. Not anymore. Thanks to you, Jess's dad listened to your message before I got a chance to delete it.' Justin's breathing becomes heavier and I jump and nearly drop the phone when he says, 'You stupid bitch. You couldn't keep your mouth shut and now you've ruined everything. The whole family have thrown me out like I'm a piece of rubbish.'

'I wanted to help her.'

'Yeah, well you're going to come to regret that, Anna.'

He laughs and then I hear the sound of a groan, a muffled groan in the background and the sound of a chair scraping.

'You hear that?'

Everything stops. My heart. My breathing.

'I've got your son with me. And if you don't turn up to the address I text you, alone, in fifteen minutes, you're going to be very sorry. And if you so much as message or call anyone and they show up, I'll kill you both then and there. I've got nothing to lose, remember? You saw to that. It's your fault, Anna.'

He ends the call.

My heart pounds and I rush for my keys and climb into my car, my phone clutched tightly in my sweaty hands.

A text comes through with the address.

The new industrial area about seven or so minutes away.

It's right in the middle of the new development and I know that nobody will be around now that it's past three. Gabriel and I drive past there on the way home from school and we always make a joke about how quickly the workers must scram out of there when it hits three because it's like a ghost town when we drive past.

I scroll for Joe's number, but remember what Justin said about coming alone. If I tell Joe and he rushes over to help us, I could wind up getting Gabriel killed.

No. I put my phone on the passenger seat and back out the driveway.

I got myself into this mess the day that I met Justin all those years ago and allowed him to take control of me, and of my life.

It's up to me to get myself, and Gabriel, out of it.

31

Daphne

Limestone crunches beneath my tyres as I pull up alongside Justin's shiny, black BMW.

Just like I predicted, there isn't another car in sight.

The shed we're parked in front of is large, and there is a huge sign bearing Jessica's father's company's logo in front of it. Justin must have still had some of the property keys in his possession when the family kicked him out.

Getting out of my vehicle as quietly as possible, I put my phone on silent and open the camera app.

Even though I can't risk Gabriel's life by calling Joe, I take a photo of the shed and the street and send it to myself, because if something happens to me, and God forbid, to Gabriel, and Justin gets rid of my phone, then at least when Joe and the police search my home and find my iPad in my bedside table, they will see this picture and know where I was before I went missing.

I shudder, and offer a silent prayer to my parents in spirit. If there has ever been a time that I needed you two to come through for me, it's now.

'Do it for Gabriel,' I whisper.

Drawing in a deep breath, I walk around the aluminium shed until I see a door.

Gabriel is behind there. I need to do this for Gabriel.

I knock on it and jump when it immediately slides open.

Justin gets out. His hair and eyes are wild. He seizes me by the wrist with a sweaty hand and glances at my car, probably to check if I came alone, then drags me in so roughly that I cut myself against the rough edge of the aluminium door frame.

I gasp, putting my free hand to the open wound that begins to bleed when I touch it.

But I gasp even harder when my eyes adjust and I see Leo tied to a chair in the centre of the shed, his head hanging down as though he's asleep.

'Oh my gosh. You've got Leo, too?'

I cast my gaze around the empty shed and panic when I don't see Gabriel.

'Where is my son!?'

Justin stares at me blankly.

'Where is my son?' I shout at him, anger and panic rising up inside of me like a volcano.

'You had better not have hurt Gabriel. Where is he?'

Justin stares at me like I've gone mad and gestures at Leo with a sharp wave of his hand.

'That is your fucking son, you daft cow. And I was just about to show him what a whore of a mother he has.'

Before I can protest that Leo is not my son, Justin takes out his phone and presses a few buttons and holds it in front of Leo's face.

Blood drips from Leo's forehead and his eyes barely focus on the screen until something catches his attention on-screen, and his green eyes widen in horror.

'That's your whore of a mother there. Look at her.'

'Where is Gabriel?' I shout, not caring who sees the video anymore. I just want my son.

'Who the fuck is Gabriel?'

I realise then what's happened and put a hand to my mouth as I stare at Leo.

'Are you telling me that this piece of shit is not even your son?' asks Justin.

I meet Leo's gaze of confusion and realise that what I say next could endanger us both. I need to be so very careful.

Justin turns off the video on his phone and shoves the device in his pocket.

'No. He's not my son.'

Justin stares at Leo and then back at me, his eyes round and bloodshot.

'Then who the fuck is he?'

I say nothing. Neither does Leo.

Justin looks at us both and then from out of nowhere, throws his head back and laughs.

'Why did you say that she was your mum?' Justin asks Leo.

Leo stares at me and his eyes tear up.

'Because I wanted her to be.'

Justin is still laughing. He slaps his hands together.

'You want a whore to be your mother?'

'She's not a whore,' says Leo, his chin quivering as tears begin to stream down his pale cheeks. 'She's amazing and she's kind and she's my friend.'

'That girl in the video I just played, well that is her. The woman you know as Daphne is nothing but a whore, just like all women are, and the sooner you learn that the better, kid.' Justin shakes his head at Leo and rushes at him, making Leo jump so that the chair scrapes against the concrete floor. He puts a hand to Leo's neck.

'I should slit your throat and bury you under a concrete pad. Nobody would look for a boy like you. I bet you're a virgin. I bet girls ignore you and I bet your own mother hates you.'

'Stop it!' I shout and I rush to stand between Justin and Leo. 'Leave him alone. He's just a boy.'

'Oh, please, he's not your son, what do you care?'

'Just leave him out of it,' I say. 'This is between me and you. Let him go.'

Justin seems to consider my words while he rubs at the stubble covering his chin. Then he reaches for the pile of rope behind him and comes towards me with it.

I step back and turn, running for the door, but he catches me by the wrist and drags me against the concrete floor.

My knees burn as my skin scrapes against the rough surface and I cry out when Justin forces me to the ground in front of Leo and pulls my arm back so hard it feels as though it's going to tear right out of my arm socket.

'Leave her alone!' Leo shouts, his tearful eyes wide. He jumps in his chair, shuffling forward a little, but that's all he can do.

I glance up at Justin just in time to see his fist meet my face before everything turns black.

32

Daphne

I wake up and it's dark and I feel warmth against my back. It's Leo. We're both on the floor with our hands tied behind our backs, the ropes binding us together.

'Are you okay?' he asks, his voice soft and childlike in the night.

'Yes, are you?' My head throbs where Justin hit it. 'I'm so sorry, Leo. I'm so sorry to have gotten you into this mess.'

'It's okay, Daphne. I don't blame you. I've been a bad person. I've done some terrible things. Things that'll make you hate me. I deserve this. I hope this guy kills me.' He stifles a sob. 'When he comes back, I'm going to tell him that. That he can kill me as long as he sets you free.'

He starts to cry, his warm body trembling against mine.

'No, Leo. Please don't say that. We are both going to survive this. Together, okay?' Even though I'm not sure that I believe my own words, I have to say them. I need to give Leo hope. 'We all make mistakes in life. But owning up to them is the first step in making things right. And it sounds like you're starting to own up to some of the things you've done. So, you're on the right track. You don't need to sacrifice yourself for me, Leo. We're going to survive this.'

Leo cries softly and my heart breaks for him.

'I filmed a guy named Brad have sex with Catelyn while she was passed out. I was angry at the time, because I'd tried to talk to her that night, at the party. I wanted to ask her out. But all she did was talk to stupid no-brains Brad, the big football star that all the teachers love at school.

'Anyway, I was sitting alone in the dark, in a spare bedroom, waiting until it was time to get picked up, when Brad and Catelyn burst into the room. Well, Brad carrying Catelyn. She couldn't even walk. I was going to walk out, but then I realised that they didn't even see me because they were both so intoxicated. So, I hid behind a desk and took out my phone and started filming. I didn't know who I hated more in that moment, Brad or Catelyn. But I filmed until they finished and Brad walked out the room.'

He pauses for a moment, to catch his breath. We hear crows outside and I wonder if it's the early morning already.

'Then it was just Catelyn and me, alone in the room. I went over to her. She was naked. Brad just left her uncovered like that and I stared down at her and all I could think about was how many times I'd found my mother just like this, passed out and naked for any man that wanted her. It made me sick. I took some photos of her, because I wanted to show them to her, to show her what she was doing to herself by allowing herself to be used by guys like Brad.

'But then Gabriel walked in the room, apparently to find me to see if we could go home early. He'd had a few shots and I think he was feeling weird. When he saw us, his eyes widened and straight away he shoved me aside and covered Catelyn up with a blanket. I could tell by the way he narrowed his eyes at me that he thought that I'd done something to her, like Brad. It made me so angry that he automatically thought I would do something like that. So, I took photos of him covering Catelyn with a blanket. The photos made it look like he was peeling the blanket back to look at her naked.'

Leo swallows thickly.

'You're going to hate me now, Daphne. But I threatened Gabriel with the photos. I told him that if he told anyone about finding me alone with Catelyn in the room that I'd send those photos out to everyone, and post them on social media for everyone to see. I told him that I would tell everyone how much of a rapist he was. That he put something in Catelyn's drink just to take advantage of her.' Leo pauses. 'You hate me, don't you?'

I think about my Gabriel, the terror in his eyes the night of the party. He must have been so frightened after discovering Catelyn naked in a room and then to have had Leo threaten him with those photos. No wonder he wasn't himself.

I take my time to answer.

'I don't hate you, Leo. But that's such a horrible thing to do. How could you?'

'I'm sorry.' He sighs. 'All my life I wanted to be liked. Like Gabriel is liked. People just naturally warm to him. And I was so jealous of him after I met you that night, when you dropped us off in the car. You both seem so connected and shared so many little in jokes and smiles. I wanted that for myself. That's another reason why I blackmailed Gabriel. I wanted to have something over him, so that he would be forced to become my friend and invite me into his life, into your lives. And then, eventually, I'd delete the photos because I wouldn't need them because Gabriel would grow to like me as a friend and you would all welcome me into your family.'

I think back to how reluctant Gabriel was to have Leo over to our place, and how when Leo did come over Gabriel seemed so tense.

'Why did you lie about where you live? And how did you get into that house? The place you've been pretending is yours?'

Leo sighs again and shifts slightly behind me.

'My mother used to clean for them, before she got so messed up on drugs, and she knows where they keep their keys. I used to help her clean the house sometimes on the school holidays, so I knew where the keys were. They're away in Croatia and they have a son my age. That was his Xbox, not mine. I've never owned anything like that. Just an iPad that the school supplies for underprivileged kids. The rich kids' parents donate them every three months because that's how often they buy their kids new stuff.'

'But why were you staying there, wasn't your mother worried that you weren't coming home?'

Leo stiffens against my back.

'She kicked me out. Well, her boyfriend did. He hits me. She doesn't care. She drinks every night until she passes out and lets him do all kinds of things to her.'

So, I let myself into that Croatian family's mansion last month and pretended to live another life. And then Gabriel said he could give me a lift to the party and everything changed from that moment onwards. It was like stepping into a fairy tale, the moment I met your kind eyes in the rear-view mirror that night. I knew that I wanted a mother like you.'

A deep sadness washes over me, for the child that Leo is.

'I'm so sorry, Leo. I'm so sorry you've felt so alone and that you've been let down by the adults in your life. No child should ever have to go through that.'

I curl my fingers around his.

'And I'm sorry that your mother is going through such a bad time too.'

'But she lets him do it. It's her own fault.'

'Leo, when a woman is passed out, she is not giving consent to what happens to her. Your mother's boyfriend is taking advantage of her while she is passed out. He's taking advantage of the fact that she's a drug addict.'

'But why doesn't she just leave? I've begged her to. She won't listen.'

I sigh.

'I was in a similar situation, Leo, and I even I can't answer that. It's a combination of things, I think. The fear of being hurt, the fear of being left alone.'

Leo tightens his fingers around mine.

'I'm sorry,' he says. 'I'm sorry you've been hurt.'

Tears prickle my eyes but I blink them away.

'So, this guy, Justin, did he hurt you in the past?'

'Yes. He hurt me in many ways, including that video he just showed you.'

'With the blonde girl?'

'That blonde girl in the video is me.'

Leo is quiet for a long time.

'Why would you do something like that? Why would you agree to do it?'

'I didn't, Leo. Did I look like I wanted to be there? Did I look like I was enjoying it?'

Leo inhales deeply and I can hear the tightness in his throat.

'I'm sorry,' he whispers.

'The man who's holding us captive is my ex. I thought he loved me once, well, maybe not love, but he used to like having me around, and when he grew tired of me, he allowed these men to rape me. He left me alone in an apartment at the age of seventeen, your age right now, and those men held me down and forced themselves onto me and filmed it for millions of men to take pleasure out of watching it.'

'Why didn't you scream and cry? Why didn't you fight them off?'

'Because before they filmed me, they threatened to hurt me, or even kill me if I didn't do what they say.'

Leo doesn't say anything. But I feel him trembling against my back. His gentle sobs echo inside the shed.

'I want to kill that guy when he comes back,' says Leo after a while. 'And after I kill him and we get out, I'm going straight to Catelyn's and I'm going to confess what I did and apologise.'

I squeeze both his hands with mine.

'Thank you, Leo. You're doing the right thing.'

'So, you mean I can kill Justin and you won't judge me?'

I smile to myself in the darkness. 'No, I mean about what you plan to do about Catelyn and the video.'

'I know.' He grows quiet for a moment. 'But I still want to kill him. If it means that you live, that we both get out alive, then I'll do it.'

'Let's hope it doesn't get to that. Let's hope that the workers turn up for an early start before Justin gets back.'

We sit in silence for a few minutes, during which I wonder where Justin has gone and what he's up to.

'I bet you hate me now,' Leo says, his voice gravelly and filled with remorse.

'No, no I don't. I don't like what you did to Catelyn, but I admire the fact that you've admitted what you did and that you want to apologise and own up to your actions.'

'I'm still a horrible person. I don't deserve to be loved. No wonder my own mum doesn't love me.'

'You're not, Leo. Everyone deserves to be loved.'

'Even Justin?'

I sigh. 'Yes, I suppose. But he still needs to be held accountable for what he's done, for how he treats people, for how he treated me. I don't want other teenage girls to have to go through what I went through.'

Leo squeezes my fingers tight and he sighs.

My mind wanders to Gabriel and Joe – they must be out of their mind with worry by now. But at least they're safe. That's my one comfort.

Leo and I fall asleep against each other until the sound of a car engine wakes us up and morning light filters through the cracks of the shed.

'We have to be quick,' Justin says, bursting into the shed with wide, crazy eyes. 'The workers are due soon.' He's wearing the same clothes and they're crumpled as though he's slept in them.

He crouches down in front of me and holds out his phone.

I crinkle my nose at the smell of him.

'I'm going to make you call my fiancée and tell her that it's all a lie and that you are the stalker and that you've been obsessed with me for years and that you cheated on me with four men and made a porno behind my back and that you just wanted me back because you're in love with me.' He pauses to take a breath. 'If you say all of that and be convincing, I'll let you go.'

'Wait. Don't say that to her, Daphne,' says Leo. He touches my fingers. 'You can't let him hurt her like he hurt you. Keep me. Let Daphne go and do what you like to me,' Leo tells Justin.

Justin gets up and I hear a whoosh and then a loud slap.

I grip Leo's fingers, but they're slack and don't grip mine back.

'Leo!' I keep squeezing his fingers until they begin to move and I hear him groan. 'Are you okay?'

'Shut up or you'll get the same backhander,' says Justin.

I wish I wasn't bound. I wish that I could protect Leo, who has already suffered so much abuse in his short life.

'It's okay, Leo. We'll be okay,' I say. 'I'll do it, Justin. I'll tell Jessica what you said.'

Leo struggles behind me and I hear a familiar whoosh again, but this time I cry out as Leo slumps to the side and I go with him.

Justin swears and then takes a pocketknife out of his trouser pocket and cuts me free. Leo slumps forward on his side against the concrete, blood dripping down his temple.

'What did you do to him?'

'He'll have a headache at most.' Justin glares at me, his nostrils flaring. 'Now, quickly, before people get here. And before I have to go hunting for your real son.'

He puts the phone to my lips and dials. Holding my arm in a death grip.

'I told you not to call,' says Jessica, her voice cold.

'It's me. Daphne.'

At first, I'm met with silence.

Then eventually she says, 'Oh. Okay.'

'I'm here with Justin,' I say, looking up at him. 'He wants me to tell you the truth about me and him.'

Justin smiles and at that moment I hear a car pull up, then several more.

I lean into the phone.

'Everything I said is true!' I shout. 'He's a monster. He has me at one of your investment properties. Number–'

Justin rips the phone away from me and tosses it across the concrete floor where it shatters.

'What the hell was that?'

Justin grips me by my hair and looks as though he's about to kill me when he's interrupted by several loud bangs against the shed door.

'This is the police.'

'Help!' I shout.

Justin's eyes bulge and he lets go of my hair. I slide over to help Leo, who groans.

'Daphne!'

'Joe!' I shout, my heart leaping to hear his voice.

Justin throws me one last look, a look that chills me to the bone, and runs out the back door. In that moment I know that he would have killed me had we not been interrupted.

'He's gone out the back!' I shout, as I cradle Leo's bleeding head on my lap.

The door bursts open and police spill in through the shed and follow in Justin's footsteps.

Joe comes in next and bends down to gather me in his arms and I cry out in relief to see him.

I start to sob when I see Gabriel and he rushes over to throw his arms around me.

'I know everything, Mum, and it's okay,' he says. 'I love you so much.'

Epilogue

Daphne

It's been six weeks since the day that Justin got caught and arrested, and my life has changed for the better already.

Justin is in custody, where he belongs, awaiting trial, and the boy from Gabriel's school, Brad, has also been charged with sexually assaulting Catelyn and for using a prohibited drug to spike her drink with.

There's been quite a bit of press and publicity in the papers and on the news. Everyone now knows that I am Anna, the girl from the video.

But I don't hang my head in shame anymore. I hold my head up high.

I feel such great empathy for myself, for Anna, the vulnerable young girl in the video. And I'm proud of her, proud of me, for finally finding the courage to speak up about what happened.

Joe and I have been going from strength to strength and our intimacy issues are slowly being resolved. We are stronger than ever and I have never felt more in love with my husband. We are truly a team and I am forever grateful for his love and support.

And Gabriel, well, he is my champion. He gives me hope for the young girls of this generation. He has great plans to fight for women's rights and for the safety of all children, boys and girls. He wants to help kids in the orphan and foster system, in honour of me, and he is in talks with the school principal about the school providing more education on the subject of consent.

He's such an inspiration and I'm so proud of him.

I've also been in touch with Leo. He and his mother have been receiving counselling. She's left her boyfriend and mother and son are starting afresh in a refuge home.

Catelyn is doing well, too. We see her often now that she and Gabriel are dating.

Me, I'm sitting in a leather seat at a hairdressing salon, for the first time in my life.

I'd always been too scared to let anyone dye my hair in case they recognised me from the video or became suspicious of my covering of my blonde roots.

I've had over twenty years of black dye stripped away, and it feels as though I've peeled back my mask and thrown it away.

And it feels so good.

I'm staring at my own reflection as the hair stylist smooths and blow-dries my new hair to perfection.

My brown eyes twinkle back at me, and it feels as though the younger me, the Anna inside of me is saying hello for the first time in years.

I've missed her so much.

The blow-dryer is turned off and set aside.

'How do you like the new you, Daphne?' the young hairdresser beams at me while holding a round mirror behind me.

My hair a rich mahogany. I've always wanted red hair. I might go blonde again one day. But I'm not quite ready for that.

I stare at myself and I see the old me and I see the new me.

I nod at my reflection.

'I love her,' I say.

The stylist nods, satisfied with my reaction. She knows who I am, what I've been through, and she smiles, her eyes shiny with emotion.

'I love her too,' she says, squeezing my hand.

If you enjoyed this book, please let others know by leaving a quick review on Amazon. Also, if you spot anything untoward in the paperback, get in touch. We strive for the best quality and appreciate reader feedback.

editor@thebookfolks.com

More fiction by Vanessa Garbin

All free with Kindle Unlimited and available in paperback!

WHAT WE DID LAST NIGHT

When a group of close friends decide to hold a partner-swapping key party one night, it is meant to be "just a bit of fun". No obligations, but no strings attached. And anything that does happen will remain under wraps. But things quickly start to unravel, with utterly deadly consequences.

YOUR EVERY MOVE

When young mother Dana discovers a bag of money under a bush, she thinks her problems may be over. Unfortunately, they are only just beginning. She starts to receive letters from someone claiming to be her "number one fan" and unless she complies with their bizarre demands, her family will be in danger.

THE STEPS WE TAKE

A mother becomes increasingly at odds with her local community when she tries to deal with the bullying of her daughter at school. Yet her daughter is trying to handle it in her own way. When one bullying schoolboy goes missing, the family will have to reach the truth to remain together.

THEIR LITTLE SECRETS

Sara's marriage is already under strain when her best friend's daughter disappears. With the parents acting strange, and her husband absent-minded and evasive, Sara starts suspecting they share a secret. When the body of a girl is found in a lake nearby, her resolve to solve the mystery will force her to question everyone.

NO FRIENDS OF MINE

Marilyn is at a low point, so when she receives an invitation to holiday with some old friends, she doesn't think she has much to lose. But old friends bring with them old memories, in particular those of a terrible event that happened ten years ago. As the past is dug up, having been bored with her life, Marilyn will now find herself fighting for it.

FOR MY OWN GOOD

Mary is on meds which make her forgetful. It's been like this ever since an incident when their baby was injured. Now her husband is being way over-protective. He insists Mary stays indoors, for her own good. He's hired a nanny. But Mary can't remember her child getting hurt. And if she can't recall what happened, how can she make things right?

www.thebookfolks.com

Made in the USA
Monee, IL
16 November 2023

46768893R00146